"The Veritas Codex is an amazing series that keeps the pages turning and your mind spinning. Suspenseful like Stuart Woods, yet thought-provoking like Dan Brown, Kulakowski has the incredible ability to weave together the threads of fact and fiction and sew them into an amazing literary tapestry that leaves you wanting more."

— BRANDON MARSH, HOST AND EXECUTIVE PRODUCER, THE PARAUNITY PODCAST

"The Veritas Codex series is a hearty paranormal narrative entree seasoned with suspense. It satisfied my craving for everything paranormal! Thank goodness there are more in the series—Betsey Kulakowski has whet my appetite and I am begging for more!"

— XANDER ZWEIG, CO-HOST OF THE XANDER & STONE SCIENCE & SUPERNATURAL PODCAST

"Realistic heroes and villains. International intrigue. More plot twists than a cup of nightcrawlers. Betsey has definitely raised the bar [in *The Jaguar Queen*]."

— J. DON WRIGHT, AUTHOR OF *BEHOLD!*

"*The Jaguar Queen* keeps the momentum going in the Veritas Codex series. I am becoming very invested in the team of Lauren, Rowan, Bahati and Jean-Rene. "

— DONNA KEY

"I couldn't put [*The Veritas Codex*] down! I knew halfway through that it was going to be a late night because I couldn't quit turning the pages. I can't wait for the next book in the series."

— LISA SMALLWOOD

"Relatable characters and crisp pace…*The Veritas Codex* combines the intrigue and chemistry of *The X-Files* with the intensity of *The Da Vinci Code*."

— JAZ PRIMO, AUTHOR OF *GWEN REAPER*

"Engaging characters and remarkable plot twists jump from these pages. They pulled me into a thrilling world I did not want to leave."

— JOHN WOOLEY, AUTHOR OF *SEVENTH SENSE*

"I enjoyed [*The Veritas Codex*]. The writing is well done. I really liked the characters. It kept me engaged to the point I was speed reading (to find out what was going to happen) and I had to slow myself down!"

— TERRI FOLKS

"

THE ALIEN ACCORD

THE ALIEN ACCORD

BETSEY KULAKOWSKI

For Barry, who made a joke that turned into a character that inspired a book.

For Jackie, who always bought me coffee, laughed at my jokes, and cried at all the appropriate moments.

Gods come, and gods go. Mortals flicker and flash and fade. Worlds don't last; and stars and galaxies are transient fleeting things that twinkle like fireflies and vanish into cold and dust. But I can pretend…

— NEIL GAIMAN, *THE SANDMAN #7*

PROLOGUE

"Extraterrestrials definitely exist," the Russian astronaut said in his thick accent. He gazed unblinking into the camera. It was his first interview for an American television documentary. While he visibly trembled with nerves, he spoke with the authority of a man who knew something he wasn't supposed to know; wasn't supposed to tell. "And they live among us … or have probably lived among us at one time." The astronaut continued. "There are billions of stars in the universe … so many that there must be different forms of life. Are they just like us? Made up of carbon and nitrogen? Do they breathe oxygen? *Nyet*. Probably not."

"Dr. Budnikov, have you … seen them?" The moderator asked. "With your own eyes?"

The gray-haired astronaut paused. "I've seen things I cannot explain. Things my government does not want me to tell."

"But you defected in 1986. Was that because you were afraid something would happen to you if you talked?"

"*Da*." He shrugged. "I had no choice. I know too much."

"You reportedly saw the wreckage of a downed alien craft

in a remote region of the Soviet Union back in the late 1970s. Can you tell us more?"

"*Da.*" He lifted his eyes towards the camera, as he spoke nervously. "I was a young soldier on my first assignment. We were told not to talk about it. I took pictures, even though it was against the rules. I never told anyone."

In the control room, techs pulled up an image that would appear as a cutout behind the astronaut before expanding to fill the whole screen. It was a grainy photo, poorly lit and the main features were not well-centered in the frame. It looked like the saucer section of the Starship Enterprise; half buried, scorched, and crumpled, in the stark Siberian landscape. Clearly, the landing hadn't been easy.

"That was 1979? Dr. Budnikov, why haven't you come forward with this information until now?"

He gazed down at his hands. "For the safety of my family, I felt it was best not to disclose what I knew. I know what can happen to someone who … talks."

"Why now?"

"Before this vessel crashed, we began receiving radio signals deep from space," he said. His eyes shifted. "Then, they just stopped." He glanced at something off camera. "But now … the signals … they're back."

"What kind of signals?" The moderator's brow furrowed.

"Alien signals …" he said. "A message from the cosmos." He lifted his hand to make an arc over his head but stopped and dropped it abruptly. His whole countenance collapsed, and he sucked in a breath as he paled.

Shouts and shuffles echoed off camera, and then the camera rocked as if it had been struck. The moderator looked away from the astronaut and fear filled his eyes. Gunshots echoed in the small space, and the camera shook violently on its tripod as it was hit hard. It fell over, the lens cracking with an audible crunch as it landed. Someone screamed. More gunshots echoed and bodies hit the floor. The astronaut fell just in the frame of the camera; a stunned expression faded to a blank stare. A single red circle marred his forehead. Blood trickled from the gaping hole.

~

MICHAEL SAT BACK FROM THE COMPUTER MONITOR. HIS HEART skipped a number of beats and his pulse vibrated in his throat. A cold sweat broke out on his upper lip. A shiver washed through him. He closed his eyes as he tried to compose himself. Nothing could have prepared him for having to watch a friend and colleague being assassinated. "When was this?" He bowed his head and took a deep breath.

"Just a couple of days ago," Dr. India Cameron said, putting a comforting hand on his shoulder as she stood behind him.

"Has this been on the news?"

"The AP ran a story about a Russian cosmonaut being shot, but the story's been white-washed," India said. "Sasha found it on the dark web. He was able to save the video before it was taken down, presumably by the government, but who knows. He sent it to me through our secure webmail system."

Michael stood and paced behind his desk, fighting for composure. He turned his back on the room, leaning heavily on the credenza by the window. A trembling breath audibly escaped his throat before he straightened and crossed his arms over his chest.

"I'm sorry I have to ask, Michael. But when was the last time you talked to Alexei?" India asked.

It took him a moment to find his voice. "Last week." Michael ran a shaky hand over his face. "He called and said he was sending me some files and asked me to look at them. I expected them to come through email, but … they never came. I tried texting him, but …"

"Did you talk to him about what we are working on? Did you mention Project Morning Star?" She lowered her voice.

"No. I didn't tell him anything." Michael glanced at her with cautious reservation. "But I did ask him about his work."

"Did you ask him about the signals he was studying?" she asked. "The ones he mentioned in this interview?"

Michael pursed his lips and looked away, still trying to wrap his brain around the fact that his colleague was dead. No one expected anything like this, least of all Michael. "Yeah," he finally said. "From what he told me, it sounds exactly like what we've been working on."

"Did you tell anyone you talked to him?"

"No." A chill washed over him. "Who would have done something like that?"

"If this were 1986, my first guess would be the KGB," India said with a smirk.

There was a long moment of silence as the project director leaned on the desk and folded her arms. Her red power suit strained over her pencil-thin frame. She poked her glasses with a manicured nail, pushing them up her equally thin nose. "Maybe it's a good thing you're going to Houston next week," Michael's boss said. "When does your flight leave?"

"Saturday night," he said. "It's a long trip from Johannesburg to Houston. I hope there are no delays."

"I just hope our grant gets renewed," India said. "God knows we couldn't function without NASA's support. We're going to need it now more than ever."

"I haven't been back to the States in a while." Michael's mind raced as he tried to figure out what to do and how to make the most of his time back in the US.

"Don't feel pressured to hurry," she said. "Make friends. Build relationships. Relationships mean money. Maybe you can get a feel for what's going on with some of the other radio-telescope teams … especially Hubble. It's a tight-knit community. Surely there's chatter."

Michael nodded. He sat gazing off into the distance for a moment. "Maybe I can get a hold of my sister …"

"Your sister?" India furrowed her brow.

"She's into the … unusual, even the bizarre," he said. "She and I have joked for years about who was going to find … well." Michael hesitated, unable to speak the words, considering what he had just witnessed. "If she'll even talk to me, she might be of some help …"

"If she'll talk to you? Why wouldn't she talk to you?" India eyed him dubiously.

"We haven't spoken in years," Michael said. "We are … not close."

"No time like the present to mend old wounds," India stated matter-of-factly as she stood. Michael thought of Alexei. He was one of those friends he could go years without talking to, but when they met up, it was like a day hadn't passed. They'd toast each other with good vodka and talk for hours about the mysteries of the universe. He would miss those conversations. India moved her hand to his arm, pulling him out of his thoughts. "Enjoy your visit to the states."

"Thanks," Michael said, turning on unsteady legs. He wasn't sure what frightened him more, the thought of the KGB or the thought of staring down his sister. He wasn't even sure where she was these days, but he had an idea of where to start.

Lauren and Rowan stepped off the plane at LAX feeling frazzled. Eight hours on a redeye flight over the Pacific Ocean was bad enough, but eight hours with a nine-month-old on an airplane had been excruciating. Henry was a good traveler, but he'd been cranky even before they'd left Hawaii, and Lauren wasn't much better off. Poor Rowan had to put up with both of them being tired and cranky.

"Let me get you some coffee then we'll go find our luggage and pick up the rental car," Rowan suggested.

"What time is our meeting at the studio?" she asked.

"Not until three." He glanced at his watch. "It's six Pacific Standard."

"Honestly, I'm not interested in coffee," she said. "I just want to lie down in a bed and sleep for a few hours before we have to go to work."

"Fair enough." Rowan shouldered his bag, taking Lauren's carry-on so she could carry the baby, who'd finally fallen asleep; a limp weight in her arms. He had his head on her shoulder. Drool left a dark stain down the back of her shirt. "Come on." He urged her down the crowded terminal.

"Tell me again why we didn't fly into San Diego?"

"I couldn't get a direct flight," he said as they headed towards the escalator, descending to the luggage pickup area. "All the flights came to LAX with a layover before going to San Diego. We'll be in San Diego before the next flight leaves from LA."

"Right." Lauren yawned. She felt as tired as Rowan looked. He had dark circles under his puffy eyes. "Did you get any sleep on the plane?"

"A little," Rowan said.

"You're not too tired to drive, are you?"

"I might need a coffee once we get on the road." He stifled his own yawn. "You had your hands full with Henry."

"I think he must have an earache." Lauren ran her hand over the sleeping baby's copper hair. "That or he's cutting teeth."

"Maybe." Rowan shrugged. "Or maybe he's still upset about what happened yesterday."

"Do we have to talk about that now?" Lauren stopped at the bottom of the escalator, stepping aside while Rowan oriented himself, before he continued. The crowds dissipated, and she followed him to an empty bench near their luggage carousel.

"We've spent the last twenty-four hours not talking about it," he said. "Heck, we've spent the last nine months not talking about it. What's going on with you, Lauren? How'd you get to Mexico? How'd you get to the farmer's market in Hilo?"

"Don't you think if I knew I would tell you?" she said, exasperated. "I have to think there are forces at play of which I have no understanding of, or any control over. You were in trouble. I was in trouble." She watched as people moved past them, shifting Henry to a more comfortable position as she sat.

"Forces? What forces?" Rowan sat beside her but neither looked at one another.

"You can keep asking as many times as you want, Rowan, but that doesn't mean I'm going to suddenly have answers." Lauren was tired, hungry, and irritable. Still she tried to keep her tone even so as not to attract any attention from the people gathering around carousel four waiting for their luggage. "I just know I had to get to you before Santiago Mateo killed you. I was in labor … I was desperate. One minute Stephanie Wentworth and I were in San Diego … the next thing I know … we were in Mexico. I don't know how it works. I don't know what else to tell you."

"Forces, huh?" he muttered under his breath. "I suppose I could understand a desperate moment, but *magically* teleporting to the Farmer's market because you forgot coconut? What forces in this universe have anything to do with forgotten coconut?"

Lauren drew up, wrapping herself around Henry. "I don't know," she said, her voice cracking. "But it's terrifying to be in one place, then suddenly be in another. Not knowing where you are or how you got there? I wish I could give you answers, and I'm sorry that I can't. But … I'm still trying to process it."

～

ROWAN SAT WITH HIS ELBOWS ON HIS KNEES, HIS BROW clamped over his eyes as he considered what Lauren had said. It terrified him, too. He'd tried asking before, after Mexico, but she never had any answers. At first she'd dodged the question, then she'd come up with some cock-and-bull story about what she thought happened. Now that it'd happened a second time, he was more determined to get answers. He glanced back at his wife, seeing the distress on her face, realizing she was no closer to that goal than he was. It upset her every time he brought it up, and they usually ended up fighting. He didn't want to fight with her, he just wanted answers.

Rowan finally gave up and left Lauren and Henry to go see about their rental car.

~

LAUREN SAT, FINDING HERSELF STARING OFF INTO SPACE. WHEN the carousel began to hum to life, she perked up and watched for their things, debating how she would manage two suit-cases, a car-seat, and a stroller. The crowd of people standing alongside the conveyors began to swarm in, and Lauren decided to keep her spot and wait until everyone else had their things before she even tried.

She spied their suitcases on the conveyor, and stood, rocking Henry side to side as she waited, happy to be able to stand up and stretch as she mentally worked through the logistics of the task before her. She noticed an olive drab rucksack on the conveyor next to their bags, just as a soldier in his military fatigues stepped up beside her. "Looks like you could use some help," he offered, reaching out and catching the handle of the stroller, pulling it off.

"Thank you," Lauren said as he reached for the car seat.

"What else?" he asked, as Lauren managed to unlock the stroller and set it up one-handed. She'd done it plenty of times before.

"The blue roller bag and the red duffle." She pointed. The soldier moved to catch them both, and set them off, before grabbing his bag too. Lauren got the baby settled in the stroller, then turned to the soldier. "Thank you so much! I wasn't certain how I was going to manage all that."

He grinned and she realized he'd recognized her. "Where's your ... husband?" He looked around. Rowan usually got recognized first.

"Getting our rental car lined up." She smiled.

"I love your show." He lowered his voice. "I especially liked the Bigfoot episode."

Lauren felt color rise in her cheeks. "Thank you, so much."

Rowan arrived while they were standing there, and the young man took a step back. "Wow." He looked up at Rowan. "You're taller than I expected."

Rowan looked blankly at the man. "Rowan Pierce." He stuck out his hand.

"Corporal Willis Armstrong," he said, shaking Rowan's hand vigorously. "Love your show."

"Thank you for your service." Rowan put his hand on his heart. "Used to wear that uniform myself."

"Thank you for your support … and your service too," Armstrong said.

"Corporal Armstrong helped me get the bags off the carousel," Lauren said. "Did you get the car?"

"I did," Rowan said.

"Are you guys doing another season of *The Veritas Codex*?" the soldier asked anxiously, grasping his hat between his hands.

"We're headed to San Diego to get our marching orders today," Rowan said.

"Cool!" He bounced on his toes, glancing over Rowan's shoulder as an announcer called his name over the PA system. "I gotta go," he said, shaking Rowan's hand again, giving Lauren a polite nod, then swooping in for a surprise hug. Lauren laughed but recoiled. "So nice to meet you both."

"Thanks for helping out," Rowan said.

"Yes, thank you," Lauren added.

"The guys aren't going to believe this." He started to turn.

"Wait," Lauren said. "Quick selfie?"

"Really?" He grinned. "Sure! That'd be great."

~

LAUREN FELT SOMEWHAT REFRESHED WHEN THEY ARRIVED AT The Network offices. Her good mood, however, didn't last long. The Network had been bouncing around ideas for the family-themed travel show they wanted to produce for The Exploration Channel's sister network, the Escape Channel, but nothing had been finalized. The idea Jacob presented now did not sit well with Lauren.

"Have you lost your ever-loving minds?" The tirade of expletives that followed — interspersed with English, but mostly in her native tongue — not only made Lauren's face turn five shades of red, but it also made Rowan blush; even though he didn't understand a word of it. The Network execs looked like they'd been hit by a ton of bricks.

Clearly, no one expected her response. Rowan caught her arm, attempting to soothe her without words. His cautious look told her he could handle this. Lauren looked like she might protest but pursed her lips and sat back in her chair, crossing her arms over her body, turning her gaze to the window.

"I think what Lauren is saying, is have you lost your ever-loving minds?" Rowan said, only a bit more calmly.

"A luxury vacation in Dubai?" She gasped, clearly affronted. "First off, I'm not taking my son to the Middle East," Lauren added, but Rowan's hand tightened on her wrist.

"Dubai isn't some third world country, Lauren." Jacob recoiled, clearly stunned by her reaction. "It's one of the wealthiest countries in the world and is generally considered safe for travel."

"Generally?" Lauren started, rising from her chair, but Rowan's hand became wrenchingly tight. She turned her angry gaze on him as she yanked her hand out of his grasp and sat back down. She turned her wrath back across the table. "I am a breast-feeding mother, and you want me to travel with my baby to a country with a strict religious code that's heavily tilted against women *in general*. Western women in particular are often targeted by government law enforcement for being ... wanton and immoral. Did you know they have women stoned for nursing in public?"

"Look, we understand your concerns," Jacob said calmly, trying to soothe her. "We've researched everything and there's no reason that, with a few precautions, you can't travel safely with your baby."

"What kind of precautions?" Rowan asked, before she could.

"It's simply a matter of being respectful of the local customs," Jacob said, sitting back in his chair.

"Have you met my wife?" Rowan stood, circling around behind his chair. "She's a modern western woman. She just dropped the f-bomb — along with a few other choice words — in a business meeting. What would happen if she did that in the middle of the mall in Dubai?"

"Well, that wouldn't be wise." Jacob stood too, walking over to the coffee service, refilling his cup. He reached over and took Lauren's cup and refilled it too, dressing it with cream and sugar just as she would, before setting it back in front of her like an olive branch. Lauren didn't reach for it. "But the social customs dictate you must comply with their modesty laws, not drink alcohol, and we're not sending you during Ramadan, so at least you won't have to worry about the fasting rules."

"They wouldn't apply to me or to Henry either," Lauren said. "I've been to Muslim countries. I know the laws, but I will not go ... nor will I take my son and that is final."

Rowan's hand went to her shoulder, and he stood in solidarity with her.

"The Dubai Travel Commission is prepared to fund your entire vacation," Jacob said.

"We're not going to *be* on vacation," Lauren said curtly. "We're working."

"A poor choice of words." Jacob conceded, holding back his hands as he sat down. "But they're offering to put you up in the finest beach-front resort properties, all the first-class accommodations, including a limo with a driver."

"How much does that cost?"

"Over $10,000," Jacob said. "But what a way to kick off the new show, right?"

"I thought the goal of this concept was to encourage the American public to take a vacation," Rowan said. "What family in the US could afford that?"

"I don't know about this concept," Lauren said. "I mean it sounded good six months ago, but I've been having second thoughts."

"Contracts have already been signed, Lauren," Jacob said. "Are you prepared to breech your contract?"

"Of course not," Lauren said. "But when we signed the contracts nothing had been decided. I'm just wondering if there's not some room for … negotiation … on our destinations or our purpose when we get there. When we agreed to this concept, we knew it was outside our roles as paranormal researchers. I get that you want something new and different for the Escape Channel. You said you wanted us to promote a longing for travel, a spirit of discovery, but if the American public is anything like Rowan and I, they're not going to want to just lay on the beach and drink rum punch all day long."

"What's wrong with laying on a beach drinking rum all day?" Jacob quipped.

"Nothing. But people want adventure in their lives. They want to explore mysteries on their own. I think that's why our shows have been so popular. People want to live a life like ours. They want to experience something new. They want to walk in the footsteps of their forefathers, explore new places and meet new people; they want to *do* something."

Jacob glanced at the other execs at the table, shaking his

head. He folded his hands and frowned at Lauren. She sat back waiting for a response.

"We did have one other concept we'd pitched before we started developing this one," Curt Jamison, one of the Escape Channel producers offered.

"Which one, Curt?" Jacob arched a brow. He didn't look pleased that his cohort would show anything but solidarity in this meeting, at least that's how Lauren read his expression.

"Well since it's a show about family, why not show them tracing their roots, and sharing in some of the adventures their ancestors faced?" Curt said. "Those ancestor research programs on public television are huge right now. The overhead isn't bad. We have a couple of sponsors already asking about a program like this. Think about it…" He turned to Rowan and Lauren, folding his hands across the table, opening them as he spoke. "We can start with your own immediate families, and then branch out through the generations."

"My mother claims we're descended from Robert the Bruce." Rowan turned to Lauren. "She's got our family tree back to the 1200's if memory serves me right."

"We can have a genealogist help track down your family tree, and then you can go to places where ... how did Lauren put it? Where your ancestors walked?"

Lauren glanced at Rowan as he sat back down beside her.

"Do you know where *my* ancestors walked?" Lauren asked sharply. "*Nu-na-hi du-na dlo-hi lu'i.*"

"Excuse me?" Jacob lifted his brow over the wide rim of his glasses.

"My ancestors walked *The Trail*." Lauren's voice went dark.

"The Trail?"

"*The Trail Where They Cried*," she said. "The Trail of Tears."

"What about your parents?" Jacob seemed unfazed, which

made Lauren all the more cross. "I mean, I have met Rowan's parents, but I've never heard you talk about yours."

"My father left before I was born," she said. "My mother and I are … not close."

"What does your mother do?"

"She teaches at the Cherokee Heritage Center … at least the last time I talked to her."

A spark appeared in Jacob's eye. "You have papers? Tribal records?"

"Excuse me?" Lauren stopped, irritated at the term. "Do you think I'm some kind of pedigreed poodle?"

"Apologies, again … another poor choice of words." Jacob couldn't seem to win today, but Lauren allowed him to hang himself with his own words.

"I know you mean well." She took a deep breath. "The Cherokee Tribe helped pay for my college tuition. I wore my tribal stole when I graduated. I'm immensely proud of my heritage, just not interested in digging up old hurts among my family. Why can't we go looking for aliens in Roswell or the Fouke Monster in Arkansas?"

Jacob seemed to surrender. He turned to Rowan, but Curt took over before he could continue. He addressed his comment to Lauren. "I'll tell you what," he said. "If you are willing to put together the pilot of your family trees, maybe we could finish off with something paranormal like past life regression. If nothing else, we might get another great two-hour special to work with. If the concept takes off, then who knows where it could go. We could even do an episode on Bahati and Jean-René. Heck, we can get all the Network stars involved."

"The way I see it, we just need to get you working and I'm willing to start off slow." Curt turned to Jacob. "I have a genealogist I worked with on another pilot that never took off. Lauren, let's start with your family tree, then we'll work on Rowan's. Maybe your mom can send what she has."

"Better yet, why don't we just go to Denver and get it? They're itching to see their grandson," Rowan said.

"Maybe after we get a start on Lauren's," Jacob said, insisting. "We have a lot more work to do tracing her roots. We'll get ahold of the genealogist and get her started. Gather Jean-René and Bahati, along with any equipment you need. You can leave as soon as you're ready."

"But …" Lauren sputtered. Everything happened so fast, her protests went unanswered.

"Don't you have a famous brother who works for NASA?" Curt asked.

Lauren's brow drew down, and Rowan heard her teeth saw against each other as she clenched her jaw. "Maybe we should call George instead," he said. "He still lives in the family home near Tahlequah. Surely he has records, pictures … things we can use."

"I don't know," Jacob said. "A brother that works for NASA is pretty cool …"

"You'd think," Lauren groused. "Michael is an …." The tirade began again.

Rowan turned to her and put a hand on her arm. "We can do this without Michael's help."

"If I have to call him or my mother, I won't do it. No way … not in a million years …" she blurted out. She glanced at the startled expressions that met her from across the table.

"I'm certain we'll find your ancestors are as strong and brilliant as you are. What harm could there be to look?" Rowan arched a brow. Lauren sat back with her arms crossed.

"Fine." She lifted her shoulder in a half-hearted shrug. "Whatever."

~

Lauren made a hasty retreat from the conference room, skipping the elevator and heading straight for the stairwell, mindless of whether or not Rowan followed behind her. She wanted to get back to Bahati and Jean-René's house. They were babysitting Henry, and it would be time for his supper when they got there. As much as she loved Bahati and Jean-René, she'd never left her baby with anyone other than Rowan.

Rowan got her door at the car, surprising her, but she thanked him with a silent nod. They didn't speak until they were in the rental car, back on the highway across town. "Did I come across as too harsh?" she asked.

"You were honest," Rowan said. "I don't know that I'd have used the same language, but I was thinking what you said. You got the message across."

"I didn't mean to swear like that." She stared at her thumbnail. "I don't know what got into me."

This wasn't like her. She seemed anxious. Rowan knew his wife to be confident, almost to the point of arrogance, but this was a new aspect of her that he found disconcerting. Rowan reached over for her hand, taking it in his. "You said what you had to say, honey. I'm only glad you said it in Cherokee."

"Only part of that was in Cherokee," she said curtly. "Bulgarian is very effective for cursing."

"Bulgarian, huh?" He mused. Another one of those *forces* in the universe that she now had at her command was an aptitude for language, not just her native tongue, but all languages. Rowan turned his attention back to the road, but in his mind, he replayed the meeting. "You didn't seem very keen on the idea of tracing your family history."

"I like the concept even less than the *vacation* in Dubai." She turned and stared out the passenger side window for a long moment. When she spoke again, Lauren turned and looked at him. "You know how I feel about my family," she said bluntly.

"Maybe we'll might find something interesting," Rowan

suggested. "Or maybe you'll learn more about why your family is the way it is."

"Oh I know why my mother is the way she is," Lauren groused. "She's mean and manipulative."

"Yeah, but why?"

"Does the devil need a reason to be evil?" The vitriol in her voice surprised even her.

"Ouch!" Rowan winced, signaling for the exit.

"The apple doesn't fall far from the tree with Michael." She turned her gaze back to the passing scenery. "Maybe my father's family is more interesting." She shrugged, pulling her sweater around her body. Rowan noticed and reached to turn down the blower on the AC. "Your family though, that is going to be fun."

"You just want to go to Scotland, don't you?" His dimples appeared in the corner of his cheek.

Her sour expression faded. "You promised me I'd get to see you in a kilt again."

"Well, it may be a while, depending on how long it takes to find something on your family tree," he said, merging into the right lane. "So what do you know about your father?"

The shadow returned over her visage and she remained silent for a long while. "John Grayson, born in Oklahoma, joined the military and served in Vietnam. I never knew him, but my older brothers did, and they adored him, but … they said he was different when he came home. One day, he went to town to get supplies to fix the kitchen sink, and he never came home."

"You never heard from him?" Rowan glanced over, as her eyes filled with tears. She fought to keep them behind her lashes.

"Promise me you'll never do that to Henry." Her voice cracked.

Rowan abruptly signaled and pulled the car into a parking lot, found a spot, and put it in park before unbuckling his seatbelt. He turned, taking her hand, gazing into her dark eyes. "I swear on everything holy in this world, I will never leave you or Henry. You know that, right?"

She bit her lip, willing tears not to escape her eyes. "I do." She sniffed. "I wouldn't have married you if I thought you'd do something like that. But ..."

"What?"

"I still don't know *why* my father left," she said. "It scares me that I might do something to make you leave your child ... your children ... I could stand you leaving me, I think, but ... Henry needs his father. You're such a good dad ... it kills me to think about a life for him … without you." Tears escaped her blockade and ran unchecked down her cheeks.

"Lauren, listen to me." He caught both her hands in his. "I will never leave you, Lauren … or Henry. Ever." Rowan pulled her into his arms and held her tightly, burying his face into her hair, breathing deeply of her, feeling her body tremble as she fought back a sob.

Michael stood at the counter in the security office at the Houston Space Center waiting for his credentials. It was mid-afternoon and he hadn't even checked in at the hotel yet. He knew he would need to renew his security pass before he could meet with anyone. He also knew there would be mandatory safety training he'd be expected to complete before he could even meet with the Finance or Engineering Departments. His first appointment with the Grant team wasn't until the following day.

"Michael? Michael Grayson?" A soft voice, with a deep Texas drawl, called from the door.

Michael felt a chill run through him, and his heart fluttered in his chest, recognizing the voice. With great effort, he composed himself, then turned slowly. "Kitty Donovan?" He nearly gasped when he saw the most beautiful woman on earth standing behind him in the lobby.

She took three steps towards him but stopped just within arm's reach. "I knew that was you! I've never known a man anywhere with hair more luxurious than yours," she gushed, reaching out and running her hand down his long ponytail. "It's gotten so long!" It hung past his belt, and it was his greatest pride. He took meticulous care of his raven locks, brushing it and keeping it well-conditioned. It hadn't been cut since he was a boy, and he hoped it would continue to grow long and thick 'til it was as white as Kitty's alabaster complexion. The thought made his stomach flip. He hadn't seen her since they'd graduated from the University of Oklahoma's engineering department.

"I didn't realize you were still working here. I thought you were at Cape Canaveral," Michael said.

"I did a brief stint there a few years ago, but it was just a short-term project I consulted on. I thought you were in California," she said, with her hand extended.

He caught it and drew her in for a polite hug.

"I was, but I got reassigned about three years ago."

"What brings you to Houston?"

"Here to renew my grant," he said.

Her brow lifted as she tucked a honey-blonde curl behind her ear. Kitty Donovan remained just as pretty as she'd been when they dated in college. She had a glow that could light up any room. "What are you working on?"

"Oh," he said. "It's a dreadfully long story."

"Your credentials, Dr. Grayson." The security officer came back to the desk and handed him the ID badge he would need to access the facility. It accompanied paperwork on rules and training he would need before his appointment. "The Southern Texas Area Safety Council is your best bet for the required training." He pointed to one of the papers. "If you go online this afternoon you might be able to get into the classes you need tomorrow morning."

"Thanks," Michael said, turning back to Kitty. "In addition to renewing our project's grant application," he said. "I also hoped someone might be able to get me access to the radio telescope on Hubble."

Kitty's brow lifted. "Hubble?" she all but stuttered it. "But, you could have done that from anywhere," she said, with a curl in her cheeks. "Why come to Houston?"

"It's a long story," he said. As much as he wanted to tell her everything – well, everything that he could – he needed sleep.

"I'm free for dinner if you want to tell me the whole story."

"I just spent the last thirty-four hours in transit." Michael blushed, running a hand over his weary brow. "Tomorrow night maybe? When I'm not so travel-worn?" It wasn't exactly the truth. The long lay-over in Boston had been sufficient to allow him to get a hotel and spend the night in a real bed. This morning, he'd gotten up early and been back at the airport in time for his 8:15 flight. Another layover in Dallas had given him a chance to have lunch, before the final leg of his trip into Houston.

"Why don't you call me when you finish your classes tomorrow morning?" She reached into her suitcoat, then took a step closer. Gently snaking her hand beneath his jacket, she tucked her business card into the pocket of his white dress shirt. The touch sent sparks through him, and he all but shivered. She paused a moment to straighten his tie. The message in her eyes suggested if he called her, she might do him the great favor of un-straightening it.

There had been this amazing chemistry between the two of them back in college, the kind of chemistry that spontaneously combusted. It had burned hot and fast. Clearly the flames still flickered.

"I'll call you first thing," Michael said.

Kitty beamed and her tongue ran over her perfectly straight, incredibly white teeth.

"Promise?" she said coyly. Kitty flirted overtly.

"I cross my heart." He ran his finger across his tie as he leaned in and bowed.

"You'll break my heart if you don't," she said, her tone softening. "I'll see you tomorrow."

"Yes, you will."

She gave him a sly wink as she passed, her high heels clicking on the tile floors.

Michael paused, watching the kick pleat of her skirt swaying as she went.

"Dr. Grayson." The security guard cleared his throat aggressively, practically scolding him.

Michael turned back, blushing. "Sorry." He cringed. "We dated in college."

"Uh huh," the guard grunted flatly, pushing the papers towards him.

Michael took them, then clipped the ID badge onto his lapel. He picked up his suitcase and turned. Walking out to the circle drive in front of the large office building, he left thoughts of Kitty for a later time. He reminded himself that he had another woman he hadn't talked to in twenty years that he needed to find.

Taking his cell phone out of his pocket, flipping it open, Michael called for a cab to take him to the hotel. He found a bench and sat his bag down, peeling out of his suit jacket. He folded it and lay it over his bag.

He hadn't been in the US for several years, and he didn't even know how to go about finding his sister. If anyone would know where to find her, Michael thought perhaps their oldest brother, George, might. It was a start. As he sat down beside his things, he glanced at his phone and dialed a familiar number.

"Hey George. It's Michael," he said when his brother answered. "I'm actually in Houston. Yeah. At NASA. I'm working on renewing my grant, but … that's not why I'm calling. By any chance, do you know how to get a hold of Lauren?"

~

MICHAEL HELD THE CHAIR OUT FOR KITTY. THE FLORAL perfume she always wore brought back old memories as he leaned over her hair and breathed her in. When they had parted ways after college, he certainly never thought he'd be sitting here having dinner with her. In fact, he hadn't thought of her in years. Once, he thought they'd have a future together, but life took them in different directions. He went on to MIT to work on his PhD. She came back to Texas to study at Baylor.

The waiter arrived a moment later with the wine list. "Do you prefer red or white?" Michael asked.

"Scotch, on the rocks," she said crisply.

Michael handed the menu back to the waiter. "Make that two." He held Kitty's gaze appreciatively. "Macallen 12, if you have it."

Kitty's eyes widened. "You have excellent taste in Scotch, Dr. Grayson."

"So glad to find you're not one of those pretentious snobs who only drinks an oaky *Cabernet* or *Sauvignon Blanc*." He over-accentuated the French pronunciations.

"Oh I am a pretentious snob," Kitty said. "But I happen to like Scotch."

That made Michael brighten as he sat back in his chair. Her grin mirrored his own, even as she sat stone straight in her chair. She wore a fitted green dress, just a shade darker than her eyes. It had a halter cut, with rhinestone chains connecting the front to the back. Her shoulders were bare. She'd pinned her hair up and a single curl fell over a perfectly chiseled eyebrow. "You look great, Mike. What have you been doing? It's like you haven't aged a day."

"Me? What about you? You look fantastic."

"Yoga and chocolate ice cream." Her gaze turned back to the waiter as he returned with their glasses. "More yoga than ice cream, I'll add." She lifted her eyes as she picked up her glass. "*Sláinte.*"

"God bless you," he said, lifting his glass in salute to her beauty.

The liquor was strong but smooth, perfect for sipping. It had a comforting burn that ran down the tongue and warmed the hollow of his stomach. The way she looked at him burned in his cheeks. *God! What a rare woman.*

"So, what are you working on these days?" she asked, leaning one arm on the edge of the table as she ran her finger over the top of her glass. It hummed a B flat.

"I'm a radio-telescope engineer." He simplified his title. At this point, the fewer details he could provide the better, especially in public. One never knew who might be listening in. "I design radio telescopes."

"Are you working on SETI?" She lifted a curious brow in his direction.

"No," Michael said. "Not exactly."

"Not exactly?"

Michael could tell she wanted more details. He leaned in, mirroring her. "I could tell you ..." he hesitated, looking around. "But then ... I'd have to kill you."

A bemused expression passed over her as she shook her head and sipped her Scotch. "You wouldn't kill me," she said. "I'm too pretty to kill."

Michael couldn't believe the audacity. But then again, it was the truth. She was pretty; gorgeous even. "So what have you been working on?" He changed the subject.

"I'm on the Hubble project."

Michael felt a wave of professional jealousy wash over him. "Damn! Who's a guy gotta sleep with to get access to Hubble?"

"Me." Her eyes twinkled in the candlelight as she smirked over her glass of Scotch.

Was she offering? Michael wondered, sitting back in his chair, eyeing her over his glass.

The flesh was willing, that was for certain. Suddenly, he wasn't hungry ... not for food anyway.

～

"The Hubble telescope launched on April 24, 1990 from the space shuttle Discovery," Kitty said, as they walked the halls of NASA's Johnson Space Center the next morning. "It's 43.5 feet long and weighed about 24,000 pounds at launch. It remains in low earth orbit at an altitude of about 340 miles and completes an orbit every 95 minutes. It travels at a speed of approximately 27,300 kilometers per hour."

Kitty wasn't telling Michael anything he didn't already know. Her honey-sweet drawl made her a pleasure just to listen to. He could listen to her read the phonebook, just to be near her. She didn't seem to be in any hurry to leave his side either. "Did you know that the Hubble transmits about 150 gigabytes of raw data every week?"

"I didn't," Michael said. "What's its energy source?"

"Primarily, the sun. It has two 25-foot solar panels."

"Is it true that the Hubble has no thrusters?" Michael knew the answer, of course, but he couldn't help asking, just to hear her sweet Texas drawl. "How does it navigate? Surely it needs to make minor course corrections from time to time?"

"It uses Newton's Third Law." She grinned brightly. "It spins its gyroscopic wheels in the opposite direction. It's time consuming, but it works. It takes about fifteen minutes to turn ninety degrees."

"I thought Hubble was controlled at Goddard," Michael said.

"It is, primarily," Kitty said. "I have access remotely to support my human spaceflight research project. We're working on early plans for the next manned space missions."

"I thought the shuttle program had been shuttered." Michael scratched his chin.

"It's a partnership with private industry," she said, pausing at a scale model of the Challenger that sat in the middle of the wide tiled walkway in a glass case. "Commercial space flight will happen in our lifetime, you know."

"I've heard rumors," he said.

Kitty motioned for him to follow. "Come on. I know you're anxious to get your hands on it." She turned over her shoulder and winked overtly, and memories of the night before made his stomach flutter and the heat rise in his core. But thoughts of getting access to Hubble did almost the same thing.

~

KITTY'S OFFICE WAS ON THE THIRD FLOOR OF ONE OF THE TEN buildings on the campus. She had a corner office with large windows. The blinds were open, giving Michael his first view of the large hanger where several aircraft were parked. He was disappointed there were no shuttles or top-secret space craft where he could see them.

"Michael?"

He turned, drawn to her computer. She had four large screens that arched around her desk. She pulled up a chair for him before she took a seat. He tried not to imagine the strain her hips were putting on the seams of her pencil skirt as she booted up her computer, inserting her security card into a scanner on the hard drive. His eyes floated up to the gossamer sheer white blouse she had on. He could see the outline of her pushup bra against her skin. He shivered, remembering peeling her out of the black lace lingerie she'd had on the night before.

"It takes a moment for the system to boot up," she said, noticing she had a stack of messages on her desk. She picked them up and shuffled through the thin sheets of paper. "So tell me about your project? What are you working on?"

"My project?"

"The one you're here to renew your grant for," she said.

"Oh, well, it's not exciting. Not like the Hubble."

"What's up with that?" Kitty asked.

"I am working on developing a new type of radio telescope."

"A *new* type?"

"It's not much different than what we have now already," Michael said with a weak shrug.

"Well I'm sure it's nothing like Hubble." Kitty turned to her computer, changing the subject. "This is the greatest piece of modern technology known to man, in my humble opinion. So, what would you like to see first?" The images of a distant planet came into view. It looked as if it were just a few thousand miles away. The image had been enhanced to paint a colorful picture of a dulcet orb against a black backdrop. "Here's Uranus."

A titter of laughter escaped Michael's throat. "Seriously?"

"I always like to start with that one." Kitty chortled. "Get the joke out of the way."

"Too bad we can't see the Southern Cross from here," Michael said.

A bright smile crossed Kitty's sweet face. "Hubble isn't over Houston at the moment," she said, keying in some information. It took several minutes for the image to change and the aperture to bring the new image into focus. Her beautifully manicured fingernail pointed to the screen. "There's Alpha Centauri, Beta Centauri." Her finger scanned sideways across the screen. "See the dark area of space? That's the Coalsack."

"The Coalsack." He smirked devilishly.

Kitty laughed, as she considered him a moment. "It's like you're five," she said. "It's a dark nebula, and just above the dark spot, you'll see a bright star, that's Crux, the Southern Cross. But crux isn't just one star, it's five." She zoomed in.

"Alpha Crucis," Michael found the lowest of the stars in the pattern. "321 light years from Earth."

"And up from there is Gacrux, and then Delta Crucis and then across the way, Mimosa." She finished. She scrolled over and zoomed in on a fuzzy area just below Mimosa. "This is the Jewel Box. It's an open cluster of stars."

"Wow." Michael examined the images before sitting back. "I've never seen them with such … clarity."

"Beautiful, aren't they?"

"You could say that." Michael's voice went misty as he leaned in to study the image. *"Gods come, and gods go. Mortals flicker and flash and fade. Worlds don't last; and stars and galaxies are transient, fleeting things that twinkle like fireflies and vanish into cold and dust. But I can pretend…"*

"Neil Gaiman?" she asked.

"One of my favorite authors," Michael mused.

"Do the stars gaze back? Now, that's a question…" she quoted back. The reflection of the image from the Hubble telescope sparkled in Kitty's eyes. He couldn't resist and leaned in to kiss her.

"Yes, they do …" He sighed.

3

"Lauren?" Bahati found her by the pool at the hotel, overlooking Coronado Island. She had found a secluded area to nurse the baby; sitting with a dreamy expression on her face. She glanced up when her friend approached.

"Hi," she said. "Did Rowan tell you about our new assignment?"

"There's a problem," Bahati said nervously.

"Come sit with me." Lauren patted the empty chair beside her. "What's wrong?"

"Jean-René just got a call from his mother," she began. "His father is sick."

"Oh no," Lauren reached for her hand. "What's going on?" Lauren could tell it was bad, just by the grave expression on her friend's face.

"It's not good news."

"What? What is it?"

"He's been diagnosed with cancer. Stage 3 … pancreatic."

"Oh no." Lauren's hand went to her mouth. "I'm so sorry."

"He decided it's time to tell them about us," she said.

"Wait. What? His parents don't know you got married?"

She shrugged. "We eloped," she said. "They live half a world away, and it just never seemed like a good time to call."

Lauren nodded. "I know what that's like." She did, too. Hawaii had been a convenient way to avoid her family. Just like every other trip they'd taken. Every assignment gave her an excuse not to go back to Oklahoma. Now it appeared to be unavoidable.

"His dad is having surgery tomorrow, and his mother is beside herself." Bahati shifted in her chair. "He wants to go see them."

"So go," Lauren said.

"I hate to go off and leave you and Rowan," Bahati said.

"You don't have to worry about us." Lauren lifted her hand in a dismissive wave. "Rowan knows how to operate a camera. I don't have a lot of hope for finding much of interest. The sooner the genealogist realizes that, the sooner we can move on to Rowan's family tree."

"We were thinking that we'd look into Jean-René's family history while we're there. If you want us to," she said. "Maybe we could get some video for him. You said the Network meant to do an episode on each of us."

"Oh, Bahati! That's a great idea," Lauren said. "Yes. Please do. I'm confident your families are far more interesting than mine." Lauren felt the sting at the very thought of what they would face in their investigation.

"I'm sorry we won't be able to go with you to see George," Bahati said.

"We can manage," Lauren said. "You need to go take care of his father."

"We'll meet up with you when we get back," Bahati said. "Maybe a week or two at most."

"Take all the time you need."

"Have you called your brother yet?"

"No." Lauren shook her head, looking down. "George is

easy enough to talk too, but … it's true what they say about going back home."

"That's a load of BS and you know it," Bahati clipped. "You're being a coward, and that is not the Lauren Pierce I know. Where is your phone?"

"Inside." Lauren glanced towards their hotel room nearby.

"Give me Henry. You, go call your brother."

"I'll do it later." Lauren hesitated to hand over her son. "George is probably at work."

Bahati tilted her head and eyed her warily.

"I'll do it, I swear." Lauren assured her. "I promise."

"You know you have to reconcile with your family, don't you?"

"Why do I have to?" Lauren rolled her eyes, her dread finally coming to the surface.

"Because they are your family," Bahati said. "No one knows you better or loves you more than your family."

"Why does it have to be so hard?"

"Because it requires the truth … which is practically your middle name. You can't have reconciliation without truth." Bahati said. "What did your family do to you that you are still so angry about?"

Lauren paused for a long moment before she spoke. "If it were any one thing …" she sighed. "It would be easy enough to mend. But it … it was so many things … Michael … my mother." A lump formed in her throat and she could feel the heat rise from her core.

"I think you've held on to your anger so long, it's become familiar. You use it like a shield to keep those who have hurt you from doing it again. But you also use it to punish yourself."

"To punish myself?" Lauren gasped.

"We both know that it takes two to start a war," Bahati said, taking Lauren's hand. "You can't be wholly innocent in all this. But you are too hard on yourself. You can't forgive your own mistakes, much less your brother's … or your mother's."

"You don't know anything about my family," Lauren snapped, hotly.

"Maybe not," Bahati said. "But I know you. Your anger is a fire that only you continue to feed."

Lauren chewed on that thought for a moment. Bahati knew her better than anyone, except Rowan. She always called her out when she had a stubborn streak, kind of like now. "You're right," she said. "You're always right."

"Yes, I am," Bahati said. "And the sooner you get it over with, the better."

"Yeah," Lauren said, her anger abating. "But that doesn't make it any easier."

"Fixing something that is broken is never easy," Bahati said. "But if you ever want peace, you're going to have to work for it."

Lauren had just put Henry to bed. She brushed out her long hair, pausing when her phone rang. "I just sent you some documents I found at the History Center in Oklahoma City," Eleanor said when Lauren answered. She had met the genealogist the day before. Eleanor had already been dispatched by the Network and it surprised Lauren to hear from her so soon. "I found some census records and other documents."

Lauren had her iPad open in front of her and quickly went looking for the email, opening it as soon as she found it. "Wait, my father's name was listed as John Gray Wolf's Son?"

"Yes," she said. "You didn't know that?"

"No," Lauren said. "I've never heard that. I told you, I'm not close to my family, but I'll ask George," Lauren said. "He's the one family member I trust more than anyone else."

"Didn't you say you had six brothers?" Eleanor asked. "And there's just one you trust?"

"I know," Lauren said. "It's hard to explain the dynamics of our family. I can tell you, there's nothing exciting or interesting about any of our history."

"Why not? You're interesting. Why would your ancestors be any different?" Eleanor gushed.

"I'm not all that interesting." Lauren sat back in her chair.

"Why would you say that?"

Lauren shrugged. "I'm just a scientist, trying to make a living on a cable television show."

"Do you even hear yourself talk?" Lauren knew she liked the genealogist from the minute she'd met her. She was a real person, who called it like she saw it. She didn't sugar-coat anything. "You have a PhD in Biological Anthropology. You have been to a hundred countries, and to almost every continent on the planet. You have won ... how many Emmys? Along with at least a dozen other awards. You are married to Rowan Pierce. He's one of the hottest guys on television today, if you don't mind me saying. I don't think you got to be so interesting by sitting still, and I expect your ancestors won't be much different. Every generation has a story to tell, you just have to be willing to sit and listen. Did you call your brother?"

Lauren didn't answer immediately. "I left a message earlier." It wasn't true. She told Bahati she'd called, but in truth she just couldn't bring herself to do it.

"Lauren!" Eleanor scolded. "Did you try calling back? Aren't you planning to meet him in the next few days? He doesn't even know you're coming?"

"It just means he has less time to warn my mother."

"Look, Lauren," she said, softening her tone. "I'm not certain what else I can do here without more information. I want to help you, but if you won't help me, I'm afraid you're just wasting the Network's money."

Lauren pursed her lips, her mind running at a whirring

pace. Wasting the Network's money was the least of her worries, but she did recognize the investment they were putting into her work. The least she could do was meet them halfway. "Fine." She hung up the phone and stared at it for a long moment, before pulling up George's contact information. Without thinking, she hit the button before she could chicken out.

"Hello?" The deep voice immediately warmed her. He always made her feel safe and loved.

"George, it's Lauren. Did I catch you at a bad time?"

"Lauren? Lauren who?"

"Lauren Pierce, your sister."

"I've inhaled a lot of smoke over the years," he said. "I think I remember having a sister. She never calls me though."

"I'm sorry, George," Lauren said, recognizing her oldest brother's gentle teasing. "Please don't be mad."

"How long has it been?" She could hear him pouring liquid, she could easily assume it was coffee. Her suspicions were confirmed when she heard the spoon rattle on the rim as he stirred in sugar. If there was one thing she could count on in the universe, it was there would be a fresh pot of coffee at George's at all hours of the day. She couldn't remember seeing him drink much of anything else. As the local fire chief, he kept strange hours. All those long shifts fighting fires and assisting old ladies off the floor had to be fueled by Folger's.

"Too long." She took a deep breath. "An error I'm calling to rectify."

"It's good to hear from you. I've been thinking about you a lot lately."

"Oh?" She paused.

"Well you have been on the cover of TV Guide, National Geographic and just about every other travel magazine on the bookstands at the Barnes & Noble in Tulsa. They even got copies of Nat Geo at the Tribal Visitor's Center in Tahlequah.

I read your article on the Maya. You've become a good writer."

"Rowan wrote much of it." She shrugged, being honest with him.

"But you're the one who figured out how to read the new calendar," George said. "You're becoming pretty good at languages, I hear."

Lauren lifted a shoulder. She didn't want to be talking about herself right now. "I guess so."

"So what are you doing now?" he asked. She could hear the leg of his chair grate against the hardwood floor in his kitchen. They'd grown up in the same house he still lived in, and she knew that sound well. It resonated through the house. She had flashbacks of all the kids gathering around the table, her mom plopping down a pan of *Kraft Macaroni & Cheese Dinner*, a cigarette hanging from her mouth, the smell of gin on her breath. George had always been in charge of serving up the food. She would hand him her plate first, and he always gave her a decent share. By the time he served himself there was little left. "Lauren?"

"Oh." She came out of the memory. "The Network is hell-bent on doing an episode about our family history. Rowan and I are going to be in Oklahoma. I wanted to see if you could help me find out more about our ancestors. At least two or three generations back. Can you think of anyone in our line who might have been the least bit interesting?"

"Besides you?" he asked. "And besides Michael?"

"Definitely not me or Michael," she clipped. "You don't have to answer that now. We can talk about it when we stop by."

"How long will you be here?" he asked. "I've got room if you want to stay a while."

"Maybe just a day or two, but you have to promise me … you can't tell anyone I'm going to be there … especially not our mother."

"I won't tell her your coming, if that's what you want, Lauren."

"Cross your heart and hope to die, George." Lauren insisted, just as she had when she was little. "Promise me."

"I cross my heart," he said.

After a long moment of hesitation, she spoke. "I'll text you the details as soon as I know everything."

"It'll be good to see you," he said. "I've missed you."

"I've missed you, too." Lauren found truth in her words. "Just don't go to any trouble, okay? I don't care if the house is clean or the leaves are raked, you know."

"I know," he said. "Having you home is no trouble. I've been waiting a long time for this."

Lauren pursed her lips and swallowed the lump in her throat. "I'll text you."

"See you soon," he said. "I love you."

Lauren's heart lifted.

"I love you, too." She hung up quickly. She took a deep breath as she ran a hand down her face, then texted Eleanor back. *Called my brother. Going to see him in Tahlequah.*

Good. Look over those documents I sent. She texted back a few moments later. *There are a few other things I found in the newspaper and court records. Show him. Maybe he'll have some answers to the questions I included.*

Lauren replied with a curt, *OK.*

Let me know what else you find. Call if there's anything I can help with.

Thanks. Lauren typed back and laid her phone on the table beside her iPad. She wanted to panic. She hadn't seen George but a handful of times since she left home for college. Their parting had been bittersweet. She'd left with a wave and a promise to see him soon … but he was right, it had been too long.

Rowan came in from the bedroom. He'd gone to run after dinner and had showered and put on his pajamas. She could smell his shampoo as he passed, and paused to peer into the travel crib the hotel had loaned them for the baby. He smiled then came over and sat down on the sofa beside her. She leaned against him; his hair still damp. He reached over and took up his iPad. "Let's see when the first flight to Oklahoma City is." He opened his favorite travel app.

"Not Oklahoma City." Lauren shook her head. "Tulsa. It's closer to Tahlequah."

"Oh, right," he said. "Silly me."

He surfed the web a few minutes. "It'd be a lot cheaper if you could teleport us."

She cast shade in his direction with her dark eyes. "Rowan…"

"I'm just kidding." He leaned against her. "But I won't be happy 'til you figure out what's going on and can explain it to me."

"But what if I never figure it out?" She rested her head on his shoulder, snaking her hand around his bicep.

"Knowing you, you'll figure it out."

They sat in comfortable silence for a long while, a sense of peace building between them as he rested his head on hers and sighed deeply. He finally lifted his head and returned to his search for flights to Tulsa.

"Before our wedding, when was the last time you saw your sister?" Lauren asked abruptly.

He paused to think. "Just after I came back from Afghanistan," he said. "She came home for my Dad's 60th birthday. The VFW hosted a huge soiree in his honor." Lauren sighed heavily, leaning against him. She said nothing. "Worried about seeing George?"

She shook her head. "George, no. We're good. He gave me a hard time when I talked to him and it occurred to me…" She hesitated. "If Michael had said the exact same words in the exact same tone, I'd have flown off the handle.

But it didn't bother me that much when George did it. Why is that?"

"I don't know," Rowan said. "I only have one sibling. It's never been an issue."

Lauren sighed again. "George always made my life easier. He always stuck up for me. He never dressed me down or gave me a hard time that I didn't deserve. I always knew where I stood with him. With Michael though; he always tried to pick fights. He always tried to one up me in everything. I could never win with him."

"I can see why that would be a problem," Rowan said, putting an arm around her, pulling her close to him. "Looks like there's a flight out tomorrow at 10:09 ..." he said.

"So soon?" Lauren furrowed her brow.

"What else are we going to do on a Thursday?"

"Sleep in? Take Henry to the zoo? See our friends? Get over jet lag? Raid the equipment locker at the Network? If you're going to be doing the photography, we'll need a couple of good cameras."

"Are you saying I'm a bad photographer?" He feigned being affronted.

"No," she said. "That wasn't at all what I meant."

"Well, you do have a valid point," Rowan said, updating his flight search. "Looks like there's a flight out Saturday morning at 7:30. Maybe Henry will nap on the plane. I'll book it and a rental car, and we can be to Tahlequah by supper time."

"Fine." Lauren yawned. "I'm going to bed."

"I'll be there as soon as I get the tickets and rental car taken care of," he said, kissing her head. "But you don't have to wait up for me."

"I'm not sure I could if I wanted to."

~

As they drove from the airport in Tulsa towards her childhood home in Eastern Oklahoma, Lauren's mind lingered on those last fleeting moments of peace in the face of the turmoil ahead of her.

"Did you talk to George?"

"I texted him yesterday," she said. "He said to call him when we got to Tahlequah and he'd meet us at his house."

"Is he not working today?"

"One of the benefits of being the fire chief ..." Lauren shrugged. "He can take off whenever he wants, as long as there isn't a fire to fight."

"That is convenient," Rowan said. "Should we stop and pick up dinner?"

"I think he'd be offended," Lauren said. "He's a good cook and he likes doing it."

"Will you want to visit with any of ... the rest of your family ... while we're here?" Rowan asked, hesitation in his voice.

"I sure don't want to talk to my mother, if that's what you're implying."

"And George knows this?"

"He's been sworn to secrecy. No one will even know I'm here."

"That's good," Rowan said.

Rowan squinted as they turned into the sun. "I can't see why I always thought Oklahoma was flat."

"Compared to the Rockies, it is," she said. Sunlight dappled through the flaming red maples, yellow elms and orange oak trees that lined the two-lane state highway. "These are ancient mountains, older than the Rockies, but no, they're not as flat as central and western Oklahoma. This area is known as the Cookson Hills." Rowan continued driving along the edge of the Fort Gibson Lake, out past Tahlequah to her family's land where her brother George still lived.

"Did you know Pretty Boy Floyd grew up around here?"

Rowan turned and looked at her sharply. "What?"

"Yeah."

"The famous bank robber?"

"Rumor has it, there are some of his treasures still hidden out there somewhere," she said. "Maybe farther south near Robber's Cave."

"And we've never done an episode here why?"

"Too close to home." Lauren turned and looked away. "But there's a lot of neat things in Eastern Oklahoma ... the Spiro Mounds, the Heavener Runestone ... skunk ape ..."

"Bigfoot? In Oklahoma?"

"Yeah." Lauren nodded. "There's a Bigfoot Festival every year down in Honobia."

"And we've never been?"

"We've always been on the wrong side of the planet." Lauren shrugged. "I can put it on our list of things to do, if we ever go back to monster hunting."

"Why wouldn't we go back to monster hunting?" Rowan asked.

Lauren didn't answer. She stuck out her hand, gesturing to the break in the trees ahead. "That's the turn." Lauren directed him to take a right onto the narrow road between the stand of golden and orange tinged poplar trees.

"How did you see that?"

"There's a reflector on that tree back there," she said. "George put it there when I was learning to drive, so I could find it."

Rowan turned and ducked, as if that would allow the vehicle to clear the canopy of trees. "How long has it been since you were here?"

"It was 1999," Lauren said. "May 3, 1999."

"How do you remember that?"

"It was the day the big F5 hit in Oklahoma City," she said. "There were over 100 tornados spawned up from that storm, all across the state and into Arkansas and Missouri."

"Any of them get close?" Rowan asked as they rounded the narrow bend. His question was immediately answered. The trees across the valley were broken off at the tops, some were dead, and if it weren't for the few that still bore leaves, you might have thought the twisters had just blown through a few years before ... not decades ago.

"I've never been more scared in my life," Lauren said. "Well, I have since then, but ..." Her voice trailed off as her eyes went to the horizon. They'd been scared plenty over the last year or two.

"I always thought it'd be fun to go storm chasing," Rowan said.

"It's all fun and games until the storm starts chasing you." Lauren shivered, glancing over her shoulder at Henry. The baby yawned and stretched, just waking up from his nap as the car slowed.

"Looks like word got out," Rowan said.

Lauren turned. "What the ...?" Cars lined the road, leaving no room to pull through. He drove up behind the last car and put the SUV in park.

A string of expletives, not any of them in English, rose from the back of Lauren's throat as her heart skipped in her chest. *Was her mother there? God, please no.* "Oh, Christ." Lauren groaned aloud as she found her older brother in the crowd assembled on the lawn.

A giant hand-painted sign sprawled across the yard, tied between two trees: "WELCOME HOME, LAUREN!"

"So much for keeping it on the down low," Rowan said.

Lauren felt her heart race. Her face flamed red. She reached for the door handle. "I'm going to kill George."

4

"See." George turned to his younger brothers. "I told you she would come."

"Well I'll be damned." Michael rose stiffly from his lawn chair. "Maybe I should make myself scarce before she bolts and runs."

David nodded. "That might be best." He watched as she stormed towards the house. "She looks pissed."

"George, you might wanna run too." Michael limped away from the family gathering and went to find a place to hide.

LAUREN RECOGNIZED FEW OF THE PEOPLE IN THE CROWD; A crowd that filled her brother's front yard. Lawn chairs circled the lawn. A group hovered around the giant barbecue grill, partially hidden in a cloud of smoke. Normally, this time of year marked the traditional fall harvest celebrations. Her homecoming gave them an excuse to extend the festivities. The aroma of roasting meat and corn perfumed the air as

Lauren stormed towards the house. Rowan jogged a pace behind, Henry on his hip.

"Lauren! You're home!" George opened his big arms wide, not waiting for her to lean in.

"I thought you were going to keep it a secret," she grumbled as George embraced her tightly. She melted into him, her anger abating, but not completely.

"You said not to tell Mom," he said, not letting her go. "I didn't tell Mom."

Rowan stopped, taken aback by the giant. Henry turned away and wrapped his arms around his father's neck, whimpering. The man stood almost a foot taller than Lauren's husband, who found himself looking up at his brother-in-law. "You must be Rowan," the giant said, a deep timber in his voice, but a twinkle in his eye.

"You must be George." Rowan all but panicked as the man raised an arm, and Rowan steeled himself for a blow that didn't come. Instead, George pulled him into his arms and gave him a manly, but genuine, hug. Henry fussed, and Lauren moved in to rescue him.

"Sorry I missed the wedding," he said in a deep voice. "It's hard to get away during wildfire season. That and the Tribe's Hazard Mitigation Plan was overdue."

"I totally understand," Rowan said, when the giant released him. He heaved a huge sigh of relief as he stepped back, feeling lucky to be alive. "Lauren didn't mention she was related to giants."

"Wanna guess what my nickname was when I played football?" George grinned impishly. His round face was cut with dimples even deeper than Rowan's.

"Yes, I do. I really do. Was it *Shorty*? Tell me it was *Shorty*."

George laughed. "That's a good one. No, man. They called me *Sasquatch*." He grinned, holding up a sandaled foot. "Size 17 ½. Extra wide." Rowan looked at Lauren who just lifted her shoulders and shook her head. George let out a sudden whistle that startled the baby, but if he wanted to cry, he didn't. Instead he just stuck out his lower lip. "This must be Henry? Right?" He took the baby and held him up inspecting him. "Sturdy kid. Like his dad." He put Henry up over his shoulder and turned, waving everyone over. "Our baby sister has come home!" Cheers echoed above his thundering voice. "This is our nephew, Henry!" He turned the baby around so the copper-haired child could see his relatives. "And our brother, Rowan!"

Cheers continued as Henry finally burst out bawling, his face turning red as crocodile tears welled up in his eyes. He wasn't used to so much noise, and it frightened him to see so many people all at once. Lauren pursed her lips, blushing but stepped forward and took Henry from his uncle.

He seemed happy once he had a fist full of Lauren's long hair and wrapped himself around her neck. It was a good thing. It took nearly an hour for Lauren to go around and say hello to everyone, and introduce Rowan to all her cousins, nieces, nephews, aunts, uncles, and various relations.

Once she got a chance to sit down under a shade tree, she set to nursing Henry, who'd grown fussy and wasn't happy about his supper being late. Someone brought Lauren a red Solo cup of iced tea, and all the women circled around her to visit as she fed the baby. The men returned to the grill and the coolers. She scanned the crowd as her brother took Rowan to join the men and was relieved that her mother was nowhere to be seen.

~

GEORGE THREW AN ARM AROUND ROWAN. "HOW DO YOU LIKE your venison?" he asked as they approached the grill.

"What? No rattlesnake?" Rowan smirked.

George grimaced at him for a moment. "Dude, it's not rattlesnake season." He snarked.

Rowan started hemming and hawing, realizing he'd stuck his foot in his mouth. George's glare turned to a grin. "Haha! I was just kidding you, brother. If you want rattlesnake, I think I got a couple in the freezer."

Rowan let out a breath of relief. "I don't even like rattlesnake."

"Are you sure?" One of Lauren's other brothers handed Rowan a beer. "You never had it how George makes it."

"I have eaten almost every kind of snake you could imagine, cooked a dozen different ways ... I just can't seem to get a taste for it."

"Seriously, bro?"

Rowan nodded. "Yeah," he said as he inspected the beer. Rowan thought he needed something stronger. Still, he tipped back the bottle and the cool bitter liquid slid down his throat without effort, providing some measure of comfort.

"What's the craziest thing you ever ate?"

Rowan had to think about that for a moment. "I've eaten bugs, snails, frogs, worms, grubs, you name it."

"You still didn't tell me how you take your venison." George beamed, seemingly impressed with his brother-in-law.

"Anyway I can get it," Rowan retorted, glad grubs weren't on the menu.

"I guess if our sister had to marry a white man, this one will do." Rowan's brow lifted as he forced a smile.

George glanced down at him and grinned. "You know I'm kidding you? Right, bro?"

"Sure." He wasn't, but he didn't want to let on. No one had ever given him any kind of a hassle for being an Anglo and he wasn't quite sure how to take it.

George's smile faded. "I didn't mean to offend you," he said, lowering his tone. "I was just joking around."

"I didn't take any offense." Rowan hadn't, either. "I just realized ... I never thought of Lauren and I as being any different ..."

"You're not," George said. "And that's how it should be. The way I see it, you're family and that makes us the same." He lowered his voice again. "Seriously. I am sorry."

"Please …" Rowan's smile returned. "No apology needed."

He and George made peace over venison steaks, roasted corn, squash, and ice-cold beer.

～

LAUREN SAW THE DARK SHADOW SLINKING IN THE CROWD AS someone handed her a plate and her cousin took Henry. All the kids gathered around with their plates of hot dogs, hamburgers, and everything that went with it. Lauren was pleased to find a lean venison strip, an ear of corn and potato salad on her plate. She hadn't eaten much all day and she was ravenous but seeing Michael lurking in the crowd made her stomach turn sour. She considered him for a moment and decided he wasn't worth missing out on a good meal for. She couldn't afford to miss many meals. Clearly the family had been prosperous, and the hunting had been good last year.

"How's your steak, Aunt Lauren?" One of George's daughters came over and sat down beside her.

Lauren chewed analyzing the morsel. "It's terrific," she said. "Perfectly cooked. Well-seasoned. Tender. Lean. All my favorite things."

"I shot it with my bow," she said. "My first buck."

"How old are you?" Lauren asked.

"Sixteen," she said. "Dad's been taking me hunting since I was little, but I hadn't gotten a buck 'til this year."

Lauren's gaze went to Michael. She noticed for the first time that he walked with a limp as he seemed to circle the family gathering, staying just outside of the circle, like a young wolf who had been exiled by the pack. He was a lone wolf; always had been. He'd never been one to participate in family gatherings. He was usually too busy hanging out with his friends. As the star of the football team, he had been popular; unlike his brainy little sister. While Michael had been a jock, he wasn't a dumb one. Besides making All-State and being a first round draft pick at OU, he carried a 4.0 GPA; made the honor roll, and National Honors Society.

Lauren had earned every academic accolade available and had since elementary school. There had been a time where he would help her with her homework, but he made fun of her when she struggled with math and she stopped going to him for help. By the time she went to high school, he was already off making a name for himself in the field of astrophysics and radio telescopy. Still, his legacy haunted her. Teachers judged her based on the Michael-Grayson-Scale of intellect, dedication, and drive. Even the typing teacher called her out in 8th grade because she didn't type as fast as her brother and she made twice as many errors.

Nothing she did had ever been good enough for any of the teachers who'd had Michael before her. Fortunately, the new biology and history teachers had never met Michael Grayson, and both took her under their wings, lauding her as the brightest student in the history of Tahlequah High School.

The first bragging right she earned — an accolade which outshone her brother—was scoring higher on the SAT and the ACT than Michael had. While she didn't make a perfect score, she beat him by several hundred points on the SAT, and several points on the ACT. Before she knew it, she had offers coming in from schools all over the country. It had been a toss-up which degree plan she would pursue; biology or history. Biological anthropology turned out to be the best of both worlds.

His dark eyes brought her from her thoughts as their eyes met. She stared him down. Without words, she laid out her challenge, not blinking; not turning away from his gaze.

Words at twenty paces. Would he wait 'til high noon, or would he come gunning for her sooner?

"Aunt Lauren?" She turned back to the girl beside her. "Did you ever go hunting with my dad?" She realized the child had to repeat the question.

"Oh yeah," Lauren said. "All the time." Her eye went to where Michael had stood, but he was no longer there.

"So, how many kids do you have?" Rowan asked, taking a bite of his venison steak, surprised to find it so tender.

"I have five," he said. "Jeff is twenty, Jack is eighteen, Jenny is sixteen, Jered is fourteen, and Jessica is twelve."

"And there are six boys and Lauren, right?"

"There are only five of us now," one of her brothers said. "We lost Kenneth in Afghanistan."

"When did that happen?"

"February 27, 1991," George said. "Kenneth had been in the 4th Battalion, 229th Advanced Attack Helicopter Regiment. His unit had just successfully completed the first night attack against enemy formations. His chopper returned from one run, then refueled and reattacked across the enemy lines. That's when his bird took hostile fire."

"That was the Flying Tigers," Rowan said. "Did he fly the Blackhawks?"

"How'd you know?"

"I was deployed over there for a couple of tours," Rowan said. "Medic."

"Thank you for your service," a chorus of voices said with polite respect.

"Thank you for your support," Rowan replied, his hand going to his heart in true gratitude. "So let me see if I have you all straight." Rowan pointed to each of the men that had been introduced to him as Lauren's brothers. "David, Bryce,

Andrew ... and George." He was the easy one to spot, being so tall. The others weren't little by any means, but George stood out.

"Pretty good. Most people mix me and Michael up," David said. "We're twins you know."

"Twins?" If Lauren had mentioned her siblings included a set of twins, he couldn't recall. He'd been looking for someone he might be able to pick out as her tormenting brother, but he still hadn't been introduced to him, if he were even here.

"They run in our family," one of the uncles said. "I had a twin, and my sisters were twins."

"What about you, Rowan?"

"No twins in my family, at least not that I know," Rowan said. "I have a sister though."

"Oh yeah? Older or younger?"

"Older," he said. "Cassandra is a fitness model and actress."

He had everyone's attention at that point. "Oh yeah?" David lifted a brow.

"She's also a Marine and if you mess with her, she will kick your butt," Rowan said. "If she doesn't, I will." It was said in jest, but the look on everyone's face suggested they believed him. Rowan grinned, waggling his eyebrows as he returned his attention to his dinner.

A man approached and sat down across from him, scowling with the same almond-shaped dark eyes that smiled at him from across the dinner table every night. The family resemblance was stronger between Michael and Lauren than any of the other brothers. Rowan recognized Lauren's antagonist immediately. He resembled David, but his hair had been chopped off even with his strong chin. He had a deep cut healing on his cheek; surgical tape held the flesh of his eyebrow together. He had raccoon-bruises at the inside corners of his eyes; evidence of a recently broken nose.

"I've been trying to reach my sister for a couple of weeks,"

Michael said curtly. "Have you guys been in the witness protection program or something?"

Rowan's brow arched. "No, we live in Hawaii. We just came back to the mainland for work."

"I tried calling the studio, but no one would tell me anything," Michael said. Rowan had given strong orders that they weren't to be bothered during their leave. Lauren didn't need her phone going off at all hours of the night and day with requests for interviews, or queries for speaking engagements.

"Sorry," Rowan said. "We were on sabbatical."

"I saw your show on Bigfoot."

Rowan hesitated. "What'd you think?"

"You didn't do it right," Michael said flatly.

There it was. That's the kind of comment that would set his wife on edge and his own flesh bristled on her behalf. "Do what right?" He kept his voice neutral.

"You can't catch Bigfoot … or any other wild animal … with all those people," he said. "Besides, Bigfoot's not even real."

Everyone laughed, but Rowan managed only a weak chuckle. "I'll be sure to tell him that next time we see him," he retorted. While he still couldn't explain everything that had happened in Washington State, Lauren's bond with Tsul'Kalu was real enough to her, and he'd come to accept it. It occurred to him at that moment that her recent *episodes* might be related. He hadn't considered that before and wondered if she had. "I'm sure he'll be relieved to know he's just a myth." Rowan's own sarcasm was overt, and he noticed the darting glances between the other men. Michael just scowled, holding his gaze with his angry dark eyes. "So I hear you work for NASA, huh?"

"I do contract work for them. I'm working on radio tele-scopes," he said, a wide grin spread across his copper face.

"Did Lauren tell you; I recently finished my second PhD in physics?"

"A second one? No, she didn't mention that."

"She'd have known if she'd given me her phone number." His tone suggested he was trying to be playful, but Rowan could see what Lauren meant now. His teasing wasn't light-hearted at all. "I need to talk to her."

Rowan scanned the crowd for her. "She's right there," he said. "But I should warn you, she's been traveling all day, and that's the first meal she's had since breakfast. If I were you, I'd wait 'til she wasn't tired or hungry."

"Noted." Michael got up and walked away, tossing his empty plate in the trash can that sat near the table where the food had been served.

Rowan saw Lauren glaring at her brother as he passed. She glanced back at Rowan. She shook her head, before returning her attention to the conversation around her.

5

Michael made his bed on the pull-out sofa at his brother's house. David's house wasn't as big as George's, but his wife was a gracious hostess, and a decent cook. She brought him extra blankets and pillows, and a fresh towel in case he got up and wanted a shower before she came down to make breakfast.

"You look like you're still sore," she observed as David came in. "Do you need some aspirin?"

"I got some muscle relaxers when they discharged me from the hospital," he said. "I intend to take one before I go to bed."

"You sure you're okay?" David asked. "How long has it been since the crash? A week?"

"Not quite," he said. "I'm fine. It's just been an awfully long day."

"Lauren didn't punch you in the face," David said smugly. "I was ready in case she didn't recognize I wasn't you."

"I half expected that husband of hers to take a swing at me," Michael grumbled.

"What? He seems like a pretty decent guy," David said. "I don't think he'd have slugged you."

"I don't think he would have, but I'm not so sure he didn't want too." Michael sat down on the edge of the bed, trying to rub the crick out of his stiff neck. "But Lauren still didn't come over to talk to me, even after I told him I wanted to speak with her."

"Why didn't you just go talk to her?" David sat down across from him. "She's your sister."

Michael shrugged, wincing at the effort. "I just got a bad vibe off of her. She acts like she's mad at me. She's always acted like she was mad at me."

"Maybe if you didn't give her such a hard time …"

"Pfff!" The sound came from between Michael's teeth. "I'm just kidding around, she knows that."

David stood, eyeing his twin brother. "Are you sure about that?"

Michael looked up at him, watching as David left him with something to think about. After a long moment, he reached for the pain pills in his suitcase and took two. He knew one wouldn't be enough to ease the ache in his back and body; nothing could ease the ache in his heart. He hoped two would be strong enough to still his racing thoughts.

As he bedded down for the night and flipped off the lamp by the sofa, he lay staring at the ceiling, illuminated by the yard lamp outside that cast a blue-white glow through the window. He thought about his sister and that look on her face as she eyed him from across the yard.

They hadn't been close since they were kids. He always tried to lighten the mood between them with some friendly banter, but she never took things the way he intended. He'd sent her a card for her college graduation — working at Goddard he hadn't been able to come home for the celebration. Two weeks later it came back, marked *Return to Sender* with no other message. The $100 gift card was still inside. The birthday card he sent her that year came back the same way.

He tried again the following year and wasn't surprised when the envelope returned.

He tried calling. He tried emailing. He even drove up to CalTech to see her, but the bursar's office wouldn't give him any information about how to find her. He even went to the Dean of the Department with no better luck. He sat outside the library on a Friday night, knowing his studious sister was more likely to go there than to a party.

He didn't get an invitation to her wedding. Their mother didn't get one either, but she went anyway, getting all the details from George. No one had even bothered to call him and tell him she was getting married. He'd heard about it on the entertainment news. It stung that he knew more about her from her stupid television show.

"YOU HAVE DONE NOTHING TO EARN YOUR SISTER'S LOYALTY. You know that right?" The voice came to him as he was drifting off to sleep. He startled, bolting upright in bed; except he wasn't in bed. He found himself standing barefoot at a clearing in the river bottom outside George's house. He'd spent most of his childhood running up and down this path through the river, beneath the spreading sycamores, weeping willows, and pin oaks.

He knew the voice, but that wasn't what left him feeling so disconcerted. This was not the first time he'd been taken from his bed in the night. "What did I do to piss her off?" He turned, finding an old man sitting on a fallen sycamore that lay across the stream. He sat cross-legged with his long white hair loose around his shoulders.

"You must ask her," he said. "It is not wise to allow old wounds to fester. While the pain started years ago, she has lived with it so long that she has accepted it; it has become a part of her."

"That's pretty bold, coming from you," Michael said sourly. "You left our mother … you left us. You're one to talk about mending old wounds."

His father considered him for a long while. "Your words are fair, but we each have our own wounds to mend. I have made my mistakes. In my time, I will have to make amends for them. But I recognized that I had done more damage by walking into someone's life, and making them happy."

Michael moved, noticing the moonlight as a cloud passed. It made the old man's hair almost glow. "Wait … am I … dreaming?" He realized. "Are you the one who's been doing this to me? What's going on?"

"When you are dreaming with a broken heart," the old man said. "The psyche will create a dialogue to allow your mind to process what the heart cannot."

"So I am dreaming?" Michael asked. "Have been dreaming all these past few months."

"The car wreck was real," the man smirked. "But things are not as they seem. You have come to a place you needed to be. The journey has not been easy, but you have a task before you. You must make peace with your sister. You will need her to walk at your side. You know this. That is why you have come home."

"Yeah, well, she won't even talk to me," Michael snarled, looking away. His brow knitted as he tried to contemplate his father's words and their meaning. He knew this was not actually his father. This was a dream-version of the man who had left him when he was just a boy.

"All the more reason for you to listen," John Grayson said. "Time heals many wounds, but not all. Others require tending, and careful words."

"You're talking in riddles, Dad."

His father stood, sliding down the trunk of the tree. Michael realized his feet were bare too. He turned, as if to go, but he stopped and looked back at his son. "Do your best not to create new wounds on old scars," he said. "You need her … as much as she needs you."

~

LAUREN WAS SITTING AT THE KITCHEN TABLE LATE THE following morning, eating a bowl of Cheerios, sipping her coffee, and reading the newspaper. When the front door opened, her head lifted. She froze when her brother walked into the kitchen. Her spoon slipped from her fingers and clattered in the bowl, sloshing milk all over the Cherokee Phoenix.

"Surprise." Michael snarked, strolling into the kitchen, looking smug. He'd probably come to pick a fight, and she was ready for it. She had been surprised he hadn't done it the night before.

"What are you doing here?" she snarled, picking up her spoon, saving a few beached Cheerios from the table. She returned her attention to the newspaper that was now soaked. The letters printed in the Cherokee syllabary were still legible.

"You didn't even come over and say hi to me last night." Michael looked at her stone-faced, taking a coffee cup from the pantry, filling it.

"Not like there was a force field between us, you know," she said. "You could just have easily come to me." But he hadn't.

Michael sat down across from her and watched her as she ate, not saying a word. Lauren was content to ignore him. Finally, he picked up his cup and took a sip. "Congratulations on your Emmy," he said. "Too bad you didn't find Bigfoot."

"Uh huh." Lauren wanted to throat-punch him, then pin him to the floor and give him a piece of her mind. It looked like someone had already tried.

"I met your husband last night." He continued. "Nice enough fellow, I suppose."

Lauren glared at him from beneath the curtain of her freshly washed hair.

"What do you want, Michael?" Lauren pushed her bowl away and leaned back in her chair. Her hands went to fists as they remained on the table.

"Wow," Michael said. "I didn't expect a hostile reception." A titter of laughter came from his chest. "I haven't seen you in what? Fifteen years? I thought maybe we could have a civil conversation like adults."

"We couldn't do it when we were kids," Lauren stated flatly. "What's changed in the last fifteen years?" He moved as if to speak. "I'll tell you." She cut him off. "Nothing. You've never had a kind thing to say to me my whole entire life."

"Hold on now." He put up his hands defensively. He started to feed on her anger, but the memory of last night's dreams made him hesitate. He softened. "Why so angry, Lauren? You know I like to tease you a little. That's what big brother's do."

"Teasing? You call it teasing? Nothing I did was ever good enough for you and I doubt it ever will be. I'm too old and too tired to give a flying rip about trying to one-up you or to worry about what you can or can't do better than me. So if you've come to gloat or brag, you can shove it where the sun doesn't shine, for all I care." She rose from her chair, taking her bowl to the sink. Storming out of the kitchen with her coffee cup, she went to find someplace else to drink it. She left her brother in the wake of her anger.

Rowan passed her in the hall, and she pushed passed him without a word. Coffee sloshed from her cup, but she seemed oblivious. He turned as if to follow her, but she held up a finger of caution and disappeared out the back door.

~

Rowan stood with his mouth open wondering what had just happened. When he walked into the kitchen, he knew.

"She's still mad at me," Michael said to him.

"Man, I don't know what you did to piss her off, but ... you should have sent flowers or chocolate or at least a freaking Hallmark card." Rowan stood befuddled.

Michael chortled. "Every card I sent her came back," he said. "She's been mad at me since she was six." He'd had a couple of hours, unable to sleep after waking from his odd dreams, to analyze their relationship and figure out where he'd gone wrong with her. Michael rested his head on his fist and leaned on the table, gazing into his coffee.

"What did you do to her?" Rowan poured coffee into his own cup and sat down across from him.

"I shot her in the ass with an arrow." Michael pursed his lips. Rowan noticed a bruise on the side of his face he hadn't seen the night before. "She's never forgiven me."

Rowan's brow reached for his hairline. "What the literal hell?" Rowan was affronted on her behalf.

"I didn't do it on purpose," Michael rejoined. "But you'll never convince her of that."

"All right." Rowan's mind was going a thousand miles an hour. "This is a story I have to hear. Spill it."

Michael looked perplexed. "She never told you? I mean, didn't it at least leave a scar?"

"No" Rowan frowned. "And if it did, I never noticed."

"How long did you say you've been together?"

"A long time."

Michael eyed him cautiously. "Okay, I'll tell you, but you have to swear ..."

"Cross my heart." Rowan's finger traced the cross over his chest, urging him. "Spill it."

"She'll kill us both." Lauren's brother shrugged.

"You first," Rowan assured.

"Probably true," Michael said after a moment's reflection.

"Fine." Her brother stood and went to the coffee pot, refilling his cup. He came back over and sat down. "We were all down at the river bottom late one summer evening. We'd been teaching one of George's hounds how to track raccoons. Lauren's job was to drag a coonskin along the ground, over tree stumps and up tree trunks." He sat back in his chair and gazed into his cup. "It was getting close to dusk and we were about to head back when the dogs caught the scent of a raccoon and went tearing through the woods after it. We all followed suit, but Lauren was so little, she had a hard time keeping up and she got lost. Well, it gets dark extremely fast in the river bottoms and we couldn't find her. If she was crying, the dogs bawling must have drowned it out. Hounds do that when they've treed a raccoon, you understand?"

"I saw *Where the Red Fern Grows*," Rowan said, as if that were sufficient.

"Well, I'd been telling her about this one raccoon I was going to catch. I don't think she realized I meant to kill it. I told her I was going to cut off its tail and make me a Daniel Boone hat out of it. But that dang monster had been getting into our corn crib and was eating up all our feed. She begged me not to. She tried to convince me it wasn't just any raccoon, that it was a powerful wizard."

"A wizard?"

"Not just any wizard, but a shape shifter. We have a lot of legends about wizards." Michael took a deep breath. "When the dogs found the raccoon and ran it up in a tree it was already dark, but I thought I had a good shot at it, so I drew my bow back and launched my arrow. I heard Lauren yelling from the darkness not to shoot, but ... it was too late. But what fell out of the tree wasn't a raccoon, it was Lauren with that ratty old coonskin. She had an arrow through her right butt cheek. She landed so hard she hit her head and it knocked her out cold."

"Oh my God." Rowan's face wrinkled in horror.

"I thought I'd killed her. But George gathered her up and carried her to our Aunt Mary's house. She's a healer, you know."

"I didn't," Rowan said.

"Uncle and George both chewed me out for shooting her, but I swear to God, the only thing I saw in that tree was that old raccoon. It was a big one!"

Rowan realized Lauren was leaning on the doorway at the entry of the kitchen, her arms folded over her chest and a scowl creased into her face. "Fortunately, Lauren remained unconscious through all of it."

"You *shot* me." Lauren snarled from the doorway. Her face reddened and her eyes tinged a shade lighter.

"I didn't mean to!" Michael defended. "It was an accident."

"It took all the rest of the summer before I could sit down right," she grimaced.

"I said I was sorry." Michael turned in his chair, pleading. "I wasn't trying to shoot *you*."

"You shouldn't be trying to shoot anyone, or anything," Lauren said. "That raccoon didn't do anything to you."

"I can't believe you're still mad about all that." He hung his head, shaking it.

"You. Shot. Me." Lauren punctuated each word. She came over and sat down next to Rowan, her eyes throwing daggers in Michael's direction. "What happened to your face, anyway?" It was the first time she'd acknowledged the cuts and bruises.

"Car wreck," he said. "I got t-boned by a dump truck." He lowered his eyes and gazed at the table in front of him.

"You cut your hair," she said, softening.

"I don't want to talk about my hair," Michael said. A dark cloud came over him, and Lauren wanted to feel sorry for him. She knew what it meant. It was customary for them to only cut their hair when someone died … someone close.

"Fine." Lauren's tone softened, but she wasn't ready to let him off the hook. "But I have plenty more reasons to be mad at you, and you know it."

Henry cried from the other room where he'd been sleeping, and Rowan rose to go check on him. Lauren ignored him. He could have flown to the moon and she wouldn't have missed him. Her attention was entirely on her brother.

Michael looked hurt. "I'm your brother. Like it or not, we're family."

"Just because we're related doesn't mean I have to like it," Lauren snarled under her breath. "It's all the more reason for me to be angry at you." She crossed her arms and sat back in the chair, scowling. "None of my other brothers put superglue in my hair or hid my kitten in the microwave." Michael blanched at the memory. "You were the one who told Adam Bonebrake that I liked him, when I most certainly did not. You were the one who told Sister Mary-Joseph that I had been practicing magic. I got a whooping for that, you know. You told our mother I spilled the box of nails on the steps to the back patio. She stepped on them barefooted when she came out to yell at me for making so much noise … because you were chasing me with a snake. She ended up with three nails through her foot … and … it got infected. The doctor in Tulsa wanted to cut her foot off, but she refused. Did you know that? And you were more than happy for me to take the blame …"

Her brother cut her off. "You *did* spill the nails …" Michael started, but stopped, his jaw dropping. An expression of abject horror washed over his features as sudden realization flooded through him. "You *didn't* leave the nails on the stairs." His face went ghost white. Lauren thought she noticed a shimmer in the corner of his eyes. "I did it … I meant to come back and pick them up but then I found the snake …it was just a little garden snake, you know? It wouldn't have hurt you." Michael jumped to his feet and turned his back on her. He staggered over to the wall, leaning heavily on it, hanging his head. She could see the sinew of his body quicken beneath his shirt as the magnitude of his mistake hit him. "Lauren, I swear ... I never meant to ... I mean ..."

"You convinced yourself you hadn't done it," Lauren said flatly. "You never could handle being in trouble."

"I'm so glad you understand." He half-turned.

"I understand that you are so accustomed to being the golden child, that you can't even admit your own mistakes or take responsibility for your actions. Yeah, I get *that*," Lauren said.

His injured brow furrowed, and he looked genuinely ruined. "All I can say is ... I'm sorry ... and ask for forgiveness."

"It's fifteen years too late, Michael." She stared into her cup, her dark lashes hiding the fury in her eyes.

"I made a mistake." Michael sat down across from her, reaching for her hand.

Lauren recoiled, drawing it back. "A mistake that cost me any hope of having a relationship with my mother. She's held that over my head my entire life, Michael. She's never forgiven me. Why should I forgive you?"

Lauren rose abruptly and walked out, running into Rowan and Henry in the hallway. "Come on," she snipped. "I need some air."

"Where are we going?"

"To town." She took Henry and turned toward the door. "Get your keys and the diaper bag."

6

Rowan found Lauren pacing outside the house. He could see she was still fuming. He approached cautiously as Henry fussed. She put him up on her shoulder. The baby wrapped his arms around her neck and nuzzled against her. She looked up and met Rowan's eye. "I told you this wasn't a good idea," Lauren said blankly. "Any of it."

"What?"

"This whole family tree thing." Lauren closed her eyes, leaning her head against Henry's as he patted her back. "Too many old hurts ... wounds that will never heal."

Rowan put his hand on her arm. "I can see you're struggling, but I watched you with your family yesterday. I talked to your cousins and a couple of your brothers. This is a family who loves you very much. They speak highly of you and I can tell they're proud. But being related is no guarantee of being able to get along. Neither your mother nor your brother defines who you are, Lauren. We don't even have to mention them."

Lauren turned and paced a few steps. Rowan followed behind her, sensing she needed to walk. When she spoke, her voice was heavy with exhaustion and heartache. "A long time ago, after the whole fiasco in Peru, one of the nurses at the hospital in San Diego made some comment about how what we did was all a bunch of hokum and I remember one of the others saying I was just another scientist trying to get attention." She sniffed. "I've never been one who wanted the spotlight. I guess she thought we're just on TV so we could be famous. It was never about that for me. I just wanted to find a way to do research and not have to grovel for grants. I'd rather chase monsters in the woods than put up with my brother."

"I know you and Michael have your issues, but if we can move past this, then maybe we can show others how to do it."

"Did you hear any of our conversation?" Lauren stopped, looking at him.

"I wasn't trying to eavesdrop," he said. "But yeah … I did."

She turned away. "Then you heard the lame excuse … the weak apology …"

"I heard a man have a sudden epiphany," he said. "If he ever thought he was innocent in all the trauma you faced, he knows now how wrong he was. He made a mistake, Lauren."

"You're sticking up for him?" She turned, her hair whipping around.

"I'm sticking up for you, Lauren," he said, reaching for her hand. She gazed at him a moment, before she took it. "It takes a lot for someone to say they're sorry, but it takes even more to accept an apology that's 15 years too late. You have to decide; what's more important? Being right or making peace?"

Lauren looked at him, her eyes searching as she considered his words. He put his arm around her and kissed her head. "Come on, I'll drive you to town if you still want to go."

~

Lauren had plenty of time to think about what Rowan had said. The drive was spent in silence, with only a few words as she directed him into Tahlequah. She pointed out the historic buildings and explained their significance. Rowan asked questions and she felt her anger subsiding. "So where are we going? Didn't you want to go to the History Center?"

"Yeah," she said. "I just wanted to make certain I wasn't going to run into my mother."

"I know you said she teaches classes there," Rowan said.

"I've been texting George," she said. "He's checking to make sure she's not there today."

"I realize it's a small world, but what are the chances you'll run into her?"

Lauren lifted a shoulder, picking up her phone when it buzzed. "Okay, he says we're good."

"Point the way," Rowan said, ready to take her directions.

Rowan watched her out of the corner of his eye as he drove. She was still a bundle of nerves, wound tightly around her lean frame. Conflict and chaos churned behind dark eyes. Rowan's heart broke for her. He'd never had any kind of issues with his sister, or any of his family. Not like this.

All-in-all, Rowan's family was unique; he knew that. His parents were still married. Most of his friends came from parents who'd divorced, and a few that had remarried. Rowan could proudly say he was friends with his big sister, and they looked forward to seeing each other at holidays or get-togethers. The *Pierce Pack* had a reunion every five years on the 4th of July without fail. Hundreds of aunts, uncles, cousins, and relations met in downtown Denver for food, fun, and fireworks. They'd done the whole *Walt Disney Family Vacation* more than once. They even had matching t-shirts made each time. He hoped to do that with Henry someday. The thought made him smile.

THE VISIT TO THE CHEROKEE HERITAGE CENTER WAS A successful one. Lauren had been surprised to find her cousin Jerome working in the genealogy library. She hadn't seen him since he was little. More surprising was the fact that he recognized her, but given her celebrity, it shouldn't have caught her off guard. She pleaded with him to keep her visit a secret and he seemed amicable enough to the idea. He helped her find some of the documents Eleanor had told her to look for, and before she was done, she had a stack of copies and purchased a few other books on Cherokee History.

~

HER DISAGREEMENT WITH MICHAEL SEEMED FORGOTTEN FOR most of the day, but as they got in the car to head back to George's house, Rowan could see the shadow return.

She was quiet for most of the drive. Henry fussed in his car seat and she barely even acknowledged him; she was so lost in thought. Fortunately, the car ride lulled him to sleep, and he napped for the half hour it took to get back to George's house. Lauren had nursed him before they left, so he'd likely sleep a while longer.

She came back to herself as the car stopped in the driveway. There, her worst fear was realized. She stiffened and froze, locking eyes with the one person she had no desire to see — her mother. A false smile lifted the older woman's face, as Lauren's expression fell.

"Who is that?" Rowan asked, his view of her blocked by George's truck.

"Trouble."

~

"YOU COULD HAVE CALLED AND TOLD ME YOU WERE COMING," her mother said tartly as Lauren got out of the car, slamming the door. She was angry in her bones and could feel the heat flaming in her cheeks, rising to the top of her head. "I had to hear from one of the neighbors in town."

"Well, I'm sorry, Mother," Lauren snarled. She wasn't, but she said it anyway. "We didn't think we'd be here more than a day or two."

"Nice to see you *too*, Mrs. Grayson." Rowan grimaced as he passed, carrying Henry into the house.

"Ms. Boudinot," she corrected him, but didn't seem angry about the slight. Rowan didn't know she didn't use her husband's – ex-husband's last name. "Is this my grandson?" she asked, trying to inspect the blanket-covered car seat as he passed. "Do I at least get to meet my grandson?"

Lauren crossed her arms and jutted out a hip. "He's sleeping. You can meet him *after* his nap." Michael stepped out onto the porch, catching Lauren's eye, and her ire, as he did. Diana turned and looked at her son with a nod.

"Did *you* call her?" Lauren demanded of her brother. "You did call her!"

"We need to get this settled, Lauren. If we're going to move forward, we have to sit down ... can we not have a civil conversation? We're all adults here. I need your help, but not when you're like this."

George stepped out behind his younger brother. "Come in the house," he said, when Lauren glanced his way. "It's going to rain. You'll get wet."

As if calling down the skies himself, the storm opened up, but Lauren stood fast. "Fine." Her mother turned and headed inside, pausing. "Stand in the rain all day if you want. I'm going in. Maybe George has coffee." Michael ducked inside ahead of her.

"You know I have coffee," George said, holding the door, leaning down to kiss his mother's cheek.

~

Diana Boudinot was a diminutive woman. She looked like a dwarf among her sons, and even her daughter was nearly a foot taller. Yet, for her stature, she commanded a room when she entered. Everyone stepped aside, surrendering to her whichever chair she chose to take at the kitchen table. Of course she chose the seat at the head of the table, where George usually sat. It was a place of honor, and she clearly felt worthy of it.

Lauren was soaked to the bone as she stood in the entry way, with her hair dripping, a puddle forming around her. She shivered, but the heat still burned within her, concentrating in her face. She looked angrily at the spectacle as George brought his mother coffee and the boys gathered around her at the table. She could have stayed outside in the cold, driving rain for hours. The lightning however, demanded otherwise. Now that she was inside, she almost wished she'd stayed out.

But Lauren didn't go to the kitchen with everyone else though. Instead, she went to find dry clothes. Rowan had laid down with Henry and was texting when she came in. "Coward." She sneered, pulling off her wet clothes, snatching dry ones out of her suitcase. She found the towel she'd used that morning after her shower and blotted the rain from her face, running it over her heavy damp hair. Flipping her head over, she wrapped the towel around her hair and twisted it, forming a turban.

"My mother wants to know if we're ready to come see them," he said.

"We're leaving ... first thing in the morning." Lauren had already made her mind up. "We can go to Barsoom for all I care."

"Do I need to get a flight out or what?"

"We'll discuss it when I'm done here," she said. "I may need you to bail me out of jail, but I will not spend another night *here*."

"Where are you going?" Rowan asked when she reached for the door handle.

"I'm going to bury the hatchet ..." Henry flinched. He lifted his head and looked blankly at his dad as she slammed the door behind her.

LAUREN STOPPED IN THE KITCHEN FOR A CUP OF COFFEE, surprised to find everyone had moved to the living room. Michael and Diana were conferring, clearly in cahoots. George had the newspaper and seemed oblivious to them as he kicked back in his favorite chair. Lauren stood in the dining room, sipping her coffee. She couldn't hear what was being said, but it didn't matter. She was still angry in her core, and she wouldn't go in 'til her pulse slowed.

They fell silent when she finally entered. She sat down on the sofa across from Michael and her mother. She lowered her cup and paused to free her hair from the towel, shaking it loose before taking up her cup, folding her hands around it for the warmth it provided. She leaned her elbows on her knees and waited for one of them to say something ... anything.

"So, how's the television business?" Diana finally quipped, looking smug.

"At the moment, I'm having second thoughts on my career choice." Lauren sniffed, her nose wrinkling.

"Look, Lauren ..." Michael started.

"Don't *look, Lauren me*," she retorted. George glanced up from his paper, but quickly realized this was no place for him. He folded it and tucked it under his arm and slipped out silently. "Did *you* tell Mother I was here?"

"I didn't have to," Michael said. "But I did tell her about my mistake, and I've apologized for it ... *again*."

"This?" She wagged her finger between her brother and

herself. "This has nothing to do with *her*." She pointed her nose at their mother. "This has to do with you ... and me."

"Lauren ..." he started, but her eyes flashed, and he froze.

"Here's what we're going to do," Lauren commanded. "I'm going to speak my mind and I will speak it plainly. You do not need to reply or add your commentary. You need only listen and hear me. *Hear* my words. Are we clear?"

Michael nodded; a look of terror passed over his features. Of all the boys, he was the youngest, having nearly ten years on her in age. He'd been the baby growing up until Lauren showed up and usurped his position of honor. It didn't matter that his twin was three minutes older than him. Perhaps that's why he'd always given her so much trouble; had always been the *rabbit* — the leader of them in all the mischief.

Lauren sat back a moment, choosing her words carefully, then began on an extended tirade ... all in Cherokee. She knew her mother would understand it all, but she didn't think Michael had more than a fundamental understanding of the language. With the whole dictionary of Cherokee words at her command, she let fly all her pent-up rage.

Her native tongue was extremely harsh, yet melodious with a curtness. The clipped consonants sounded like the speaker was choking. There were no P's or B's in the Cherokee language. It was one of a few rare languages that lacked bilabial stops. Instead of using the lips, Cherokee words lay primarily in the epiglottis at the back of the throat. The frequency of glottal stops provided a unique emphasis that punctuated her anger.

Throughout her tirade, her brother looked blankly at her as his brows slowly lifted; his eyes darted to his mother, pleading for rescue. Lauren's soliloquy continued, and her tone remained level, with a restraint he hadn't expected. Her deep voice never raised into the soprano range she was capable of, knowing that the alto range was much better suited to convey the intent of her words, even if he didn't understand them. The last few came with a lifted chin and flashing eyes, the words coming from deep in her throat with syllables that ended abruptly in the back of her throat, almost as if she were swallowing the sounds.

Michael looked to his mother overtly, hooking his thumb towards his sister. "Are you going to let her talk to me like that?"

Diana appeared impressed at her daughter's skill. "Lauren, I had no idea you had any *Tsalagi*. I thought they'd beaten it out of you at that fancy school I sent you to in California. As for you, Michael, you've had it coming, so yes. I am going to let her speak to you like that. Now, let's have some more coffee and we can catch up ... unless you have something else to say ..." She looked at Lauren.

"I've spoken my peace. I have no more words to say to *this one*." She turned to her brother. He looked wounded, which had been her intent. He didn't have to know what she said to understand the magnitude and depth of her anger.

"Michael?" Diana challenged.

"I have given my apologies. I have nothing else to say." Michael held up empty hands, unsure what else he could do or say to defuse her ire or bring an end to the long-standing feud he hadn't realized was on-going.

This was not the first time either had said these words to one another. Their mother had interceded in their squabbles like this before, and rarely had the peace lasted more than a few minutes. "I need a fresh cup of coffee. Anyone else?" Diana announced, holding her cup out to Michael.

"I take mine with cream and one sugar." Lauren held up her cup. She sat back and crossed her arms, watching her brother move like a whipped dog. He was wounded, physically, but he'd taken her scolding, begrudgingly.

Rowan's words came back to her. Maybe he had come to some kind of epiphany about his failings in their relationship. For a moment, Lauren considered her own. As Bahati had pointed out, she had allowed herself to carry her anger like a stone in her heart, and while she wasn't confident she was ready to let it go, its presence was suddenly a burden she hadn't realized was there. She was willing to give him a moment's grace; provisionally.

7

"Last night you told Rowan you wanted to talk to me," Lauren said. Henry had woken up from his nap and was now being introduced to his grandmother as she and Michael sat at the kitchen table with fresh cups of coffee. Her pulse was still racing, and the anger that had burned so hot just minutes before was only slightly cooler than the coffee.

"I've got a project I'm working on I've been wanting to talk with you about ..." he began, sitting down across from her. Their old wounds would take a long time to heal.

"Something else you want to rub in my face?" she asked. "Did you find aliens?"

Michael looked sharply at her, clearly surprised by the vitriol in her voice. "Maybe."

"Maybe you want to rub it in my face?"

"No," he said, hesitating. He stood, shaking his head. "I've never tried to rub anything in your face, Lauren."

"I beg to differ," she snarked under her breath as she took a sip from her cup.

"Lauren." He turned. "I ... I think I found aliens."

Her cup lowered from her lips to the table. "What?"

"I'm still not sure what I found." He sat back down. "I can tell you what I *think* I found, but …"

"But what?"

"I can't be sure," he said.

Lauren sat looking blankly at him for a moment. "What evidence do you have?"

"Signals," he said. "Fast radio bursts to be more precise."

"FRBs are nothing new." Lauren crossed her arms as she sat back. "You'll have to do better than that."

"It's not the fact that we found FRBs that's so exciting," Michael hesitated as Rowan came in to get a cup of coffee, pausing as he overheard the conversation.

"Honey." Lauren motioned him over. "You're going to want to hear this."

Rowan came over and sat down at the end of the table. "FRBs?"

"Maybe I should back up and tell you a little more about my work."

"Uh yeah, because in case you've forgotten, I am no rocket scientist," Lauren said.

A wide grin made Michael's teeth glow against his russet skin. He had a crooked canine that gave him a slightly snaggle-toothed smile. "Good thing I am, then," he added. Even that made Lauren smile, and she gave a wave of capitulation. "So, six years ago, I was asked to design a satellite system to pick up incoming radio waves from the cosmos."

"A receiver?" Lauren asked.

"It wasn't that hard," he said. "Radio technology has changed little since it's invention." He paused, considering his words carefully. "You understand the principle of capacitive induction, right?"

"My PhD may be in biological anthropology, but we deal with radios and communications systems all the time. I don't know the intimate details of how it works, but yes, I do understand the principle."

"Well, radio waves in a vacuum travel at light speed, so radio waves through space travel lightning fast," Michael continued. "About three years ago, I was working at the radio telescope when … for less than a millisecond … a barrage of radio waves arrived from space."

"What was it? The Beatles?" She found herself channeling Rowan's sarcasm. Even Rowan chortled at her joke.

Michael stared at her for a moment. Clearly, he was in no mood for her jokes. "We got lucky. We had all 38 of the antennae that make up the array pointed in the same direction in the sky. This was a stroke of luck that allowed us to take all that data and use it to basically triangulate where in the universe the signal came from, and how far away it was from us. You wanna take a guess?"

"Well, I'm pretty sure it wasn't a text from Mr. Spock on Vulcan." Lauren drained her cup.

"The bursts came from approximately 13,000 light years near the center of its home galaxy … 4 billion light years from earth."

"Damn!" Rowan gasped. "I'd hate to pay the long-distance bill on that call."

"Don't you understand the technological significance of this event? It's like … it's like …" he fumbled for an analogy. "It's like standing on a mountain in Colorado and the Yeti shouting at us from Bhutan. And us not only being able to hear that Yeti as clearly as you hear me now, but to tell you exactly where the call came from." Lauren's gaze was fixed on him intently. "But here's where it gets good. The signals have become more frequent. Radio telescopes all over the planet have been able to pick up these … these … shrieks. Preliminary data suggested these messages are all coming from the same general area of the cosmos."

"Same message? What did it say?"

"That's the problem." Michael shook his head. "We don't speak the Yeti's language, so we don't know what he's saying.

It's not making any sense to anyone in the lab. We're all arguing about what we did ... or didn't see; what we did ... or didn't hear."

"But why do you need me?" She rose to refill her cup.

"Your choice of career fields has always puzzled me," Michael said. "Anthropology by itself is fascinating, yet you've never studied apes."

"Unless you include the currently unidentified species of the North American Wood Ape, or the other unidentified greater apes, like your hypothetical Yeti." Lauren conceded with a nod.

Michael's left eye twitched when he realized what she was suggesting. "But biological anthropology? It's an interesting mix of social and biological studies, I'll give you that, but human evolution hasn't followed the same path as our knuckle-dragging cousins."

"Just because they're bigger than we are doesn't mean they're stupid," Lauren said before she could stop herself. "The evidence suggests they could be quite intelligent." She recovered quickly enough.

"If Bigfoot was real, you mean." Michael turned in his chair. His gaze followed her as she added creamer to her coffee.

Lauren fought to control her face. It would have been easy for her to reignite the feud at that moment. Her ire was rising, along with her pulse and probably her blood pressure. This was the kind of behavior that made him infuriating. He was so self-assured; so cocky. She wanted to blow up at him, but she took a deep breath, then took the high road. "I believe you were about to make a point as to *why* you need *my* help."

"I was reading one of your blog posts on human biosocial variation and extrapolating the data and applying it to supposed Bigfoot populations ... and it got me thinking about biosocial variations of alien life forms," he said. "Then it hit me. If you could theorize thusly about a mythical creature like

Bigfoot, maybe you could help me come up with a hypothesis on … on …. on alien life. Something that might be able to help me explain this signal at least until someone can translate it. And if your grasp of languages are as strong as everyone says, I hoped you might be willing to … help me figure out the message." It seemed to pain him to admit she might be able to do something so very remarkable. Maybe it was more the idea of alien life that stuck in his craw as he glanced up at her nervously.

Lauren wasn't exactly sure how the All-Language of the ancient gods applied to extraterrestrial languages, but he might have a point. "Is anyone currently working on translating it?"

"One scientist was, but … he's dead," Michael said. "Which brings up the next issue we need to discuss."

Lauren sat down with her coffee cup. "Oh?" She glanced at Rowan who leaned forward, resting his elbows on the table around his cup.

"Two scientists are dead," he said. "One was assassinated. The other was killed in a car wreck. We don't know if the two are connected, or if the second was a coincidence."

Lauren's own words resonated in her ears. "I don't believe in coincidences." The words slipped off her lips as she tried to make sense of it all. "What do these two scientists have in common?"

"Me," Michael said. "First, my mentor Alexei … then … Kitty."

"You were in the same wreck?" Lauren put the pieces together. "Wait … Kitty? Kitty Donovan? Your old girlfriend?"

He nodded. "It's a long story, but …we got hit by a truck," he said, and it clearly pained him. "The car flipped into a ravine." He struggled to continue. "I don't know how, but I made it out. I woke up in the hospital … they never found her."

Lauren reached across the table for his hand. He gave it to her and looked up, meeting her eye. "I'm deeply sorry to hear about Kitty."

He pinched his lips tightly, fighting back emotions, then slid his hand from his sister's.

He stood and paced behind his chair. "I came to you because I didn't think anyone else would believe me, but I'm afraid getting you involved might put you in danger."

"Not just me, Michael. My husband … my son …" She looked to Rowan. "Even George and our mother. But you're in danger too, you know that, right?"

He nodded. "I had been trying to convince myself that I was just being paranoid, but I know that's not true." He paced behind the table, running a trembling hand over his cropped hair.

"Look, I had no idea you were such an amazing linguist, but I've never been chewed out by anyone in such fluent Cherokee, and that includes our mother. And after you translated the Maya calendar, I can only imagine that if anyone could decrypt this … alien code, it would be you. I'm still convinced it has to be you. I wouldn't ask if I didn't think you couldn't do it."

"But Michael." She sat back, trying to reconcile her fears with her professional interest. "This isn't two kids trying to one up each other …"

Michael hesitated and sat back down, letting out an exasperated groan. "Look," he said. "I've got something I need to tell you … and I really need you to keep an open mind about this …" Lauren felt like she'd heard something like this before. "Some incredibly strange things have been happening to me …"

"You too?" Rowan nearly choked.

"Me too?" Michael looked at his brother-in-law blankly. Then he looked at Lauren. "You too?"

"What's going on, Michael?" Lauren asked.

"I … I think … I think I've been … abducted," he spat the words out as if they were vile. "I think I've been abducted by aliens." He tried it again, and the words flowed out so fast Lauren wasn't sure she'd understood a word of it.

Rowan sat back; a stunned expression painted over his features. He looked to Lauren. "Were *you* abducted by aliens?"

"Me?" Lauren's face contorted. "No." She didn't sound convinced. She set her jaw and shook her head, running a hand over her brow. "I don't know what's going on with me, but *I* definitely have *not* been abducted by aliens."

"What's happening to you?" Michael asked.

"What makes you think you've been abducted by aliens?"

"You go first," Michael recoiled.

"You brought it up," Lauren said. "You go first."

Rowan's gaze flipped back and forth as they volleyed queries at one another, like a spectator at a tennis match. "Michael, what's going on?"

Michael seemed to deflate then ball up his courage. He explained it had started about three years ago. He'd go to bed and as he fell asleep, bright flashing lights would wake him, and he'd find himself somewhere else … sometimes it was in what looked like a lab or a spaceship, sometimes he'd find himself standing out in the streets. Rowan and Lauren exchanged a glance that didn't escape Michael's notice. "Last night … it happened again," he said. "Last night, something … different happened; something I've never experienced before."

"Last night?" Lauren asked.

"Yeah," he said. "Last night … I found myself down in the river bottom behind the house. Sitting on the fallen sycamore tree … was our father."

"Our father?" Lauren asked. "John Gray Wolf's Son?"

"Huh?" Michael's face contorted.

"The genealogist we're working with found his name listed

that way on some records …" Lauren said. "That's what we're working on … an episode on our family history."

"He looked older," Michael said. "Not like he did when I was a kid."

"I wouldn't know," Lauren said. She'd never even seen pictures of her father. There were few pictures of any of the family when she was a baby. There were pictures lining the hallways now, but they started when she was about seven or eight. By then George had already gone off to college. He'd earned his degree in Fire Protection & Safety Engineering Technology from OSU in Stillwater before she'd graduated high school.

"What are the chances you've been dreaming?" Rowan asked.

"I'd considered that," Michael said. "Especially since I've been on pain meds, but … well, the wreck is part of the problem."

"Oh?"

"Yeah," he said. "I remember the initial impact, the feeling of the truck being born aloft and flipping … and then I wasn't in the truck anymore. I was standing in front of the Administration Building at NASA."

"That sounds more like what Lauren has been experiencing," Rowan said.

Michael looked to his sister. She realized she had to tell him. She told him about the first episode of the — *teleportation* — that had taken her to Rowan in Mexico. "I had to think it was an act of desperation. How I did it, I don't know. I thought that was the end of it … until last week when it happened again."

"What happened?"

"Henry and I went to the Farmer's Market in Hilo to get fresh produce before we came back to the mainland. I wanted to make one last tropical fruit salad before we left. I got so spoiled having fresh pineapple and coconut every day," she said. "But I forgot the coconut. I turned to put the pineapple in the refrigerator, and the next thing I know, I'm standing in the middle of the Farmer's Market. Henry was still in the sling on my chest; still sleeping peacefully."

"That's it?" Michael asked.

"No, there was one other time." She admitted, looking at Rowan with trepidation. She hadn't told him of the other time.

"What?" Rowan gasped.

"I didn't tell you because I thought maybe I was sleep walking … and I didn't want to worry you."

"So what happened?" Michael asked.

"Rowan was reading Henry a bedtime story." She looked to Rowan. "Baby Honu." She turned back to Michael. "It's Henry's favorite book … about a baby sea turtle. Anyway, I must have fallen asleep while he was putting Henry to bed. A few hours later, I woke up in my pajamas, standing on the black sand beach in the rain … baby sea turtles all around me. I had to find my way home in a blinding storm. I was soaked to the bone and half frozen. I got in the shower and warmed up before Rowan or Henry woke up. I don't know what happened, but I'm quite certain I was not abducted by aliens. What makes you think you were?"

Michael sat a moment, taking it all in, seeming to plan his words. "I remember seeing … *them*."

"Them?" Rowan asked. "Who's *them*?"

"The aliens," he said.

"Are you sure it's not the pain meds talking?" Lauren stood, turning her back on the pretense of refilling her cup. She sat her cup down, her head lowered as she leaned on the counter.

"I know what I saw," Michael said. His tone suggested she'd hurt his feelings.

She turned. "I'm sorry," she said. "I don't mean to

discount your experience, Michael. I just don't think it has anything to do with what *I've* been experiencing."

"Tell him about your sudden ability to understand every language on the planet," Rowan said. She turned and looked at him sharply.

"What?" Michael asked.

Lauren took a deep breath, looking at the toe of her sneaker as she tried to calm herself and not blow up at Rowan. He'd come to accept that part of her, even though he still didn't understand it. "When I got abducted by the fake Bigfoot in Washington, I had a bad head injury. I don't know how, but somehow I was able to communicate with the shaman of the Bigfoot tribe, Tsul'Kalu. He told me the ancient gods had bestowed a gift upon me; the ability to speak the All-Language."

Michael looked at Rowan, who shrugged. "I don't understand it either."

"Wait," Michael said. "You found Bigfoot?"

THE CONVERSATION CAME TO AN ABRUPT HALT THE MOMENT their mother walked in with Henry in her arms. The child didn't seem pleased about it. She sat down with him and he reached for his mother, but Diana turned him away from Lauren. "He's kind of big for his age, don't you think?" Diana asked her. It was like nails on a chalkboard and Lauren fought the urge to cringe.

"Have you seen the size of my brothers?" Lauren reached for him, but Diana protested with a glare, drawing the child away from his mother. Lauren withdrew her hands with an apologetic look to her son. "His father isn't exactly short either."

"George was a fat baby," she said. "But the others,

including that one …" her nod went to Michael, "weren't overly large."

"He's in the 85th percentile for his weight," Lauren said. She didn't mention he was over the 95th percentile for height.

"Was our father very tall?" Michael asked.

Diana's eyes darted towards Lauren to gauge her reaction, then went back to her son's. "Oh, I suppose so," she said, shifting Henry in her lap. Henry let out a screech so sharp Lauren flinched. She reached over and took him before her mother could protest.

"Henry's probably hungry," Lauren said, putting him to her shoulder as he fussed. She cast a wicked glare at her mother. "If he gets off his schedule, he gets cranky."

"He's not the only one," Lauren heard Diana mutter under her breath as she rose, intending to take him to the other room where she could get comfortable and nurse him in peace.

"Well, I guess I better be going," Diana said, shouldering her purse. "I have to teach a class at the Heritage Center in an hour."

"What are you teaching?" Lauren paused at the doorway.

"I teach the girls to sew ribbon skirts," Diana said. "Do you remember how?"

"Yes," Lauren said. "But I don't have much time for sewing these days."

"Well, I will make you a new skirt to wear when you come back."

"Come back?" Lauren quipped. "I don't know when or if we'll be back any time soon."

"Perhaps not, but I will send it to you so you will have it." Lauren held her face as neutral as she could muster. Her mother leaned in to kiss her cheek. Lauren did not return the gesture but allowed it. "*Sigwu da na da gwa do'hv,*" Diana said, and nodded to her son as she headed out the door.

"What did she say?" Michael asked, blankly.

"*Sigwu da na dagwa do'hv?*" Lauren turned to him. "You really have forgotten any Cherokee you might have learned as a child, haven't you?"

"I'm out of practice." He admitted. "It's a use-or-lose skill."

"In Cherokee, there isn't a word for *goodbye*." Her eyes went to the window, watching as her mother got into the car. "We simply say *we'll see one another again soon*."

8

Lauren was sitting in the living room, nursing Henry, and trying to gather her thoughts when Rowan came back in. "I guess we're not leaving tonight then?"

She looked at him, biting her lip. "I don't know what to do," she said. "I wasn't expecting something like this could happen to him too."

"Why didn't you tell me about the second time," Rowan said. "The turtles?"

She let out an exasperated breath. "What could you have done about it? Worry about something else I can't explain … can't change?" she asked. "No, there was no sense in scaring both of us."

"Lauren, if you're scared, I need to know about it …" he said. "No matter how bad something is, I am here to help you through it; to help take the burden off you."

"That's just it." Lauren turned her gaze to the baby at her breast. "My burden would be no lighter if you knew. If anything, it's heavier now."

Rowan considered her a long moment. "You want to help Michael try to figure out what the signals are, don't you?"

Lauren looked sharply at him. "I do," she said. "But if it's going to put us at risk … I just don't see how I can."

"Not how *you* can … how *we* can."

"But …" Lauren sputtered, glancing at Henry. He had her braid wrapped in his chubby fist and was smiling up at her. He was done with his supper. She smiled back at him, sitting him up, tugging her shirt back down. "What about Henry?"

"I'd offer to take Henry and go to my parents," he said. "But I'm not sending you on this knight's errand alone."

"It wouldn't work anyway," she said. "You can't just go cold turkey to wean a baby. It's not good for me or Henry. The baby cuddled up against her chest, grinning at his daddy.

"Ma …" he rocked against her, head butting her, playfully. "Mama."

She wrapped her arms around him and kissed his head. "Hi, sweet boy."

"Mama," he gurgled.

"Can you say Dada?" Rowan bopped his nose.

Henry squirmed, wiggling in Lauren's lap, reaching for his Dad. "Dada," he cooed.

Rowan scooped him up, tossing him up in the air. Henry giggled a high-pitch squeal. "Dada!" He repeated.

"That's my boy!"

Lauren sat back, smiling sadly as she watched her boys play. She leaned a weary head on her fist, her thoughts going to all the potential hazards they might face, and how they would mitigate the risks if they did pursue this folly.

Michael stood in the doorway, hesitating. Lauren lifted her head and motioned him in. "I didn't want to intrude if Henry was still nursing."

"No, you're fine." She wasn't shy about nursing her son anywhere. "Come sit down," she said. "We're not done talking."

"I didn't want to say anything in front of Mom."

"I'm glad you didn't," she said. "So, tell us more about your work. How would we help? What's involved?"

"And how do we do it safely?" Rowan added, as Henry sat down in his lap, patting his hands on his knees.

Michael gave them as much insight as he could on his work. "It's a top secret project," he cautioned. "I can only tell you so much. I've probably said too much already, but … you're my sister. I trust you."

That made Lauren feel somewhat better about this sudden détente they'd come to. "You know we'd never say anything … but we're supposed to be making a television show. How can we accomplish both? Our Network was particularly interested in you. They wanted me to do the episode on my famous brother who works for NASA."

"Well, technically, I am not an employee of NASA. I work for the private sector. I only have a grant from NASA to help fund my research. Even NASA doesn't know about this part of our project. They think I'm developing a new radio telescope that may someday replace Hubble, and I am, but … I have access to a large radio telescope array in South Africa. I mean, we can go under the pretense of doing something on the Morning Star Telescope, the MST isn't a classified project."

"Do you think your crash was an accident? I mean, it could have been a coincidence," Rowan said.

"I don't believe in coincidences either," he responded. Lauren smiled faintly. "That's one of the reasons why I'm so wary. We have security, not just our offices, but our housing too. We have armed guards and live in a gated community. I can arrange for housing. I have a driver and a security guard at my beck and call."

"Does anyone know where you're working?" Lauren asked.

Michael shrugged. "I don't think it's any secret."

They sat looking at one another. No one seemed to be

able to come up with the right answer. "If it makes any difference," Michael started but hesitated. "Our father told me I had to make it right with you … that I needed you to solve this."

"Me?" Lauren recoiled.

"I think his exact words were, *you need her as much as she needs you.*"

~

LAUREN LAY IN BED THINKING THROUGH THE EVENTS OF THE day, long after Rowan had gone to sleep. She was still angry at Michael; her mother too. But she was also angry at her father. He'd come to Michael but not her. How dare he? She had to think it was a dream. Michael had known their father and perhaps had manifested him into a dream-vision. Perhaps John Grayson was Michael's Tsul'Kalu … his vision guide. Tsul'Kalu had come to her at a time when she needed help. She was willing to allow that the dreams she had of him now were just that; dreams.

After several hours of laying watching the moonlight through the swaying trees, she finally surrendered and got up, pulling on a t-shirt and pair of shorts, slipping into her sneakers. Quietly she went downstairs, avoiding the floorboard by the back door that often gave her away when she snuck out as a kid. She found the door still stuck just a bit, and forced it open, escaping quietly into the moonlit night. It was cooler than she expected, and she wished she'd grabbed her jacket. Still, she walked out onto the deck and gazed out over the valley behind the house. A light breeze lifted the branches and she noted they moved like waves on the tide. The night air smelled damp; subtle notes of lilac and honeysuckle reminded Lauren of her youth.

She walked out across the yard toward the familiar path that was still there. It wound through the trees and down to the river. She stopped only when she reached the old hollow tree where the raccoon wizard had lived.

"You didn't bring me any candy." She turned at the sound of a familiar voice. The old raccoon was practically white. It was still huge, but it moved slowly; a waddling, limping gate as it came down the path behind her. It climbed up on the fallen sycamore tree with great effort, pausing as it sat on its haunches. "You haven't brought me candy for many years." The voice was trembling and faltered. "You have grown."

Lauren stood with her mouth open as she tried to figure out if she was hallucinating. No, she was dreaming; had to be. "It's been a long time," she said. "I didn't think you'd still be here."

"I have been waiting for your return," he said. "I knew you would come home."

"How did you know this?"

"I know many things," he said. "I am a wizard after all."

"I think I always knew that," Lauren said, giving in to the dream.

"Do you know the meaning of the word, wizard?"

Lauren pondered for a moment, rolling the word around in her mind, seeking the word in the ancient language. "From Middle English," she said. "The origin word was *wys* meaning wise … in Lithuanian *žynystė*, meaning magic, or *žynys* meaning sorcerer."

"Well done," he said. "We are all wizards, each in our own way."

Lauren's brow lifted.

"What do you know of God?" He asked.

"You're a raccoon. What do you know of God?"

"Thou art God. I am god. All that groks is God."

Lauren's face contorted and she all but did a double take as she drank in what he was saying. "A raccoon who knows Robert Heinlein?"

"A wizard who is well-read," he chuckled, scratching

behind his ear with one paw. "But what makes me wise … you as well, child … is our ability to *grok* all."

"It's been a couple of decades since I read Heinlein for school. Remind me again what the whole *grok* thing means."

"When Heinlein was writing *Stranger in A Strange Land* the world was a much different place." He stretched out on the log and yawned before he continued. "It was the dawning of the age of Aquarius, the height of the counter-culture movement. *This* world was at war, and the warriors were blamed for the turmoil. He meant to speak to the times and making sense of the world on a higher level. So, *grok* means to understand intuitively or by empathy, but there was much more to it. It meant to fully comprehend on a higher level. Heinlein used the line *thou art God*, it is logically derived from the concept inherent to the term *grok*."

"At the moment, I am not so sure I'm not hallucinating," she said. "I'm standing under a full moon, talking to a raccoon … about God." She ran a weary hand over her face. "I'm definitely dreaming."

The raccoon rolled over on his back and laughed. "To sleep, perchance to dream …" the raccoon quoted, lifting up a paw, pressing the other to his chest as he lay on his back. "Aye, there's the rub. Yes, Lauren, you are dreaming, but dreams are just the consciousness functioning on a different level of existence. Here, we *are* god."

Lauren puzzled on this a moment. "But … *I* am no god." Lauren shook her head. "No way."

"But neither are you a mere mortal," he said. "You have long known this."

"Oh? I have? Have I?" She bowed up, ready for a fight.

"We are all gods," the raccoon said, sitting back up, crossing his hind legs, resting his front paws on his knees. "In an ancient text, a teacher once said, *You are gods; you are sons and daughters of the Most High, but you will die like mere mortals; you will fall like every other ruler*."

Lauren's heart flipped in her chest. "Thou art god …" she muttered, her head swimming as the words ran through the back of her mind in every language her mind could comprehend. She stumbled backwards, feeling a force catch her and redirect her to the log. She recovered her balance, feeling faint. Visions of ancient texts blurred past the backs of her eyes and she came to fully understand not only the words but the deepest meanings of each of them.

"Thou art god," a familiar voice brought her back to the moonlit field, but this one had Mount St. Helen's in the backdrop. Lauren turned to find Tsul'Kalu sitting beside her. The old raccoon was gone, and the kindly Bigfoot shaman she'd come to love rested his massive hand on her arm.

Without a word, she rose, throwing her arms around the beast, resting her head on his shoulder. He embraced her in the circle of his massive arms, and she felt warm and safe. When she finally turned him loose she stepped back, standing in front of him, drinking in the scene. "Is this a dream?"

"A single dream is worth a thousand realities," he quoted, a beatific expression gracing his aged visage. A scar cut across the beast's great face, and she remembered the day it was made, though it seemed like a lifetime ago.

"This one is," she said. "I think of you all the time. I know you said you couldn't be with me always, but it seems like … like somehow, you always are."

A grizzled smile broke across his face. "I missed you too."

"Tsul'Kalu," Lauren started to say, but stopped, not sure how to ask the questions running through her mind. "Do you know what's going on? What's happening to me?"

That all-knowing gaze returned to his face as he nodded with his whole body. "You are chosen," he said. "Your gifts grow as the ancient gods find you worthy."

"But … I'm not the only one, am I?"

"We all have our gifts," he said. "But not everyone pauses to listen, nor are willing to accept them."

"And my brother?"

"Michael has earned his own gifts," Tsul'Kalu said. "His path is not the same as yours, but … when the two of you work together, there is no force in the universe that can stop you."

"So is he the one that …" Lauren was still struggling. "I mean … you know … one minute I'm here, one minute … *poof*! I'm somewhere else." She blinked and they were in the standing in front of the El Castillo in Mexico. The air was suddenly warm and humid, and the sky was ablaze with stars. A yelp escaped Lauren's throat as she tottered a moment, disoriented. Tsul'Kalu caught her arm and steadied her, gently.

"Like that?" Tsul'Kalu asked.

Lauren gulped hard, nodding. "Yeah. That."

"I must tell you, this is not your gift alone," he said. "You are the vessel, but a catalyst is needed."

"Michael?"

"Among others," he said.

"So … you got me here when Rowan was hurt? Before Henry was born?"

He stepped back and raised a finger. "That was not me," he said. "That was a union of forces, forces that continue to grow stronger. Forces you will need as your journey continues."

"My journey?"

"You will travel far and answer many questions," he said. "You, Truth Seeker. But a word of caution." He lifted his hand. "Believe those who are seeking the truth. Doubt those who claim to have found it."

"Why must you always speak in riddles?"

"Because you always seek the truth in my words," he said. "And because you seek, you will find."

Lauren started to speak but found herself in lying in her own bed at George's house. She sat up, gasping. Rowan reached for her, his hand finding her bare arm, pulling her back down beside him, drawing her into him. He was warm and comforting and she melted into him as he curled his body around hers. She rested her head on his arm and took a deep breath realizing it was still the middle of the night.

Rowan's lips found her neck and she found his hands were searching her skin beneath the blankets. She sat up abruptly, pulling away. She got up and pulled on her sweatshirt. "Come back to bed," Rowan said dreamily. "Lauren?"

"I can't sleep." She paused to check on Henry. He was warm enough and sleeping soundly.

"Lauren?" He reached for her as she came around the bed, headed for the door. She took his hand. He tried tugging her back to him, but she resisted.

"Sleep," she said. "I need to talk to my brother."

"At two in the morning?" Rowan called softly after her, but she left him to sleep.

Lauren grabbed her purse and keys from behind the sofa table. She threw open the front door while she was still trying to get her shoes on, and froze, nearly falling over, finding Michael reaching for the door. A yelp escaped her throat, and he jumped back.

"Jesus, Lauren! What the …" he gasped, his hand going to his chest.

"What are you doing here?"

"I need to talk to you," he said. "Where are you going at two in the morning?"

"I needed to talk to *you*," she said, recovering, kicking off her shoes. She opened the screen door and held it for him. "Come in."

"Is there coffee?" he asked.

"I'll make some," she said. "Want food?"

"God, yes."

9

"It happened again," Michael said over a plate of pancakes.

Lauren knew exactly what he was talking about. He'd been *taken*. She took a moment to consider how similar their experiences were, but how different their explanations were. He was *abducted*, she was *teleported*.

"To me, too," Lauren said. "Except ... I didn't see our father ..."

"Oh?"

"Remember that old raccoon?"

"The one that got you shot in the ass?" Michael smirked.

"He told me he was a wizard."

"A wizard, huh? Like Harry Potter?"

Lauren shrugged as she sat down across from him with the coffee pot. "But it wasn't really a raccoon." She held his gaze a moment, debating whether or not she trusted him enough to tell him what she needed to. The anticipation on his face encouraged her. "It was ... a Bigfoot."

"I thought you said it was a raccoon."

She took a deep breath. "Well it started out as a raccoon, and then turned into a Bigfoot."

"Oh," he lifted his brow. "A Bigfoot."

"Not just any Bigfoot. Tsul'Kalu."

"Tsul'Kalu?" He sat back. "You mentioned him last night."

"I met him in Washington State … almost three years ago," she said. "He saved me when I had been kidnapped by a … a hoax monger in a monkey suit," Lauren said.

The words rolled off her tongue once he gave the slightest impression that he believed her. She told him everything, from the ancient god child in Peru to the gift of the ancient All-language. Her pancakes went cold in the telling of the events that led to Henry's birth in Mexico, and the discovery of the lost calendar of the Maya and the treasure-trove of lost gold and the missing Wentworth ransom money.

THE SUN WAS RISING WHEN ROWAN PADDED BAREFOOT INTO the kitchen. Lauren, with her back to the entryway, heard him yawn as Henry fussed. "Mama." She heard the baby's little voice and rose to take him from his weary father. "Mama," he laid his head on her shoulder and wrapped his arms around her neck.

"You're up early," Rowan said to Michael, reaching for the coffee pot.

Michael glanced at his watch. "You, too."

"Henry's always been an early bird," she said.

"Lauren and I needed to talk," Michael said. "She makes good pancakes, too."

"Yes she does." Rowan beamed.

"There's more in the oven," Lauren said over her shoulder, as she sat down. Henry leaned back against her, reaching for the plate. He was just big enough now to start eating soft solid foods, and he loved pancakes. He had four little teeth, with a promise of more, and Lauren broke him off a piece of her food and handed it to him. He wrapped his chubby little hand around it and gnawed on it.

"Sit down, join us," Michael invited Rowan over. He brought his plate and sat down. "We need to talk."

Rowan looked at Lauren dubiously. "What's up?"

"We have to find a way to make this work," he said. "Lauren and me. We've got to solve this puzzle …"

"Together," Lauren said. She couldn't believe that, for once in her life she was agreeing with her brother. "I know there are risks, but I also know … I know we'll all do everything within our powers to protect each other."

"Within *our* powers?" Michael raised an eyebrow. "That's saying a lot."

Rowan sat back in his chair, his jaw slack; his eyes wide. "Are … are you … are you sure?" He gazed sternly at Lauren.

"I'm scared, but this … this is the right thing. Michael needs my help … and I need yours, Rowan." She held his gaze. "I can't go without Henry, but I can't go without you either."

Rowan broke her gaze, glancing at her brother. "I can't believe I'm hearing this," he said. He looked back at Lauren. "Are you sure about all of this?"

"Trust me," she said, reaching for his hand. "No one is more surprised by the recent turn of events than I am. But … I have to do this. I have to. I have to find a way to make it safe, for you, for Henry; for all of us. I can't explain it, but …"

"Is this about your life-long feud to find aliens?" Rowan's brows reached for his hairline. "Because it seems like Michael may have beat you to it."

Lauren turned and looked at Michael, one edge of her lip curled up, and she softened, running a hand over Henry's head. "You know what? I don't even care who was first."

Rowan shook his head. "Un-freakin-believable."

~

Long after George left for work and the kids headed off to school, Lauren, Michael, and Rowan sat at the kitchen table, volleying *what ifs* at each other, trying to work out how they would accomplish the task at hand. Henry slept in the crook of his father's arm now that his tummy was full, and he was content.

"How are we going to explain it to the Network?" Rowan finally came to the one question he was certain they wouldn't be able to answer.

"You've got your camera equipment," Michael said. "Right?"

"We'll tell my boss you're doing a documentary on the new radio telescope I'm designing," Michael said.

"Why don't we tell your boss the truth?" Lauren said.

"The truth?" Michael's brow lifted, intrigued.

"That's what we're all about," Lauren said. "The truth is … and yes I hear myself, and I can't believe I'm saying it … we're making a show about our family history and my most interesting brother. Does it get any more innocent than that?"

Rowan had an epiphany of his own. Lauren had finally made peace with their mission. Finally, he could see, they might actually get to make a television show. And not just any show. This had the potential to be something really big; huge, in fact. A broad grin spread over his face. "Okay," he said, with a nod of his head. "Let's make it happen."

10

It took three days to get the details worked out and the travel arrangements made. They caught an early flight out of Tulsa and flew into LaGuardia where they had a long layover. Henry had slept most of the flight and was rambunctious; ready to take in all the excitement of the bustling airport. Rowan was ready to stretch his legs and offered to take him on a walk down the terminal. Michael went to find the restroom and left Lauren at their gate. She'd been up since three in the morning. It was almost noon. They had three hours to find some lunch and prepare for the long red-eye flight over the Atlantic into Heathrow.

"Coffee?" Michael startled her as he approached with a cup in her face. "I hope you like mocha."

The perfume of coffee and chocolate hit her as she reached for the tall cup. "Oh, God bless you," Lauren gasped, taking it, wrapping her hands around the cup. It was hot and comforting and she anticipated the effects of the caffeine bringing her to life.

The cup was nearly empty when Rowan returned with a fussy baby. "Someone needs a clean diaper and some lunch," he said, reaching over her for the diaper bag.

"Want me to change him?" she asked, setting her cup down.

"No, I got it," he said. "You cook. I clean."

Lauren smirked and let him handle the messy business. When he returned, Henry was somewhat happier, but he reached for his mother babbling, "Mama mama," as she took him. He wrapped his fists in her hair and hung on for dear life.

"Are you good here?" Rowan glanced around. The crowd had dispersed, and this part of the terminal seemed quiet.

"Yeah," she said. "Go look around and find us some place good for lunch."

"Sure," Rowan said. "Michael? Need to stretch your legs?"

"Yeah," he said, unfolding his long lean frame, glancing back at his sister, who nodded for him to go on as she settled in to nurse the baby.

After lunch, Lauren found an empty seating area near their gate and put one of Henry's blankets down on the floor by the window so he could play and watch the airplanes. Rowan's phone needed to charge, so he went to find a place to plug in the power cord. Michael seemed content to shadow his brother-in-law. Lauren decided it would be good for the two of them to get to know each other.

Lauren smiled as she watched Henry pushing up on his arms. He looked like he might scoot off the blanket. He was ready to take off crawling in earnest at any time, and Lauren knew it wouldn't be long before he started walking. Before she was ready, she'd be chasing a toddler up and down airport terminals. Maybe she'd let Rowan do that. She smiled to herself. He could use the exercise.

Henry startled her by squealing in delight, and she realized she had drifted off into thought. She looked at him, then followed his view, and realized the security officer was walking through the area with the largest German Shepherd she had ever seen in her life. It was dark and looked vicious. Henry, however, rocked on his hands and knees grinning brightly, drool running down his chin as he lifted one hand to reach for the dog, even though it was too far away to touch.

Lauren smiled but scooped him up and snatched up his blanket as the security officer moved closer. Henry had caught his attention and he made eye-contact with Lauren as she caught Henry's hand and leaned in and said, "We mustn't touch. He's working. He's a good dog though."

"Ma ma ma ma…" Henry began to babble, looking up at her then reaching out towards the dog wagging his fingers to get the beast to come closer.

"We can't pet the puppy," she said, taking his hands.

He frowned at her. "Pup pup …"

Lauren smiled as his voice raised louder and higher in pitch. "Pup pup," he screeched. The dog had seen Henry and looked like it wanted to come over, but his handler seemed oblivious as they continued walking through the chairs. The dog returned to sniffing bags, his eyes still on Henry. Finally, the handler figured out what was going on when Henry screeched so loud the whole terminal looked his way.

The handler stopped just a few feet from Lauren so Henry could see the dog. He squirmed his hand loose and reached for the canine, but Lauren held him back, and his giggles turned to whimpers. "No touchy, sweetheart."

Henry stuck out his lip but sat back against her, as if he understood. The handler managed a faint smile towards Henry, nodded to Lauren, but went on his way with his dog. Henry whimpered again. He turned and looked up at his mom, frowning as the dog left. "It's okay, Henry. We'll find a puppy we can pet."

Henry slammed back against her chest and reached up, grabbing her hair, yanking her braid. He was brooding. It made Lauren smile, even though it hurt. His personality was beginning to shine, and clearly, he was an animal lover. She couldn't wait to take him to Yellowstone when he was older and introduce him to the wolves. She spent over a year studying them so long ago, and he might just follow in her footsteps if he didn't become the next Indiana Jones, like his dad hoped he might be.

Henry yanked her hair, hard. "Ouch!" Lauren snatched it from his grasp. Then looked down at Henry who laughed at her, his chubby cheeks dimpled deeply. "You are mean." She teased, tickling his tummy. "Yes you are! You are a mean baby! You pulled your mommy's hair. That's not nice." She scolded him, but it was playful, and she tossed her braid over her shoulder. She picked him up, turning to stand him up on her knees. He stood and grinned at her, sticking his finger in his mouth, slobbering down his shirt. The hint of a new shiny white tooth she hadn't noticed before appeared from his lower gums. "What's this?" she asked, craning her head to get a better look. "No wonder you've been so slobbery."

"What's going on?" Rowan asked as he approached with two coffees.

"He's got a new tooth," she said, turning him where Rowan could see. Rowan made faces at him to get him to smile and gurgle, and he saw it too.

"Well it's about time!" he said. "Maybe that's why he's been so fussy. I figured he'd have a couple more by now."

"This isn't fussy," Lauren said. "Henry's a good baby."

THEY MADE IT TO LONDON WITHOUT ANY ISSUES. LAUREN caught a few hours of sleep with Henry on her chest. They made the most of the layover, to eat, refresh and stretch their legs, but Lauren was tired. Henry was tired, too. She knew how hard it was for him when he got off his schedule.

Lauren lifted her head, cocking an ear to try and make sense of the PA announcement. She groaned, sitting back in her chair.

"What was that?" Rowan asked.

"Our flight's been delayed," she said. "Mechanical issue."

After a four hour delay, the flight from Heathrow finally boarded. For their final leg of their trip, Michael had the seat to her left, Rowan and Henry had the seat across the aisle to her right. This time, it was Rowan's turn to nap with the baby, and as soon as they were cleared to do so, he leaned his seat back as far as it would go. Soon, he was snoring softly with the baby laying across his chest.

"Have you ever heard the sounds made by stars?" Michael asked, leaning against her.

"I didn't realize they made sounds," Lauren said.

Michael held up a finger, then reached for his phone. He paused and handed her his headphones which were connected. He pulled up an audio file and hit play as she put the earbuds into her ears, cupping her hands over them to block out the sound of the plane's engines. She didn't know what to expect, but she certainly didn't expect what she heard. If she could compare it to anything, it would have been the tones made by running a finger around the rim of a water glass. The sounds were varying, deeper at first then higher the next. Two tones came together blending in almost a pulsating rhythm then splitting as one faded off in one ear; the other lingering a moment longer.

"Oh my gosh," Lauren gasped. "That's beautiful." She handed the headphones back as the recording ended.

"That was captured by the Hubble telescope," he said.

"Hubble did that?"

"Yeah," he said. "I recorded it while I was visiting at NASA."

Lauren detected the sadness in his voice. She put a hand

on his arm and leaned against him. "Michael, I'm so sorry for your loss."

He leaned against her in return. "Thanks. Kitty and I hadn't been seeing each other that long."

"I can tell it was … special," Lauren said.

"We dated in college and only reconnected a few days before …" He paused. "So, my team … we weren't looking for, you know." He pointed up, his eyes darting towards the heavens, so he didn't have to say the word. *Aliens*. He hesitated, clearly fighting to let his emotions go. "Finding this signal was just a pleasant happenstance. We were testing an upgrade I designed that had just been installed on the dishes in the array."

"That's amazing," Lauren said. "So you're looking for more sounds like that?"

"More or less," Michael said. "Some of the things we're listening for are the return signals sent by Voyager, and other probes sent into deep space." He hesitated, then continued. "What I want to do is figure out what is noise, and what is sound."

"What's the difference?" Lauren puzzled.

"Noise is just the unwanted sound in the background," he said. "If you listen now, you'll hear a lot of noise …" He paused a moment for her to hear to the rumble of the engines, the sounds in the cabin of the flight attendants preparing for beverage service, etcetera. "Sound has substance, there's a meaning behind it. Speech, signals … communications."

"I don't guess I ever thought of it that way," Lauren admitted.

"One of the things I accomplished was getting permission to use the Hubble to listen for these radio bursts in the area we pinpointed. It's a region of space marked by the Southern Cross, or the constellation known as *Crux*."

"You are allowed to use the Hubble?"

"Kitty gave me a day with it, but I put in an official

request for more time before I left," Michael said. "If my request is approved, I can access it from my lab. I haven't heard back yet.."

"And if you don't get your request approved?" Michael pursed his lips and raised his brow, lifting his shoulders. No words were needed.

Space ... the final frontier. Lauren knew little about it. She'd spent her career investigating the mysteries of *this* world. She hadn't had time to worry about the mysteries of *other* worlds. The *ancient gods*, she had surmised, were not of *this* world, but they had given her an amazing gift. She'd had little time to wonder where they were from or why they were here. She was grateful for their blessing; happy to have helped them find their missing child, even though it was too late to save its life.

"There was a physicist named Lem Stanislaw." Michael brought her back from her thoughts. "He theorized that there might be two reasons why we couldn't translate messages from outer space: the linguistics gap and the intelligence gap."

"I'm not sure I understand," Lauren said.

"Lem suggests that because our languages come from two different evolutionary paths, we don't share enough reference points for us to be able to understand what the message means. There's no Rosetta Stone, so to speak."

"Okay, that I can comprehend."

"The other factor is intelligence—not so much that we're too stupid to understand, just that intelligent life on Earth might not look or behave similarly. I went to a presentation at Cambridge a few years ago. Two of the speakers made the argument that there is a universal grammar of languages on earth and that this grammar should exist in extraterrestrial languages too, especially their syntax. I don't think I buy that, but I'm just an engineer. What do I know of languages?"

What do I know of languages? Lauren thought to herself. While she knew many languages, she was not a linguistics expert. She had studied ancient migration patterns and how they influenced cultures in one of her college courses. Rowan had said that his guide at Chichén Itzà had undergone DNA testing and found that many of them descended from Mongolians. There had been many debates about the existence of a land bridge between Asia and Alaska, and as far as she was concerned, the Maya's very existence was proof of that. The ancient gods may have intervened at some point, but there was no evidence to convince her of that, even with everything she knew.

It was a point that occupied her mind throughout the night as she gazed out over the dark blue sky, dotted with soft clouds illuminated by moonshine and starlight.

11

Michael's lab wasn't at all what Lauren expected. First off, the main telescope was on a mountaintop some fifty miles away. The rest of the array were scattered about the tip of Africa, including some as far away as Australia. There were thirty-eight in all. Each of the giant dishes pointed towards the sky and could be controlled from the remote location; which was an obscure office building on a campus, next to a military installation.

Michael had the limo bring them to the lab first so they could go through an orientation on safety and security protocols; as well as how the operations worked. They had nondisclosure forms that had to be signed. It meant the lab had final say on what information could be released. It would be easy enough to film the show, with the waivers they were granted, but all video would become property of the project and subject to tight scrutiny before it could be aired on television. Lauren had expected there would be some kind of NDA, but the strictness of it caught her a bit off guard.

"Legal's not going to like this," she said under her breath as they were loading back into the limo to head to their apartment.

Lauren hadn't slept since the flight to London and was practically dead on her feet. Somehow, she managed to keep going. "I'm sad we didn't get to see the actual telescopes," Lauren said to her brother as he came to bid them adieu for the day. He had work to do but promised the driver would deliver them to the apartment and he'd come to see them that evening after they'd gotten some rest.

"There's plenty of time to see them while you're here," Michael said.

Lauren would just have to be happy with that, for now.

If the lab was a letdown, the apartment most certainly was not. The bellman met them at the door of the hired car and helped them with their things. Inside the lobby, the concierge stopped to greet them and had the bellman take their things to their apartment while they took care of some paperwork. The bellman said something to the concierge in Afrikaans, and Lauren looked up at the concierge, her brow lifting.

"What?" Rowan asked.

"You speak the local dialect, mum?" The concierge grinned brightly. Lauren answered in Afrikaans.

"Your accent is beautiful." The concierge complimented her, then looked to Rowan, holding Henry. "We have a crib being brought in for your son."

"Oh," Rowan said. "Thanks." He looked at Lauren as they turned for the elevator. "Swahili too?"

"Afrikaans," Lauren said. "It's one of the dozen or so languages spoken here."

Rowan looked at her skeptically. "Really?"

"Most of the people in South Africa speak English and another language," she said, matter of factly. "Most are true polyglots."

"Like you?"

"Well." She shrugged with a lifted hand. "No one is really like me. Are they?"

"True enough," he said, shaking his head. Lauren yawned,

and Henry followed suit. "Come on." He put an arm around his wife. "Let's get settled so we can get some rest. I'm sure your brother will want to get started as soon as possible."

"Me, too," Lauren said.

DESPITE FINDING THEIR ACCOMMODATIONS LUXURIOUSLY comfortable and only a few brief hours of sleep in transit, Lauren was restless. She lay across the middle of the king-size bed in boneless relaxation, but her mind was racing a million miles an hour. The sudden comfort of having come to terms with her brother and, to a lesser degree, her mother, was oddly pleasant. She had her reservations about her mother's motives, more so than her brother's. Lauren had come to consider her mean and manipulative, and just down-right evil. She always felt like it was her own fault that her father had left; like he hadn't wanted another child, least of all a girl. Six sons would be enough for any man, right?

Would Rowan want that many kids? They hadn't talked about a limit, but he'd been thrilled to have Henry and she suspected he'd be ready for a second if the time ever came, even though she was perfectly content. The most she'd ever heard him say on the subject was, "I've always wanted to be a dad." Or "I've always wanted kids." *Kids, plural. More than one.* Lauren had never even planned to have one. Before Henry, they'd taken steps to prevent parenthood — steps that proved ineffective. In hindsight, she'd been grateful. Henry was a blessing and if their children were all as good as Henry, she'd consider having another one. *After all, what were a few more stretch marks at this point?*

Then there was Michael's mysterious screams from outer space. Now that she had heard the stars, she couldn't imagine what might be screaming through the cosmos. Perhaps she'd seen too many episodes of Star Trek. She'd always imagined space to be a very peaceful place, like a quiet dark ocean of nothing but happy little comets and peaceful floating asteroids. Now she lay wondering if the shrieks were coming from dark matter or wormholes, or little green men from Mars — or Crux — or wherever it was.

Finally, her stomach began making more noise than extraterrestrial signals possibly could, and she decided sleep was beyond her reach for the rest of the afternoon. Food was now the priority.

She rose and shook off her thoughts, wandering through the spacious suite, finding Rowan sitting in the living room floor with Henry; all his toys scattered on the blanket around him. They were watching Sesame Street, in English, on the television and sharing a box of Cheerios.

"Ah, Snuffleupagus." Lauren beamed, leaning on the back of the sofa, taking it all in.

"Pup pup!" Henry cooed, gurgling as he kicked his feet and shook his toy shark. "Pup pup!"

"Snuffy," Rowan corrected, handing him another Cheerio.

"Pup pup!"

"Henry wanted me to remind you," Rowan said. "You did promise we could have a dog."

Lauren grimaced, shaking her head. "But not a Snuffleupagus."

"True, but I saw Henry with the dog in the airport," he said. "This boy needs a dog."

"You and I both know…" Lauren started.

Rowan raised a hand and she paused.

"I know," he said. "We're going to be on the road for a while, but at some point, we have to get this kid a dog."

"We're in agreement on that." She came over and sat down. "When the time is right, it'll happen."

Rowan nodded. "So, how was your nap?"

"I didn't sleep," she said, running a weary hand over her face. "Is there anything to eat? I'm starving."

"They sent up some snacks for us," Rowan said. "But your brother said to call him when we were ready for dinner."

"Dinner?"

"It's after five," Rowan said. "You may not have been asleep; but you've been in there for hours."

"Hours?"

"Maybe you nodded off and don't remember it," he said. "Text Michael and we'll go eat. Henry and I are hungry too."

AFTER DINNER, THEY WENT TO A CAFÉ MICHAEL KNEW NEAR the lab and insisted was safe enough. There they had coffees and desserts. As they sat at the walled-in patio in the warm evening air, the perfume of flowers drifted by. "They call this the *City of Roses*," Michael explained. "It's supposed to be spring here, but as you can tell, it's a lot like Oklahoma."

"It's a beautiful city," Lauren said, sipping on her coffee, pushing her cake around with her fork.

"I have made arrangements for us to get a tour of the planetarium," he said. "It's the only digital planetarium here. I work with the head astronomer and I got us access to their telescope."

"When? Tonight?"

"If you want to," he said. "I just need to text him and let him know we're coming. They're working every night this week."

"I'm sure Lauren's ..." Rowan started to decline, but Lauren cut him off.

"Tonight's good for me," she said. "I'm not sleepy." She glanced over at Henry who was nodding off in his Dad's lap, slobbering all over the side of his hand as he gnawed on Rowan's knuckle. He was teething and it must have felt good. Rowan didn't seem to mind. "But if you wanted to go back to the apartment ..."

"No," Rowan shook his head. "I caught a nap when Henry napped. He can sleep anywhere."

"Then let's go."

~

THE PLANETARIUM REMINDED HER A LOT OF THE SCIENCE museum in Oklahoma City. Her school had gone there on a field trip once when she was a kid. She'd loved that museum, but she'd forgotten about it ... until now. Now the memories flooded back. They had a theater for star shows and a variety of science experiments tailored to kids or just kids at heart. The Tesla Coil had been one of her favorites, but what she genuinely loved were the star shows.

"Lubanzi, this is my sister, Lauren and her husband, Rowan." Michael introduced her to the director and head astronomer. "Lauren this is Dr. Lubanzi Dlamani."

The man had skin as dark as coal, so dark his lips were almost blue. He was slender, if not downright gaunt; his yellowed teeth were crooked, but he had a quick smile. He rose from his desk to greet them. "Welcome, welcome," he said in a thick accent, taking Rowan's hand but not hers. Instead he bowed deeply. "Dr. Grayson, I am most honored."

"It's Pierce now," she corrected politely. Her hand went to Rowan's arm. "I took my husband's name. I just use Grayson on television."

"We are honored to have you both." He bowed again. "Welcome. I will show you ... the cosmos." He waved his hand towards the ceiling where tiny pinpricks of lights representing the constellations shown through the dark blue ceiling overhead.

Lauren and Rowan exchanged pleased expressions as Rowan put his sleepy son up on his shoulder and fell in behind their melodramatic host. Michael leaned into Lauren. "I think he has a crush on you."

"What?" She mouthed silently.

"Ever since I mentioned you were my sister; he's been asking to see pictures of you. I honestly don't think he believed me that *you* were my sister."

"You did mention that if he made a pass at me, Rowan would beat him up, right?"

"There would be a long line of Graysons standing behind him waiting for a turn." Michael took her arm as they followed Dr. Dlamani through the dimly lit museum. After hours, there was almost no one there, and even the janitors had finished their work and gone home for the night. It wasn't quite ten, and despite the differences in time zones and the long travel, Lauren felt as spry as a teenager.

"Are you familiar with the work of Dr. Raymond Code?" Lubanzi asked.

Lauren shook her head. "I can't say that I am."

"He was my mentor," Lubanzi said. "This was the telescope he gave me after completing my dissertation." He led them into a small room with a retractable ceiling. The telescope he indicated, was sitting on the table. It was about the same size as one of the old-fashioned movie projectors Rowan's mother had given him, the one that still sat in his office back home; half a world away.

"I had the honor of working with him before he died about seven or eight years ago," Michael explained to his sister. "He was brilliant. A lot of the work we're doing today is based on some of his groundbreaking research."

"He was the founding director of the Radio Telescope Science Institute," Lubanzi said. "He helped pave the road for the Hubble telescope."

She leaned in to look in the scope, at Lubanzi's silent behest. It took a moment for her eyes to focus, but she finally got the resolution to clear enough to make out the patterns of stars. "You should be able to see the Southern Cross," he explained and guided her eye toward the constellation marked by four bright stars and one slightly dimmer one.

"This is the particular area of space I was telling you about," Michael said. His tone told her this was the area the signal he'd been tracking had come from. Lauren stepped back and let Rowan have a turn, taking the sleeping baby. "Dr. Code told me stories about his time in the navy back during World War II. He built a number of radio receivers, but he was the first to suggest the receivers needed to be in space, not on earth."

"He said that having receivers on earth was like watching birds from the bottom of the ocean," Dr. Dlamani said. "Or something like that."

"Yes and it was sheer genius," Michael said, looking in the telescope himself.

Lubanzi waved them along behind him. "Come, let's see the bigger telescope."

The room where the *bigger telescope* resided was a huge domed area. They entered a small control room with a wide arching glass view port. "This telescope has a multitude of uses. It has all the features of an apochromatic telescope. It can disperse light into three wave lengths at one time; but also has the achromatic lenses that contains liquid between the lenses to aid in dispersion."

"Is that the bigger telescope?" Rowan pointed to the large tube pointed towards the ceiling. Lubanzi reached over and hit a switch and the ceiling began to part like a cyclop's eye after a long nap.

"No," Lubanzi said. "This is the *biggest* telescope."

"Has to be one of the biggest I've ever seen." Rowan shrugged.

"The only one bigger is on the summit of Mauna Kea," Michael said. "That is a twin ten-meter lens in Hawaii. This one is just a single lens."

"That's not that far from our house." Lauren nodded,

smiling at Rowan, suddenly feeling far from home. The bungalow outside of Hilo sat empty. She could imagine sitting out on the lanai watching the wind and the waves play against the rocky shore. She could smell the bouquet of flowers in the humid night air. She could taste the Kona coffee on her lips, and the sweetness of the pineapples she often snacked on. A wave of homesickness washed over her, then passed just as quickly as the astronomer brought her out of the moment.

"Here. Take a look," Lubanzi said, getting the telescope set up, pointing to a screen. "Here is the Southern Cross." He zoomed in on the area, naming each of the stars that made up the constellation. "But we can see so much more ..." he said, zooming in even deeper. The dark void was filled with pinpricks of light as invisible stars became visible.

"Wow!" Rowan exclaimed. "That's amazing."

"Somewhere here, someone is calling to us," Michael said.

Lauren turned and looked at her brother. "That's a pretty bold statement ... for a scientist."

"What do you mean?" Rowan asked. "I thought you were in on Michael's theory that it was a message from ... someone." Lauren was so accustomed to being mocked and ridiculed that it was easy for her to get defensive. Finding the Maya artifacts in Mexico had helped minimize some of the hazing from the scientific community, but some of the chatter he'd heard had called their discovery a stroke of luck. He wanted as much to make a significant find again just to prove them wrong, but Lauren took it all way too personally.

"On the contrary." She shrugged. "It's one thing to acknowledge that someone is sending a message, and that we might be able to translate it, but it's terribly vain to believe they're sending it specifically to us."

"Why not us?" Michael's eyes narrowed and the wrinkles around his eyes deepened.

"To use your analogy, that's like the Yeti in Bhutan yelling, *Hey Michael, I'm over here!* There's a difference."

"But isn't the point of science to observe and theorize?"

"Yes, but not speculate. Theory has to be based on data," Lauren said, surprised to be having this conversation with, of all people, her brother. "You haven't isolated the possibility that it's a natural phenomenon. You don't have any evidence that they're trying to contact Earth specifically. You haven't ruled out other possibilities. You just automatically jump to the conclusion that it's little green men from Mars or… Crux …whatever."

"But Occam's Razor? Besides, I'm more interested in the Fermi Paradox," he started, but Lauren's eyes narrowed, and he stopped. "Hey, I never said they were green," Michael retorted like a wounded school-boy. "Honestly, Lauren. Of all people, I would expect *you* to be a little more open to the idea, considering what *you* do for a living ... chasing ghosts and things that go bump in the night," Michael quipped. "Can you even walk into a room full of scientists and not get laughed at?"

His sudden turn caught her completely off guard. She looked around with a limp hand raised. "No one is laughing here," Lauren said. "Besides, *you* asked for *my* help, but if you'd rather stand here and mock me, I can go home."

"Okay. Okay." Rowan stepped in between them before either of them said anything else they would regret. "It's late and we're all tired. Let's just agree to disagree at the moment."

Lauren moved past him to stare at her brother, but Rowan took a step to block her, drawing her gaze to his eye instead. He took the brunt of her raven fury. "You haven't slept in two days. He's not mocking you, just let it go."

Her color seemed to lighten as her countenance melted. "You're right." She leaned into his chest and let out a deep sigh. "I'm sorry, Michael. Rowan is right. I'm too tired to fight tonight."

"So what? Words at twenty paces at high noon tomorrow?" He quipped sharply. Rowan recognized a smart aleck when he met one. He *was* one. But Lauren balled up and moved to get past him.

Rowan caught her arm. "Lauren. Let it go." He drew her eyes to his by lifting her chin. "It takes two to fight."

"Come on," she said. "Let's go back to the apartment."

THE NEXT MORNING, THE CONCIERGE HELPED LAUREN ORDER some groceries to serve as their breakfast and lunches. They napped in short spurts and by dinnertime, they were better rested, and hungry for a good meal. The concierge had dinner brought in. She was pleased to find that a bottle of wine was included in the order. Rowan fed Henry a bowl of his rice cereal and some pureed peas while Lauren set the table and plated their dinner. Henry was covered in baby food when she came over with the corkscrew, opening the bottle. She poured two glasses of chardonnay, then brought over their plates. She sat down and set to work on her food, while Rowan finished feeding Henry, then lay out some Cheerios on the table of his highchair so he could entertain himself while Rowan turned to his own dinner.

Lauren watched him from beneath the veil of her bangs but said nothing. They'd spoken little since leaving the lab and she was still trying to decide if she should be mad at him or if Michael should bear the whole brunt of her anger. Rowan had stuck up for her brother, and she wanted to use that as an excuse to take it out on him, but in truth, she knew better. Rowan was a peacemaker if anything. If she and Michael were ever going to find a path through and make things work, she needed that. She'd spent the better part of the last decade being mad and not speaking to her brother. Now, she'd had her chance to speak her mind and she'd spoken it. If there was justice in the universe, and Lauren knew there was, she had to let it go. He'd offered his apologies for his past transgressions, and she'd accepted them. She had to be the one. She had to trust the Universe. She had to forgive. No one else could do it for her.

"You okay?" Rowan's voice drew her from her thoughts.

"Yeah." She stabbed at her food with her fork, but she'd spent more time pushing it around than eating it.

"I can see how you and your brother have been at odds for so long," Rowan said.

"Yeah," she repeated, picking up her glass and draining it, reaching for the bottle for another pour.

"What are you going to do?" He reached for his own glass.

One of Lauren's shoulders lifted. "I've given my word," Lauren said. "I have forgiven his past, but … that doesn't mean I'll let him treat me like that in the future."

"Fair enough," Rowan said.

"Tsul'Kalu's words keep coming back to me." Lauren didn't look up as she spoke. She could feel his eyes on her and sensed his reservation. He didn't like it when she talked about Tsul'Kalu. "Justice demands repayment for the trouble he's created."

"Because the rabbit was the leader in all the mischief?" Rowan asked, surprising her as she looked up at him. "I get it. Michael is your *rabbit*."

Lauren's face lightened, and the corners of her lips turned up. He had been paying attention. He had been listening. "Yes," Lauren said. Bahati's words came back to here, too. "But the rabbit is not wholly wrong in this case. I've played my own part. It has to be me that makes peace work."

Rowan considered her a moment, as if trying to read her. "Do you think he's changed?"

She considered this for a long time. "Perhaps, but … that doesn't matter." She returned her attention to her plate. "I have."

~

"Lauren, look, I'm sorry about yesterday," Michael said before Lauren could get a word in edgewise. "I was a jerk, and you didn't deserve that."

"I guess I was, too." Lauren conceded.

"You guess?"

"Michael, I want us to be able to work together, and I don't want us to bicker."

He hesitated a moment, then nodded. "I want that for us, too," Michael said. "So, remember on the plane, I played you the signal I recorded from Hubble?"

"Yes," Lauren said, as he led her back to his office.

"That's not exactly the same signal we've been monitoring from here," he said. "The repeating signal is different. Whereas the signal I played for you is sublime, this one is ...enfeebling."

Lauren's brow arched and she gazed at him. He pulled a chair out for her at one of the workstations, indicating for her to sit. She did and watched as he squatted beside her. He turned the keyboard around and typed in his password. It took a moment for the terminal to boot up, and while it did, he handed her a pair of headphones. She pulled the headphones on over her ears. When the computer woke, he cued up a file and sat back on his heels.

"First, you'll hear the same types of sounds you heard earlier," he said, as she lifted the muff to hear him. "You'll know it when you hear the signal I'm concerned about."

Lauren's hands cupped the headphones as she closed her eyes waiting for the recording to play.

"This is at normal speed," Michael said. The music of the stars filled her ears and a wave of peacefulness washed over her. She listened for the signals she expected to hear, but there was nothing unusual. If he hadn't told her, she might have thought it was the same file he'd played for her on the plane. It was beautiful and rich like whales' voices in the deep cold sea. She remembered Rowan talking about the whales he'd seen diving off the lava fields south of Hilo, and she suddenly felt a pang of jealousy for having missed out.

She opened her eyes and looked to Michael. "Pretty, but I don't hear anything out of the ordinary."

"Let me speed it up," he said, messing with the controls. He hit the play button and the cosmic song came out as more of an aria. The notes shortened as they chased each other in growing crescendos; then, it hit her. A sharp high pitch screech nearly shattered her ear drums. She couldn't get the headphones off fast enough. Michael looked startled. "Sorry," he hit the controls. "I didn't realize I had it that loud."

"Jesus Christ, Michael!" she said loudly, then stuck a finger in her ear and shook it trying to get the ringing to stop. The room tilted and one hand went to the edge of the desk to hold herself upright. "That was loud."

"Sorry," he said. "But see what I mean about the difference?"

"Sheesh!" She shook her head. The ringing began to subside. "That's insane."

"It's like screaming," he said. "Right?"

"Uh huh," Lauren's ears were still ringing.

"Can you make any sense of it?" he asked. "Does it sound like … language? You'd know if it was a language right?"

Lauren's face remained pinched as she considered him. "I think I would, but … but I don't hear anything in the recording …" She stuck her finger in her ear again. "Probably because I can't hear anything other than ringing."

"Look." He pulled up a chair and took her hand, pulling her into him. "I told you you'd think I was crazy, but …in these dreams I've been having I told you I would wake up some place different, right?"

"Yeah," Lauren puzzled, wondering where this was going.

"And I told you I thought I'd been abducted by aliens."

"Uh huh?"

"I saw them," he said. "They talked to me. They told me things. Things that come back to me in bits and pieces. Things I don't understand, but yet, somehow I know that in this signal there is a message, and it is important that I find it. That *we* find it."

"Why is it so important?" she asked.

"I wish to the gods I knew," he said.

Lauren gazed at him a moment. "I'll listen to them, on one condition." She held up a finger.

"Sure," Michael said. "Anything."

"You're going to have to show me where the volume control is."

"There are fundamental laws which apply to the entire universe," Dr. India Cameron explained as they sat at the conference table. Michael had introduced his sister to his boss, and the conversation had taken most of the afternoon. "It's because of these fundamental laws that we have to believe that if life developed on Earth, intelligent life must have developed elsewhere, too," she reasoned. Michael had made certain she knew that her boss was in on his secret project and they could talk freely with her about it.

"Fermi's paradox," Lauren agreed. "It's my understanding, just from the limited information Michael has given me, you believe these signals come from a sentient species."

"Has he filled you in on *Project Morning Star* then?"

"*Project Morning Star*? That's the name of your telescope that you're working on, right?" Lauren asked.

"It's also the name of the secret project," Michael said. "These signals…" He looked to his boss. "I figured the less I told them, the better," Michael explained.

"Probably for the best," India said. "Just know this, we are looking for life in the universe outside our own solar system. We believe we may have found it within our own galaxy."

Lauren felt like Mr. Spock as her brow lifted and she spoke. "Fascinating." She thought on this idea for a moment. "So let's talk serious science. How would one go about looking for life in the galaxy? I mean, what kind of scientific process are you using. What's your methodology? Surely you're not relying on these *screams* from space alone, are you?"

"Of course not," India's face lit up. "We use radio-waves to scan for exo-planets around stars similar to our own. We're looking for several things. First is an exo-planet in an area we call *The Goldilocks Zone* … not too cold, not too hot … just right."

"Cute." Lauren mused.

"Then we look for evidence of an atmosphere," she said.

"Can you tell that with a radio telescope?"

"We can," she said. "More or less. If we had access to Hubble, we could verify the preliminary data."

"I didn't get enough time with Hubble when I was in Houston to check." Michael looked sheepishly at India. "Assuming our technology continues to improve, we think we'll be able to examine over a million stars in the next twenty years or so. We think that at least one in a million will have a habitable exo-planet." Michael continued. "But if this signal is sentient, if it's a message, we could save twenty to thirty years of work, if we can identify the source."

"Have you ever considered that they might not be all that much like us? They might not even be carbon-based. In fact, they're more likely to be silicon-based; it's the next sequence in the periodic table."

"Valid point. We are definitely a product of our evolution. But there are theories that we might have been influenced, or formed and shaped by outside sources," India said.

"Alien DNA," Lauren muttered to herself. She'd heard this theory before. She had discredited it at the time.

"What's your blood type, Lauren?" Michael asked.

"A-negative, but what's that got to do with anything?"

"I'm A-negative as well," Michael noted. "There's some who think that negative factor is indicative of alien DNA."

Lauren sniffed. "It's a simple genetic mutation that occurred sometime in our evolutionary past. *You* might be an alien, but *I* certainly am not."

"Rude." Michael protested. Lauren gave him a wink to show she was joking. He was not. "Did you know that 15% of the modern population have the negative Rh factor?"

"So?"

"Did you know the majority of those people live, or have genetic connection to the Iberian Peninsula?"

"What's that got to do with it?"

"Ever heard of the Astronaut of Cesar?"

"Any relationship to the Astronaut of Palenque?"

"Actually, yes." Michael surprised her. "It's a carving found in the Iberian Peninsula, of what appears to be an alien. The stone dates back thousands of years. Archaeological and linguistics analysis of the astronaut shows unusual features that cannot be explained with the knowledge that we have now of the cultures and languages of ancient Iberia. The going theory is visitation by extra-terrestrials."

"Aliens are responsible for human's having a negative Rh factor. Is that what you're saying?"

"It's one of the theories," Michael said.

Lauren turned to say something but paused with her mouth agape. She closed it abruptly but hesitated to speak again. "Fine. Where can I find more on the linguistics of the region and this Astronaut of Cesar?"

Rowan arrived at the lab with a wailing baby on his hip. Henry's face was red and crocodile tears welled up in his eyes and ran down his face, along with slobber that darkened his shirt. Every once in a while, he'd add a wailing, "Ma ma ma!" to his tirade.

Lauren turned when the door opened and was halfway across the room as Rowan thrust the boy into her arms. "Oh, baby! What's the matter? Huh?"

"Do you have any idea what time it is?" Rowan demanded, clearly frustrated. "I've been trying to call you for hours."

Lauren glanced up at the clock and her whole countenance collapsed. "Oh, honey." She took Henry over to a chair at the conference table and sat down with him. "I'm so sorry. I completely lost track of the time."

"I gave him his last bottle four hours ago," Rowan said. "I tried cereal, Cheerios, peaches, but he didn't want any of them. He's been inconsolable for the last forty-five minutes. When you didn't answer, I didn't know what else to do."

"No, you're fine." Lauren settled in to nurse him and he heaved one last sob before he relaxed and calmed. "I don't know what happened. I must have laid my phone down somewhere."

Rowan took a chair across from her and put a hand on her knee. "It's okay. I knew where to find you."

"I'm sorry," she said, for the first time to him. "I meant to call you when we stopped for lunch."

"So, why didn't you?"

"We never did," she said, looking around. "Michael!" she called out.

A moment later, Michael came in carrying a stack of books. The tomes were large, old leather-bound volumes of information. He fumbled one, and Rowan jumped up to catch it before it hit the floor. He took half the stack and set it on the table. "Hey, Rowan," Michael said. "When'd you get here?"

"Just a few minutes ago," he said. "What's the big idea?"

Michael froze, looking wounded. "What?"

"Make my wife work all day without lunch," Rowan

grumbled. "She's still eating for two, you know." He nodded to Henry.

"Huh?" Michael looked up at the clock, wincing as he realized it was after seven p.m. "Oh, dang. Lauren, so sorry. You too, Rowan. I don't know what happened."

Rowan shook his head. He knew dang well what had happened, by the sheer number of reference books on the conference table. Lauren was like a hound dog with a treed raccoon when it came to figuring out a mystery. He mused, remembering Michael's story of her and the raccoon. Clearly she'd found a hint to the mysterious signals and was on the hunt. She wouldn't quit 'til she dropped, if left to her own devices. "Well," he huffed. "You two are clearly cut from the same cloth. I don't care what you're working on, wrap it up. As soon as Henry finishes his dinner, I'm taking my wife out to eat. You're more than welcome to join us."

"I know just the place," he said.

THE RESTAURANT MUST HAVE BEEN ONE MICHAEL FREQUENTED often. The owner greeted him with a kiss on each cheek and called him by name. "Amari, this is my sister," he introduced Lauren. "And my brother-in-law Rowan, and their son Henry."

"Welcome. Welcome." The rotund woman wore a brightly colored caftan and a matching turban tied around her head in the traditional style. "Come. The private dining room is ready for you." Michael had called ahead in the car.

"Thank you, Amari," he said. "Is Jamal on duty today?"

"Of course," she said. "Don't worry. No one will bother you here. All my boys are on duty today."

"Thank you, Amari."

"Now come, I put a bottle of your favorite wine on to chill

when you called. I'll pour you a glass. Lauren? Rowan? Wine?"

"God, yes," Lauren said.

At the same time, Rowan answered. "I'll pass."

"Can I get anything for the little man?" She cooed over Henry, pinching his cheek, and ran a dark hand over the curls at the nape of his neck.

"He's been fed," Lauren said as they entered the dining room. "Maybe some water. Bottled, if you don't mind."

"Of course." She nodded. "How old is he?"

"Not quite a year," Lauren said.

"He favors his father." She patted his head one last time as they were seated. "I'll be back with a highchair and some water for him. Please take a moment to look over the menu and I'll take your order when I come back."

"So what did you guys do all day today?" Lauren asked as Henry wrapped his chubby little fists in her braid and stretched to try and reach her earring. A tilt of her head kept the charm safe from his grasp.

"We took a bubble bath, and we went to the park in the middle of the apartment complex. We saw a genet in the park. Henry shrieked so loud, if anyone had been around, they'd have called the police."

"A genet? Really?" Lauren gasped. A genet was a feline native to the area, larger than a ferret, but smaller than a housecat. She'd heard about them but hadn't seen one herself.

"They're usually nocturnal." Michael's expression mirrored his sister's. "I think they're known carriers of rabies."

"It was more scared of Henry than anything." Rowan shrugged. "But you know how he is with animals. The kid is crazy about them."

"They seem to like him too," Lauren said to her brother. "He's charmed half the cats and at least three chickens on the Big Island of Hawaii."

Michael folded his menu and set it aside. "Why Hawaii? I can think of about thirty other places to live that cost less and are easier to get to."

"We wanted to stay in San Diego," Rowan said. "But we couldn't find a place. Hawaii was a compromise. We figured we'd eventually rent it out through Air B&B, but we needed a place to call home."

"Well what about you, Michael? South Africa? Really?"

"This was where the work was," he said. "I have an apartment, kind of like yours. If our grant doesn't get renewed, I might have to find another project, and there's no guarantee it'll be here."

"We have a guest room if it's at Mauna Kea," Lauren said.

"I'll keep that in mind," he said. "Speaking of which, this would be a great night to do some star gazing, if you're not too tired."

Rowan's glass lowered mid-sip. "As if she hasn't had a long enough day already?"

"Surprisingly, I'm not all that tired," she said. "Why don't you and Henry come with us."

"But Henry ..."

"He can sleep anywhere," Lauren said. "I'll put him in my sling, and I'll be right there if he needs me."

"I've got a small telescope I can take with us," Michael said. "I know a nice spot just outside of the city where the light pollution isn't so bad."

"I'm game," Lauren said, turning to Rowan. His features were heavy with concern, but she gazed at him, her eyes pleading.

"Okay," he said, conceding.

"Let's eat so we can go see some stars," she said as much to Henry as to anyone else.

~

LAUREN SPREAD A LARGE BLANKET DOWN ON THE GRASSY HILL far outside the city. It was darker than she'd expected, but she had a small flashlight she used to inspect the star chart Michael had brought along. She used the light sparingly to save their eyes, as Rowan stretched out on his back and tucked one hand behind his head. Lauren sat cross-legged with Henry in her lap, her braid wrapped in his fist. He reached for the light with the other hand, but Lauren held it and the map out of his reach. Michael set up the small telescope he'd brought with them on a tripod, then, pointed it towards the sky.

Stars bedazzled the dark above. Lauren scanned the sky, orienting herself. With her excellent sense of direction, she always knew which way was north, but outside of the northern hemisphere, the stars were of no help in navigating, at least – not initially. Given time to orient, she'd be just as efficient in wayfinding as always.

Michael spent a little over an hour giving them a tutorial on the constellations of the southern night sky. Lauren thought again of the star shows they'd seen at the Science Museum in Oklahoma City as kids. Michael had been fifteen, she had been five. He'd sat beside her and listened to the docent just as intently as she had, and it was one of the few fond memories she'd had of their time together as children. He would have been an excellent docent at the museum. His deep voice was warm, familiar.

Finally, he went silent for a long moment. He cleared his throat before he continued. "The signals we're studying have come from the general direction, somewhere between Crux and the Southern Pleiades," Michael said, as if that should have been obvious. "But it's a broad area of space, so it's been nearly impossible to pinpoint. We've triangulated multiple occurrences. At one point, it seemed to come from the Southern Pleiades, whether it's moving or we're off in our triangulation, it's hard to say."

"The Pleiades?" Lauren's brow twitched.

"Mean something to you?"

"The Pleiades play a central role in the stories of the Annunaki, the ancient Sumerians," she muttered.

"The Annunaki?" Michael asked. "I think I've heard some stories about them, but I always discounted them as myth."

Lauren ran a hand over her son's head as he cooed, gurgling in his chest; content. "The word itself means *those of royal blood*," Lauren began. "They were believed to be immortal gods that lived on the earth in ancient Mesopotamia. They were said to be advanced beings with currency, astronomy and even things as simple as farming."

"Ah," Michael said. "The Pleiades play a role in ancient Egyptian myths and even in Cherokee legends too, you know."

"I remember Aunt Mary's stories about the Seven Sisters when I was a kid." Lauren nodded, leaning back. "What I find so curious is the similarities in the ancient legends from the Annunaki to even the stories you read about in the bible."

Now it was Michael's brow that flinched. "Oh?"

"There were two primary hero-gods in the Annunaki legends," Lauren said. "Enlil and Enki, they were half-brothers. Enki was the *protector of mankind*, while Enlil was thought to be the *creator of mankind*, but with a less-than-benevolent purpose. He made men from clay, but only to enslave them. As the story goes, they needed gold, and so humans were made to provide that for the gods." Lauren paused, thinking, then continued. "Enlil was also the guardian of the *Tablets of Destiny*."

"What's that?" Michael asked.

"Nothing more than a clay tablet, marked with writing similar to cuneiform; a Rosetta stone, if you will."

"Okay." Michael drew the word out, encouraging her to continue.

"Sorry, I digress." Lauren stood, hoisting Henry up onto

her shoulder. He lay his head down and wrapped his arms around her neck. "Enlil was the oppressor of mankind. He was not a *good guy*, to say the least. He was a *bad guy* through and through. But Enki was practically the opposite; mankind's benefactor and hero."

Michael allowed her to pace and ramble through her thoughts as she processed them. He watched her, but said nothing, allowing her his undivided attention.

"Enki sticks up for humans in conflict with the gods. But Enki wasn't too pleased when he discovered Enlil planned to wipe out the very race he had created. So he warned Utnapishtim to construct an ark."

"Like Noah?"

"Exactly like Noah, and he commanded him to load up the Ark with the animals."

"Interesting," Michael nodded, templing his fingers in front of him as he thought.

"But the correlation between this story and Noah isn't what I think is so fascinating about these two." Lauren hesitated, glancing up at the sky as a shooting star streaked high overhead.

"Oh?"

"Who came up with the name Project Morning Star?" Lauren asked, seemingly catching Michael off guard. He did a double take.

"Huh? I did. Why is that important?"

"Why? Why did you name it that?"

Michael stuffed his hands into the pockets of his jacket and shrugged. "Sounded good."

"Who is the Morning Star? In the Bible? Do you know?"

"You'd think after all those Sunday mornings of Mom dragging us to church I'd remember some of that, but … I don't."

"It's okay," Lauren said with a mischievous grin. "I do. The Bible refers to Jesus as the Morning Star."

"Oh," Michael said, sheepishly.

"Ironically, the Bible also refers to Lucifer as the Morning Star."

"Wait, what?" Michael quipped. "Lucifer? And Jesus?"

"The twin hero gods of Christian religion." Lauren's voice went misty as she thought aloud. She rocked Henry who's limp weight grew heavy as he dozed off, still patting his mother's back as she wrapped a blanket around him.

"Enki and Enlil … the twin hero gods of the Sumerians," Michael added.

"Hero and anti-hero." She glanced at her brother.

"One the god of death, the other the god of life …" he said. "Like Demeter and Hades in Greek mythology."

"Thor and Loki of the Norse mythos. Xbalanque and Hunahpu of the ancient Maya." Lauren paused a moment. "There's even some who have compared Enki and Enlil with Adam and Eve."

"How so?"

"Both were the sons of Anu, the supreme god in the Sumerian pantheon. Both were sent to the Earth," Lauren said. "But that's where the correlation ends, if you ask me. Enlil was given dominion over mankind, but he was a cruel taskmaster. Enki was not happy about his brother's promotion and became the defender of man. Eventually, a rift formed, and the brothers grew at odds with one another."

"Kind of like us," Michael said. "I never meant for that to happen; you know?"

Lauren looked at him, realizing she had apologies of her own to make. "I realize I have not been wholly innocent in our rift," she admitted. "I'm sorry I let it go as long as I did. I didn't see a path through, so … I just quit trying. It never occurred to me that I'd placed just as many of the barricades between us. I regret that now."

There was a long pause between them. "Can I ask you a very serious question and get a serious answer?" Michael asked as she went over and sat back down by Rowan who snored softly. She tucked Henry up against his father as the baby dozed off peacefully.

Lauren looked up at Michael. "I guess so."

"Do you believe in aliens?" he asked. "I mean truly believe they're out there." His eyes went back to the heavens above.

"Why Michael? Why would you ask that now? You teased me for years about finding them before I did. What gives?"

"It's just … I never thought to ask." He paused. "I have watched every episode of your television show, every special, every video of your public appearances on YouTube. I've read every one of your blogs. I have a subscription to the Exploration Channel's magazine, and I read it cover-to-cover. I don't think I've ever heard you say, or seen it in print, that you believe in any of the things you've spent your life looking for. I think it's a fair question."

Lauren forced her thoughts aside as she rose and walked over to the telescope, leaning down to gaze into it. The move gave her a moment to think. She chose her words with extreme care. "I believe in statistics," she said, curtly. Her eyes went to the sky and she lifted a hand to the cosmos. "Billions and billions of stars…" She turned back to Michael. "If it can happen here, it has to happen out there too … at least in some form."

"Okay." Michael took a moment, seemingly to absorb what she was saying. "I just …I really needed to hear you say that."

"Really?" She puzzled, contorting her face in confusion. "Why?"

His shoulder lifted. "Why seek aliens when you don't believe in them?"

"Because I'm curious about my world … and the worlds beyond. I want to know what's out there and how we relate to our universe." She hesitated, taking a deep breath. "Hunting for extraterrestrial biology differs from most science … in that its hypothesis can't be disproven. You can't tell me I'm wrong if I say *aliens definitely exist*. Can you?"

"Do you believe aliens definitely exist?"

A bemused expression passed over Lauren's visage. "I want to believe."

"And do you believe me when I tell you I've seen them? That I've somehow been teleported to their ship?" His voice seemed to tremble as he came over and stood beside her.

"I do," she said. "Because … while you are many things, Michael, you are not a liar."

A wave of relief seemed to wash over him, and he all but melted right then and there. "Thank the gods," he said, running his hand over his face. "I needed to hear you say that."

"What's going on, Michael?" She could sense he was worried about something.

"Since all this started, I haven't been sleeping. Even though I've never been harmed, it terrified me to think that they were coming for me. I mean, at first … I thought it was just a dream," he said. "Then, I tried to convince myself it was my imagination. That I'd been watching too much of your stuff. That episode from Peru … my God. I still get chills thinking about that body you found."

"Me too," Lauren said.

"Then I convinced myself I was going crazy," Michael said. "India made me see a counselor, a shrink."

"How …" Lauren's mind was racing, and she couldn't form a logical question. "How often?"

"It was sporadic at first, once or twice in the span of a few months," he said. "But it became more frequent. I'd listen to the signals all day, then go to bed … and wake up … somewhere else." He looked up, his hands tightening in hers. "I really needed to hear you say you believed me."

"Michael." She softened. The look in his eyes sent an ache through her core. She felt for him. She truly did. "I believe …

I … I believe something is happening to you and I'm here to help you. What can I do?"

"Help me figure out this mystery." His eyes pleaded.

"That's why I'm here," Lauren said holding his gaze, seeing the exhaustion in his eyes. "When was the last time you slept more than just a few hours?"

Michael withdrew, tucking his hands under his thighs, shivering, even though the night was warm enough. "Too long."

She glanced over at her husband and son. "Come stay with us tonight," she said. "I'll watch over you so you can rest."

"You can't stop it." He suddenly looked terrified. "I've tried."

"If they come for you," Lauren said. "Then they'll have to get past me."

WHEN MICHAEL AND LAUREN RETURNED TO THE LAB LATE THE next morning, he was bright-eyed and rested. He hadn't slept so well in such a long time. Lauren, still functioning on almost no sleep, had kept her word. She curled up in the recliner beside the sofa where he slept and spent the whole night doing research. She was anxious to keep at it.

She hoped Rowan wouldn't be too upset about being left behind with the baby, but they'd come here to work, and work was what she needed — almost as much as she needed sleep. But sleep could wait, for now.

First up, was a review of the history of the Iberian Penin-sula and the Sumerian texts that coincided with the tales of alien space crafts and gods from the stars. Michael left her at the computer. He had a meeting with India and the team.

The *Tablets of Destiny*, she quickly learned, was believed to be little more than a mythical item. In the Mesopotamian mythology it was nothing more than a clay tablet inscribed with cuneiform writing, impressed with cylinder seals, and served as a permanent legal document conferred upon the god Enlil, giving him supreme authority as ruler of the universe. The legend went on to say that whoever possessed the tablets, ruled the universe. Yet another legend contradicted the first.

Instead, the tablets were made from precious metals or stone. The tablets weren't a contract, but instead described in detail the forces of nature that would enable the world to exist, or how to destroy it. Enlil had lost the tablets when they were stolen by Anzu who created seven monsters, one with each of the seven tablets. The monsters were to guard them from the wrath of Enlil, and included a dragon, a bison-beast, a scorpion-man, a seven-headed serpent, and a giant hairy beast to rule over the creatures of the earth, including man.

The Beryl Tablet, responsible for creating the giant beast, had been fashioned of chrysoberyl, also known as Cat's Eye. It was originally a statue of Utu, the Sumerian god of Justice. Lauren's hand went over her mouth as she tried to process what she was reading.

The text went on to tell about an epic battle between Enlil and Enki, as the brothers battled for authority over the Heavens and the Earth. When Enlil lost his tablets – whether there was just one, or seven – he lost the strength to defeat Enki, and the battle ended as he was cast out of the heavens. He called out to his brother a dire warning, that he would return, reclaim his power, and destroy not only the humans he created to serve as his slaves, but the entire Earth, just to spite his brother.

When Michael returned, she spent nearly twenty minutes telling him everything she had learned. "So, where are the tablets now? And why is that important?"

"What if it's some kind of … of Rosetta Stone. Something

to help me translate the screams. What if it's a signal from Enlil? What if he's coming back to follow up on his threat?"

Michael put a hand on his shoulder. "This isn't like you, Lauren."

"What?" She protested. "Science requires we pose a hypothesis, then work to prove or disprove it. I am trying to prove the hypothesis that there's a message in these signals. Think about it, communication is a system of imparting or exchanging information or ideas through common symbols, signs, or behaviors. I currently have no frame of reference for this theorized language, if it truly is there. Short of divine intervention, I need a Rosetta Stone if I am to make sense of it all."

That gave him a moment's pause. "Okay, so … where is the tablet or tablets?"

"One of the texts I read said they'd been placed in the Ark of the Covenant," she said.

Michael recoiled, and stood, pacing. "Now I know you're off your rocker. First you name your kid after Indiana Jones, and now this?"

Lauren's upper lip contorted and her eye twitched. "Think about it, Michael. In all of human history there has been only two sets of tablets that empower man with the words of God … or the gods. The tablets of the Ten Commandments and the Tablets of Destiny. Could it be that the Tablets of Destiny are the real power behind the Tablets that Moses returns with from Mount Sinai?"

"Or maybe the Tablets of Destiny are just the Annunaki version of the Ten Commandments," Michael proposed.

"Possibly. I mean, these tablets were said to hold the secrets of the Universe on them. It gave the holder their knowledge that had allowed the Annunaki to live for ages, to levitate and travel huge distances at great speeds. This is the knowledge that has been hidden from mankind because with it, any man … any human … could become a god. It is this knowledge that separates man from the gods. In the Book of Enoch it tells of this knowledge that was to be kept hidden from man."

Lauren stood and went over to the window, turning her back to him as she processed everything she'd learned in the short time he'd left her alone. "As far as I know, the use of the word ark occurs twice in the history of man. Noah builds an ark to salvage mankind and many of earth's animals from the deluge of the flood; a story also told in the Sumerian text about Enlil trying to destroy mankind … and the Ark of the Covenant. The question is why was the Ark of the Covenant called an ark?"

"Linguistics is your department." Michael shrugged.

Lauren turned, looking over her shoulder. She hesitated a moment glancing towards the door, hearing voices in the hallway.

"Michael." She came over and sat down in front of him. "Last night, you asked me if I believed in aliens …" she began.

"Lauren, Michael, come quickly," India said, clearly ruffled. Though Lauren had just met her, she'd never seen Michael's boss appear disheveled. Her hair was sliding from its pins, her glasses had been cockeyed on her face, and her blouse had come untucked from her kick-pleated skirt. Her stiletto heels had been abandoned and she ran barefoot in just her silk stockings.

Michael rose, looking puzzled. "What is it?" He followed his boss, leaving his sister behind. Dr. Lubanzi met him at the door of India's office. "Do you know what's going on?" Lauren heard as she rose to follow. When she came into Dr. Cameron's office, the astronomer was rattling on about some pattern of prime numbers. It took Lauren a moment to realize he had made an amazing discovery.

"The signal is repeating in regular patterns," Lubanzi gushed. Lauren realized his yellowing teeth almost matched his yellowed eyes. "Prime numbers, Dr. Grayson! That's the pattern!" He came over and took her hand between his, shaking her hand as he spoke. "There's math!"

Michael sat back and seemed to stare at the tip of his nose. Lauren looked from him to India to Lubanzi. "Is that significant?"

Michael turned and looked at her. "Is it significant? Of course it's significant."

"Mathematics is the language God has written the Universe in," Lubanzi said. "You are familiar with the Fibonacci sequence?"

"I've heard of it," Lauren said. "The Golden Ratio, right?"

"Correct," he said. "Fibonacci primes when graphed out, create a graduated spiral … the golden spiral, or whatever you will call it. The signal is repeating in these numbers."

"Spoken like a true mathematician." India beamed.

"Galileo said, the laws of nature are written by the Hand of God in the language of mathematics," Michael said as realization appeared on his features. "It's math! Of course it is! Why didn't I see that?"

Michael and Lubanzi began babbling on in a dialogue, speaking of things that left Lauren lost and alone. She was a brilliant scientist, proficient in advanced mathematics and physics, but this exchange was beyond even her ken. She locked eyes with Dr. Cameron who gave her a bemused grin, then nodded her head as she rose, summoning Lauren to follow.

"I don't know about you, but I could use some coffee," she said, when Lauren came out behind her.

"Yes," Lauren said. "Coffee would be good."

"You look tired, Lauren," she said when they reached the coffee service in the break area down the hall. "Jet lag?"

"Hmm?" She looked down as India pressed a cup into her hands. "Yeah, jet lag."

"Half-and-half?" She reached into a micro-fridge beneath the cabinet and produced a small carton. Lauren stuck out her cup. "Sugar is over there." She pointed to a covered bowl. Lauren added two cubes to her cup and stirred it with a bamboo stirrer.

"Mmm," Lauren took a long sip, appreciating the strong brew. "I needed that."

"The Syrians and the Chinese thought of math as a language, a written one more so than a spoken one," Lubanzi was saying to Michael as they came out of the conference room, walking towards Lauren and India.

"I brought Lauren in because she has a penchant for languages," Michael said, stopping Lauren as she raised her cup to her lips. "Lauren, have you ever thought about math as a language?"

Lauren hesitated, leaning against the cabinet as Michael poured himself a coffee. "Well, if you think about it, language is defined as communication by the use of sounds or conventional symbols," she thought aloud. "A code we use to express ourselves and communicate with others…" They walked back to Michael's office as they talked.

"Sometimes, formulas can't be understood without some kind of explanation," India said.

"Like a Rosetta Stone," Michael said. "As my sister so eloquently put it."

"True, but the information can easily get lost in translation." Lauren shook her head. "I'm a biological anthropologist, not a mathematician."

"Then let us think upon the grammar of mathematics," Lubanzi said, as they walked back to the conference room. "The mathematical notation is not dependent on a specific natural language. Many are shared internationally regardless of their mother tongues." He went over to a white board and picked up a marker. "In mathematics, universally, formulas are written predominantly left-to-right, even when the writing system of the substrate language is right-to-left, and the Latin alphabet is commonly used for simple variables and parameters." He began scribbling.

Sin x + a cos 2x ≥ 0

"This formula is recognized by Chinese and Syrian mathematicians alike."

"Okay," Lauren said. "I'm still puzzled how this can translate into anything meaningful to an alien species, other than being a simple quadratic expression?"

"Trigonometry like this, is all about plotting locations …" Michael's voice went misty, and Lauren turned. "Do you think they're sending us … coordinates?"

Lubanzi's expression went blank. "Soundwaves …" they suddenly said in unison.

Lauren looked to one then the other, seeking explanation. "I don't get it."

Lubanzi drew a straight line across the board, then bisected it with a line that arched up then down. "A soundwave, like the rapid bursts." He pointed at the wavy line. He put a dot on it each time it crossed the straight line. "Fibonacci prime numbers." He added 1-1-2-3-5-8-13 to the six dots he'd drawn. "Assign either a mathematical or alphabetical value to each of these points … and you could have some kind of a Morse Code." He added A-A-B-C-E-H-M above the numbers. "This could be a basic cypher, or perhaps, there's another factor involved."

Michael stood and grabbed a blue pen, drawing out a three dimensional cube, then took a red pen and drew a curving wave through the three dimensional plane. "Frequency, tempo, pitch … anything could be a variable."

Lauren looked to Michael. "Now that's something I can work with."

13

Kitty Donovan sat in the Region VI Area Director's office, with her hands in her lap, her gaze directed at the broken nail that was visible between the wrappings of her splinted thumb. She was furious at the organization for the method used to extract her from her previous assignment. The team put her at risk, and while she hadn't been seriously injured, she hadn't escaped completely unscathed. A broken thumb wasn't the worst of it. Her whole body ached, and she'd spent nearly a week flat on her back in bed.

"Dr. Donovan." The Area Director came in behind her, but she couldn't even turn her head to look at him. He came around and sat down at his desk with a file that was nearly two inches thick. "Do you realize your actions have put this whole organization in jeopardy?"

"My actions?" she snarled. "You nearly killed two people. One of those was your best field operative … me!"

"I can assure you, we carefully planned everything," he said, sitting back in his high-back leather chair. "Your safety was our top priority. Dr. Grayson was treated and released from the hospital within twenty-four-hours of the event."

"Safety my Aunt Fanny! I've been laid up for a week," she said. "You broke my finger!"

"Broken bones heal," he said. "But you nearly blew your cover. What were you thinking? A sexual liaison with your intended mark was not authorized."

"It got the job done," Kitty stated. She didn't mention she and Michael had hooked up in collegeand were sweethearts, if truth be told. Had she not been in the position she was in, it would have been easy to allow herself to fall in love with him all over again. Using her body to accomplish her objective was a move James Bond wouldn't have given a second thought to. She'd done what she had to do.

"And you're confident he's studying the same signals as Dr. Budnikov?"

"I'm positive," she said.

"What did he tell you?"

Kitty hesitated. "It wasn't what he said that convinced me," she admitted.

"Gawdammit, Donovan! I need specifics."

"I can't give you specifics," Kitty said. "But, from our discussions, and the time he had access to Hubble, I am absolutely positive."

"You gave him access to Hubble?"

"Not long enough for him to confirm anything," she said. "Just long enough for me to confirm my suspicions."

The director stared down his nose at her a long moment. "You're dismissed," he said. "That'll be all."

Kitty didn't move. "But ..." she all but squeaked. "His data needs to be collected. We need to shut that project down."

"You're correct," he said. "We'll take it from here."

Kitty scooted forward in her seat. "This is *my* assignment. *I'm* the Senior Coordinator. It's *my* job."

He shook his head. "I don't think so," he said. "Your position has been compromised."

"My position at NASA has been compromised," she said. "But as far as anyone there knows I'm out on medical leave."

"Which is another reason for you to just go home," he said. "You have no business in the field."

"I'll go over your head," Kitty said. "My orders come from the Secretary of Homeland Security. My job is to control the dialogue and control any first contact with an alien species. Our mission is sanctioned by NATO as part of an international accord. I don't report to you."

She expected that to infuriate him, but he sat expressionless as he considered her. "I don't respond well to threats, Dr. Donovan."

"It wasn't a threat," Kitty said, crossing her arms, at great pain to her back and neck.

He considered her a moment. "What do you propose, Dr. Donovan?"

That was more like it.

TWELVE HOURS LATER, KITTY SAT IN THE EMERGENCY Operations Center at Quantico with the head of Homeland Security, Secretary Frank White, sitting beside her. On the video screen that took up the full wall in front of her, representatives from each of the countries represented in the NATO First Contact Task Force, or FCTF, appeared like blocks on the Brady Bunch. Kitty allowed Secretary White to brief the nations of their findings and planned efforts.

"And where is this scientist who has the data you need to contain?" The German liaison asked.

"That's something we're working to determine, sir." Kitty spoke up. "I have a plan to find him. When I do, I'll go collect the data."

"He needs to be silenced," the rep from Great Britain said, with a huff in his voice.

"Like Dr. Budnikov was silenced?" The Canadian representative retorted. "I thought you were supposed to be working on who killed Alexei Budnikov."

"The CIA *is* working on it," Frank said. "Trust me, we want to know that as much as you do. His murder occurred on American soil. The last thing we want is for another scientist to fall victim to this unknown assailant."

"Our scientist's safety is my first priority," Kitty said, hearing the Area Director's voice in her head. "The sooner I can find him, the better I can protect him." Kitty still couldn't believe that the Area Director had authorized so violent a method of extraction. She wouldn't rest until she knew Michael was safe, and certain he hadn't been seriously harmed. If the Area Director thought her injuries were minor, she couldn't imagine what he considered to be significant.

"We agreed when we formed this accord that no one country would act alone," the head of the Estonian Security Council said. "Do you intend to violate our charter and go it alone, Dr. Donovan?"

"On the contrary," she said. "I welcome any nation to send a counterpart to join me, once I know where to find my target."

"What kind of resources are you asking for?" The Italian representative demanded. "These operations tend to be expensive, not to mention … messy."

Kitty let the secretary field that question. "The US has funds to support one nation's participation in this operation. Since the gentleman from Estonia seems most concerned about this operation, I suggest Estonia send their agent."

The group broke out into a raucous debate. The volley of arguments escalated into a shouting match. The secretary looked over at Kitty, who eyed him without turning her stiff neck. "You sure you're up to this?" he asked once he'd muted the mic.

"I'll get the job done," she said. "I don't know how I feel

about an Estonian escort, but ... it doesn't look like the committee likes that idea either."

The two sat and waited for the committee to govern itself. In the end, a vote was taken, and it was agreed, the agent from Estonia would join her after all. Kitty had never met her Estonian counterpart, but they had been introduced via email on at least one occasion.

"Now the only question that remains," Frank said, turning to her after the video call ended. "How are you going to flush out Dr. Grayson?"

"I've woven my web," she said. "Now it's just a matter of time before the fly falls into my trap."

"In that case, let *Operation: Black Widow* commence," the secretary said, basically writing her a blank check.

"Thank you, sir." She rose slowly and stiffly.

"Dr. Donovan," he said behind her.

She paused, turning her whole body. "Yes, sir?"

"Take some damned pain meds and get some rest until your trap is sprung. I'm not sending an agent into the field if she can't even look over her own shoulder and watch her own six."

Kitty bit her lip. "Yes, sir."

After she'd fed Henry, Lauren put his blanket down on the floor and went to retrieve his toys from his diaper bag.

"Here's Fishy." She handed him his shark, bemused by his reaction when he saw it.

"F-fishy!" He squealed and clutched it to his chest, hugging it and resting his head against it. He babbled to himself as he drooled and blew raspberries, as she put his things on the blanket, then sat him down in the middle of them, making sure he was content before she returned to her work.

She glanced over at Rowan, who had his nose in a book, but looked completely bored. His dinner plate in front of him was empty and she wasn't unaccustomed to seeing him nod off over a good book in the evenings after dinner at home. Now, his eye lids drooped as he leaned his elbow on the table, resting his chin on his fist. He had the patience of Job, she had to give it to him. They'd been at it all day, and he hadn't complained or fidgeted. He jumped in and went to work, doing his best to help with the Sumerian myths or wrangling their son, who seemed just as content.

Going back to Michael's desk, she fumbled beneath a stack of papers for a tablet to write on. The last few hours had been spent listening to recordings forward and backwards, trying to make sense of the bizarre rapid pulses that were becoming as clear as the beating of her own pulse in her throbbing temples.

As she retrieved the tablet, an envelope on the desk fell with a thud from the stack of folders, unopened mail and other papers piled up on the desk, awaiting Michael's attention. Lauren called him over as she picked it up.

He'd been pouring over tomes at the table across from Rowan. He rose and came over to see what she was holding. "What's this?"

Rowan's head lifted and she realized he'd fallen asleep. He looked over at her blankly.

"It was on your desk under this stack of papers," she said, handing it to her brother, returning her attention to him.

Michael inspected it, but his hand barely covered his mouth before a gasp escaped his throat.

"What?" Lauren looked at him, concerned by his odd reaction.

"It's … it's from Alexei …" he said under his breath. "He said he was going to send something …" Michael slipped down into the chair beside her, his hands visibly trembling. "I assumed he was going to email it, but … I never got it." He inspected it. "Where did you find this?"

"In that stack of mail," she said.

Rowan rose and came over to see what was going on.

Michael ran a hand over his face, and she realized he'd broken out into a sweat. "This is what I get for not checking my mail …" His voice trailed off.

"Aren't you going to open it?" Rowan asked.

The manilla paper had been roughed up in delivery, and a dozen stamps had been affixed to the top right corner. The flap had been sealed with masking tape. It was addressed in black marker — written in an unsteady hand — to Dr. Michael Grayson and a red stamped declared CONFIDEN-TIAL DOCUMENTS ENCLOSED. There was no return address.

"I'm not sure I want to," Michael said in a weak voice.

Lauren's hand went to his. "You owe your friend that much. He risked his own safety for you to have this information."

Michael nodded and reached for a letter opener. He slit the opposite end of the envelope and a cell phone fell out and landed in the palm of his hand. He inspected it, glancing up at his sister, before he turned it around, looking for the button. "It's an Apple. I don't know how to work it."

"Let me guess, you're an Android user," she snarked as she took it and tried to activate it. "Rowan, do you have your charger? It's dead."

Rowan retrieved his power cord from Henry's diaper bag and plugged it into an outlet on the conference table, then handed the other end to Lauren. She connected it, putting the phone down. "It won't take long," Rowan, said, then pointed to her plate. "You didn't finish your food. Come sit down. Eat."

Lauren didn't argue.

When the phone had enough of a charge on it, Rowan did

Michael the courtesy of booting it up before he handed it to him. Lauren came to watch over his shoulder.

Michael thumbed through the programs. The only apps still left on the phone were the ones that came with it. There wasn't a single email account connected with the program, so there were no emails. Location services had been disabled; Wi-Fi disconnected. The Bluetooth was disabled as well. There was one audio file in the music program. Michael cued it up and recognized the recording.

It was remarkably similar to the one he had played for Lauren earlier…at least at first. But something was different. Lauren sat back in her chair and closed her eyes. The swirling waterglass music resonated in her core as Michael turned it up. As the music transformed, the notes appeared behind her eyes, marking their places on the scales. The image moved into three dimensions as the Golden Ratio of the Fibonacci sequence came into view and morphed into four dimensions. The mathematical spiral expanded in her mind's eye. A minute into the recording, the tempo increased, and became more like a symphony than hums from water glasses. The music rose to a quick crash then fell in a stunning decrescendo … and ended.

They sat looking at one another as Lauren's mind raced. "Play it again, Sam."

She took up the paper and pen once, jotting down notes as it played again. She'd never studied music, but it was a language, much like English or Cherokee; a code to communicate meaning.

Michael let the audio loop as he tapped on the icon for photos. There was only one file. He tapped on it, opening it. It appeared to be an old photograph of the crash scene Alexei had discussed during the television interview; the interview where he died. Michael attempted to zoom in and was impressed when the image came into focus. "Lauren…" His hand went to her wrist. "Look … Lauren. Look!"

Rowan and Lauren both did as he asked. There, on the side of the wreckage, was a series of symbols — each a variation of a triangular shape — each marked with a number of dots over them. One dot over the first two symbols, then two dots over the next two, three dots over the next, five dots over the next, eleven dots, then thirteen dots, all lined up in rows above the symbols.

"It looks like Sumerian," Rowan noted.

"This is what we've been looking for!" Lauren exclaimed, startling Henry who was crawling off the blanket. He froze, looking to his mother. Rowan took him up.

"That *is* your Rosetta Stone." Michael beamed. "And look … Fibonacci prime numbers."

She took the phone to study the markings, scribbling down what she could make from the distorted image. The notes and their location on the scale appeared as a code, then in the back of her mind, the symbols morphed into something she could read; something her brain could comprehend. The epiphany hit her hard, and she sat back, as her mind raced a thousand miles an hour. "Music … harmony, melody, rhythm …" She paused, deep in thought as she worked to validate the data. "Discordant harmony though …" she muttered.

"Discordant?"

She pointed to her notes. "These … tones, these notes … they're discordant, meaning they stand out because they don't sound pleasant. They create a sense of imbalance …they make the listener feel … off kilter."

She tore off the page and jotted down the markings from the spaceship, aligning them in the same grid pattern from the ship. "I think this is a code … a cypher … in Sumerian. This is what we've been looking for!"

Both men gazed at her. Michael's brow knitted. Rowan leaned back; his expression blank.

"Rowan," she said. "Play Michael's recording again?"

"Sure." He looked at her, puzzled. He put Henry back

down on the floor and went over to the computer and cued up the signal Michael's team had recorded.

"Can you slow it down?"

He made the adjustment she requested and watched to see what she had up her sleeve. Lauren closed her eyes listening. The music came through, feeling more somber, more ominous. As the recording continued, she realized it was a repeating message. The rapid bursts indicating the end of the message, like a telegram ending in *stop*. After the third shriek, which was now a somber trembling staccato, she began jotting down the information that consumed every inch of her brain. She wrote like a woman possessed, oblivious to all else.

"What's this?" Michael asked, as she scribbled feverishly, the language finally making sense in her brain.

"Again," she said when the recording stopped. After the third round, she lay her pen down, and looked up blankly at her husband. "I think I did it."

Michael glanced at the tablet. "It just looks like chicken scratch to me, Lauren."

She pointed to her notes from Michael's recording. "It's … the flood story," she said. "It talks about how the gods … Enlil, primarily, were angry, and a flood was sent to destroy the earth. There are similar versions in the Epic of Gilgamesh and the Bible." She grabbed the paper she'd torn off the tablet. "This is from the message Alexei recorded."

Michael crossed his arms and furrowed his brow. "What's it say?"

Lauren hesitated. "I don't know if I've translated it correctly."

"What do you think it says?" Rowan looked concerned.

"*The Dark One returns to destroy the World of Man. Comes with it, a war among the gods from the heavens. No Man is to survive … or maybe that is … will survive … the destruction. When the Dark One's tablet is made whole …*"

Rowan looked to Michael, then to Lauren. "Seriously? It reminds me of something Nostradamus would write."

"It does have that sing-song feeling of the Seer's quatrains," Lauren allowed.

"So does this go back to the Tablet of Destiny?" Rowan puzzled.

"I don't think so," she said. "The Dark One … I can only assume that refers to Enlil, and while he did have possession of the Tablet of Destiny — and it made him the supreme ruler of the universe — in some of the legends, the tablet, if it is real, changed hands a number of times."

Rowan sat up, lifting a finger. "I saw something in one of these books …" He reached for the stack and thumbed through one of them. "There is a Sumerian poem titled *Ninurta and the Turtle* which mentions that Enki possessed the Tablet."

"So if Enki represents Jesus, or *good*, and Enlil is Lucifer, or *evil*," Michael thought out loud. "Do you suppose there are forces … factions … battling for control and we're just innocent bystanders in a cosmic war that is coming? Does this mean Enlil is coming here … to destroy the world?"

"So you're thinking this message is a warning." Rowan pointed to the page with Lauren's notes from Alexei's recording.

"If this is a cautionary tale," Lauren said, holding up the page from Michael's recording, the one retelling the flood story. "Then this one is a threat." She held up the one from Alexei's recording. "If we're to believe these messages … and if my translations are correct … then a war *is* coming; a war we may not be able to win without divine intervention."

14

As they sat trying to process their revelation, Michael's phone chirped in his pocket. He went back over to the computer and pulled up the email. "It's from NASA," he said, drawing everyone's attention. "Oh my gods …" His hand went to his mouth. "I've been granted access to Hubble."

"That's terrific," Lauren said.

He nodded. "Competition for time with Hubble is extremely intense, you know."

"What'd you have to do to get it?" Rowan asked.

"I had to show my observations could only be accomplished with Hubble's unique capabilities and are beyond those of ground-based telescopes." Michael paced, running his hand over his head, trying to steel his excitement.

"That's terrific!" Lauren said. "When? How?"

"They sent me a code …" he said. "It looks like I can access it from any computer." He paused, sinking into a chair, scooping up Henry who crawled over and sat, lifting his hands to his uncle. Henry settled into his lap with his toy shark under his arm and looked at Lauren as if he wanted in on the conversation. "Telescope observing time is measured by the number of orbits required for a successful observation.

Programs that request multiple orbits get much greater scrutiny. The observations must address a significant astronomical mystery. I requested six orbits, just to make sure I could triangulate the source of the signals."

"And?"

"They gave me what's called a *snapshot observation*."

"What's that?" Lauren asked.

"Snapshot observations are used to fill in gaps in the telescope schedule which cannot be filled by regular programs," Michael said. "They basically gave me forty-five minutes of telescope time. That's not even a full orbit."

"Is that enough?" Rowan asked.

"It'll have to be," he said.

IT WAS MIDNIGHT WHEN THE TELESCOPE'S ORBIT PUT IT IN optimal position for Michael's purposes. He had everything set up, the code entered, and the programming set for the scans he needed. With Hubble traveling at five miles per second, he needed to be efficient. There were a lot of variables; a lot of moving parts. Ideally, he'd have had a month, maybe two, to figure out all the necessary factors and set up the perfect scan. This situation was not ideal.

"Everything ready?" Lauren asked. Rowan came up behind her.

Michael nodded. "As ready as it'll ever be," he said with trepidation. He shivered as he held his finger over the *ENTER* key. "And we're live in 5…4…3…2…1." He hit the button.

A graph popped up on the bottom of the screen with a timer.

"Is that it?" Rowan asked. "How long 'til we get the results?"

"We have forty-five minutes of scanning, then the data has to be extrapolated into something we can analyze." He sat back, crossing his arms, swiveling the chair around. "It'll probably be tomorrow before we can dive in."

"Tomorrow?" Lauren's brows knitted. She'd been ready to work through the night, despite having had practically no sleep since arriving. She blamed it on the multiple time zone changes they'd been through since leaving Hilo a little over a week before.

"We might as well go back to the apartment then," Rowan said. "I'm exhausted."

Lauren nodded, glancing over at Henry asleep on his blanket on the floor. Lauren suddenly felt sorry for her son. He'd been so good through all of this; the travel, the time changes, the strange places, strange people. Still he'd been cheerful and playful all day. He'd crawled all over Michael's office and they'd cheered this new milestone, much to his delight. He'd worn himself out. He deserved a better bed than the floor in an office. He needed his rest, even if Lauren couldn't sleep.

As Lauren thought about a warm bubble bath, she collected him, and his shark from the floor. She wrapped him in the blanket as she hoisted him to her shoulder. He was getting so big; so heavy. He wouldn't be a baby much longer. She would miss this phase of their lives together, but she smiled thinking of his future. Would he be more like her, or more like Rowan? Perhaps the perfect blend of the two of them.

Henry stirred as she shouldered her purse and took her cell phone from the table. He put his arms around her neck, patting her back. "Mama," he muttered in his sleep. "Mama … go …"

One minute she was in Michael's office, the next, she was standing in the bedroom in their apartment. The abruptness of the transition was disorienting, and her head spun. She staggered back, making it to the edge of the bed before she fell over. Henry sat up and looked at her, grinning. She inspected him, suddenly more worried for him than for herself. "Are you okay?"

"Mama," he giggled. "Go." His hand patted her cheek, then snuggled into her. "Mama."

Lauren wrapped her arms around him and held him tightly. Her heart was still racing, a wave of nausea passed over her. "Christ," she muttered, patting him. She nearly leapt out of her skin when her phone in her hip pocket buzzed.

She fished it out with trembling hands. It was Rowan. She hit the button, preparing for the inquisition.

"Where the hell did you go?" he demanded.

"I'm at the apartment," she said, running a hand over her face.

"How … how did you get there?" His voice was trembling too.

"I'm not sure," she said. "I was standing there thinking about getting Henry tucked in and debating about a bubble bath before I went to bed … the next thing I know … we're here."

"Just like Hilo?"

"Just like Hilo." She confirmed. "Just like Mexico."

"I'll be there in twenty minutes," Rowan said.

LAUREN MANAGED TO COMPOSE HERSELF AND CHANGED HENRY into his pajamas and put him to bed. He drifted off peacefully. The sudden change of location didn't seem to faze him one bit. Clearly it upset Lauren more than she realized. She found herself agitated, unable to sit still. She went to the kitchen and found the half-empty bottle of wine in the fridge. She took it out and poured herself a dose. Leaning on the counter, she lifted the glass to her lips with a trembling hand. It shook so bad the liquid splashed down her chin and the front of her shirt.

She nearly dropped the delicate wine-glass before she could set it down.

Suddenly, all the emotions she'd been fighting not to acknowledge came flooding over her. The excitement of breaking the alien code, the fear of all the unknown and the risks they faced, blended with the uneasy feeling of sudden displacement and the disorientation that came with it. For a woman who always knew her spatial alignment with the Universe, to suddenly be in a different place, it took her brain a long while to re-orient to her new surroundings. Combined, it was all too much. She sunk to the floor, burying her face in her unsteady hands as the flood poured from her eyes. A pitiful sob escaped her throat as she struggled for control; failing miserably.

This was where Rowan found her when he blew through the door. "Rowan," she sobbed, as he dropped to a knee beside her, she threw her arms around him. He sank to the floor and drew her in, wrapping her in the safety of his arms. Burying his face in her hair, he held her.

"Thank God," he muttered, kissing her head. "That scared the life out of me."

She sniffed. "Me, too." Her voice cracked. "I don't know what happened."

"You didn't do it on purpose? Or inadvertently?" She shook her head, unable to find the words. His hand ran down her hair, and he kissed her again. "Henry?" He was having a hard time formulating logical thoughts too.

"In bed," she said. "He's fine. It didn't seem to bother him one bit."

Rowan nodded, relieved. "It's okay," he said, brushing her hair off her face. "We're going to figure this all out. You're okay." She heaved a heavy sigh, letting it out with a ragged breath as she melted against him. "Come on," he moved to get up, offering her a hand once he found his feet. "We're tired and we have a lot of work to do tomorrow. You need some sleep."

"I haven't slept since we got here," she said weakly, swaying with the exhaustion she'd been fighting through for days now.

"You're going to sleep tonight, if I have to make you," he said.

"Like you can force me to sleep," she said as he took her hand and led her to the bedroom.

"Maybe, but if I need to wear you out to make you sleep, I will," he said, the innuendo overt. He looked back at her with a wicked grin.

~

"Yes, sir," Kitty said into the phone tucked under ear. "I'll take care of it. Yes, sir. I understand."

She hung up the phone and gazed out over the crowded terminal. She was expecting her contact to arrive any minute. No delays had been announced, but she checked the time on her phone again as she nervously waited.

"Dr. Catherine Donovan?" A voice behind her in a thick accent startled her from her thoughts. She turned and glanced over her shoulder. A tall, stoutly built man stood in an expertly tailored black suit. He was completely bald but had thick gray eyebrows. She stood to greet him.

"I am Dr. Donovan," she said. "Please, call me Kitty."

His brow arched. "Yevgeny Malakoff, Estonian National Security Council." He bowed politely.

"Have you been briefed on our mission?" she asked.

"I have," he said.

Kitty picked up her duffle bag, putting it over her shoulder. "Good," she said. "I'll go over some recent updates in the car."

"I drive," he said. "My rule. I always drive."

"Is that some kind of male macho crap? Because that doesn't go over well with me."

"I like to drive," he said. "That's all."

She nodded, flashing him a Texas-size smile. "In that case, the wheel is yours."

He fell in behind her as she headed down the terminal. His dress shoes slapped against the tile floors as they walked. She had a on a suit but had slipped on her favorite pair of Chuck Taylors for the journey. High heels looked pretty, but they weren't functional while working in the field. If she needed to escape a crashed airplane or chase a bad-guy down the street, she needed shoes she could run in. She didn't expect to have to do either, but if the need arose, she was prepared.

"Your accent is quite unique," Kitty said. "What part of Estonia are you from?

"Narva," he said. "It's near the border."

"The border with Latvia?" she asked, wondering if he was testing her.

"Russia," he said. "About two hours from St. Petersburg … eight hours to Moscow."

"Ah," Kitty said. "Northern Estonia then."

"You know your geography then," he commented with a nod. "Dr. Donovan," he stopped, and Kitty did the same a moment later. "I'm here to do a job. Not to make friends." He eyed her down. "Less talk. More global security."

Kitty considered him a moment. "Strong silent type. Fine, suit yourself."

They reconvened early the next morning at Michael's office. Lauren had been anxious to get back to the results of his pass with Hubble. Michael had a cup of coffee ready for her. "You scared me last night," he said, leaning in to kiss her cheek as she handed Henry off to Rowan.

"Me, too," Lauren said, taking the cup from him. "I am starting to think it happens more when I'm tired."

"Did you get some sleep?" he asked.

Her eye went to Rowan who avoided looking at her, but a dimple tightened in his cheek. "Yeah," she said, hoping she wasn't blushing. "I slept like a baby." Rowan *had* made certain of it.

"And did my adorable nephew sleep well, too?" Michael went over to his brother-in-law. Henry reached for him. Michael took him and tickled his cheek. Henry giggled and reached for Michael's hair.

"Hey, little man," Michael said, backing his head up. "Grow your own hair."

"Mama!" Henry giggled.

"I am not your mama," Michael said. "Michael. Can you say Michael?"

"M...m..." Henry babbled, then blew a raspberry at his uncle.

"Close enough." Michael grinned.

Lauren took the baby back. "What's the word on Hubble this morning?"

"I was waiting for you to get here to see," he said. "If we're going to find definitive proof of alien life today, we'll find it together."

That made Lauren smile. She nodded and pulled up a chair by Michael's at the computer station. Rowan brought his chair over and took his place behind them. Lauren glanced back over her shoulder, scooting her chair over so he could see.

The computer took over a minute to boot up. Michael logged in and keyed in some information. They waited another few minutes for the images and data to populate on the computer screen. Before Lauren knew it, they were looking at a dark field dotted with brilliant stars in a wide-screen panorama. Michael typed in some information and clicked on the image. A grid laid over the scene, along with a few markers identifying the primary stars in the field. A few more clicks and a roll of the mouse, and the image zoomed in. "Ordinarily, I'd start with the first block in the grid on the top and work my way through it block by block," he said. "But I know the region where my signals came falls in this block," he pointed to the center of the screen. "There's the Southern Cross ... there's the Pleiades." He used the pointer on his mouse to direct her eye.

"What about Alexei's signal?" Lauren asked, picking up the cell phone the Russian scientist had sent her brother.

Michael shrugged. "I don't know."

Lauren nodded, putting the phone down, turning her attention back to the screen as Michael continued to zoom in ... and in ... and in. Soon, the dark field was filled with a large glowing star, set in a field of what looked like blue smoke.

Lauren gasped at the beauty of it. "I had no idea the cosmos was so … colorful."

"The computer is doing that," Michael said. "So it's easier to make out the variations in the darkness."

"Oh," Lauren said, a bit disappointed.

Michael continued zooming in on one star in particular. "Okay, this is Mimosa." He leaned in on the desk. A few more clicks and the bright light took over the screen. Dark dots blurred around it. "Exo-planets," Michael pointed at the dots. He clicked again, zooming in on one. "This one … see the aura around it?"

"Yeah," Rowan said. "What is that?"

"It's a planet …" Michael flashed a bright smile over his shoulder. "With an atmosphere." The tone in his voice told Rowan and Lauren how significant the find was.

A knock at the door was followed by the arrival of Michael's boss. "Dr. Cameron," Lauren greeted her with a nod.

"India," Michael said. "Come see … we got access to Hubble. Look! Exo-planets."

"What?" India hurried over, putting a hand on Michael's shoulder as she leaned in. "Is that? An atmosphere?"

"Yeah," Michael said. "Mimosa has at least five planets … five we can see anyway. At least one … has an atmosphere."

"Does that mean there could be life on … what would you even call that planet?" Rowan asked.

"Mimosa 1?" Lauren offered, bemused by the name.

"There's a whole naming convention, established by the International Astronomical Union," Michael said. "The Working Group for Planetary System Nomenclature maintains that naming convention. It isn't up to us."

"They do allow teams to offer suggestions, but Michael is

right," Dr. Cameron said. "We don't get to name the exoplanets."

"So much for Grayson Mimosa," Michael chortled.

"Grayson-Pierce Mimosa," Rowan added.

Lauren glanced at Rowan, then Michael. "Has a nice ring to it," Michael said.

"I just want a mimosa right now," Lauren came back.

Rowan put a hand on her knee. "When we are done here, I'll take you to brunch, and you can have all the mimosas you want."

"Deal," Lauren chirped.

"I should call Dr. Dlamani," India said. "He's going to want to see this."

"Yes," Michael said. "Call him."

LUBANZI PUSHED MICHAEL OUT OF THE WAY TO TAKE CONTROL of the telescope's images on the computer. He acted, at first, as if he didn't believe what had been accomplished. He zoomed in on Gacrux, counting the number of visible exoplanets, then moved on to Alpha Crucis.

Michael sat back, taking it all in with a pang of melancholy; the moment, bittersweet. The last time he'd gazed at Alpha Crucis, Kitty had been sitting beside him and he'd quoted Neil Gaiman. It broke his heart now. He hadn't realized until that morning in the lobby at NASA how much he'd missed her. They'd parted ways amicably enough, but he had always regretted that he didn't fight harder for her; hadn't chased her down and begged her not to go. He could have given up his intended path but hadn't done that either. He'd tried to go on with the life he'd planned for himself, without a second thought. Now, it was too late.

He forced back his emotions when he realized his sister's gaze had fallen on him. She offered him an encouraging smile, and a strong sense of peace washed over him. He reached over and took her hand and squeezed it hard. "Thank you," he said. "I couldn't have done it without you." Lauren leaned into him, resting her head against his shoulder.

"We did it together." Lauren sighed.

"This is it." Lubanzi pointed at one of the exo-planets that the computer had painted green, with a blue halo around it. The image was as fuzzy as a picture of Bigfoot, but it was 321 lightyears away, so it would have to do. "This is a planet in Acrux or Alpha Crucis, a cluster of three stars at the bottom of the Southern Cross. I think this may be where your signal is coming from, Michael."

"How can you be so confident?" Rowan asked.

"I can't, but I've run the calculations a dozen times. This is the only exo-planet we can see with the data we have. I suspected it came from this region, and while it is possible that I am wrong, statistically speaking, this is the most likely source."

Michael looked at Lauren, wide-eyed. "You believe in statistics, right?"

Her eyes lit up. "Yes. I do."

"Then there you go …" Michael beamed. "We've done it!"

Rowan, tending to Henry, looked up. "Done what?"

"We translated the messages, and now … it looks like we've found a potential point of origin," Michael said. "For at least one of the signals, that is."

"You won't need to find any others." A voice in the doorway caught the team off guard. Lauren turned. The woman at the door had a badge, and she came with back up. Lauren glanced back at Michael who'd gone ashen. "I'm afraid this project is officially terminated," the woman said.

"Kitty?" Michael gasped.

Lauren turned back and recognized her immediately. Kitty Donovan was most definitely not dead.

"What the hell?" Michael demanded. Lauren could see his confusion turning to anger. "They told me …"

"I don't care what they told you, but I'm here to secure all the data from this project. This is a cease and desist order issued by the US Department of Homeland Security and NATO." She held out an envelope with two government seals on it.

"You died …" Michael muttered. Lauren reached up and caught his arm to steady him.

"You've got some nerve coming here," India spoke, snatching the envelope out of her hand. "Just who do you think you are?"

"Dr. Catherine Donovan, US Office of Homeland Security and the NATO First Contact Task Force. This is my counterpart from Estonia, Yevgeny Malakoff. He's an agent with the Estonian National Security Council. He's here to ensure these orders are carried out as issued."

"First Contact Task Force?" Lauren demanded. "I've never heard of this … NATO First Contact Task Force." She glanced at Michael, and noticed he was trembling.

"Our mission is to ensure a unified approach to First Contact with any extraterrestrial life forms."

"A little late for that, don't you think? What makes you think you're entitled to confiscate *my* work?" Michael's words were harsh, his voice raking. "I thought you worked for NASA?"

"Think about it Michael …" Kitty turned on him. "If your research proves the existence of extraterrestrial life, what will that do to life on *this* planet?"

Michael paused a moment to consider it. "We will become enlightened," he said optimistically.

"Wrong," Lauren said, her tone dark. "A person is smart. People are dumb, panicky, dangerous animals … and you know it." She directed the statement to Michael; it was a line from the movie, *Men In Black,* and it rolled off her tongue before she could stop herself.

Kitty turned to her. "Your sister?" she asked Michael. He nodded. "We met before, right?"

"A long time ago," Lauren said, staring her down. Lauren didn't know what her game was, or why she'd faked her own death, but clearly Michael was upset with her, so Lauren was ready to hate her too.

"Well, your sister is smart," Kitty said. "This world is filled with frightened, uneducated people. People fear what they do not understand. What they don't understand, they try to destroy. It's our job to prepare for that day and ensure a peaceful outcome."

"Why have we never heard of this NATO First Contact Task Force before?" Rowan asked. "Is this something new?"

"Our project has been around since the mid 1980's," she said. "The nations represented by NATO were concerned with how the globe would manage first contact with an alien species *when* it occurs."

"When?" Rowan asked.

"Not if," she confirmed. "When. Think about it. In every era of human existence, the dominant culture moves in, takes over, and destroys the lesser. It happened with the Romans, the Turks … the Vikings, the British." She glanced at Lauren. "Even when the Europeans came to the Americas, the indigenous tribes were over-powered, destroyed by conflict and infection. When *they* come," her eyes went to the ceiling. "*We* become the lesser species. Our own fear, our own panic could do more damage than anything… if *we* don't manage the situation, it could set into motion a chain of events that could lead to the destruction of the human race." Kitty looked to Michael. "It's my job … our job … to prevent that consequence. If our goal is to become an outward-looking, space-faring species, equal to any race we might encounter, we have to work together to even the playing field."

"Equal to? Or greater than?" Rowan queried. "So you can destroy them before they destroy us."

Kitty shook her head. "Since the incident at Roswell, we've known it was just a matter of time, and began working towards managing the public's perception of contact with alien life forms so we could avoid panic and infighting. The goal is a unified and managed response, globally …"

"Well we didn't do a very good job of it, did we?" Lauren simpered, standing. Michael stood too, but she noticed him sway, and glanced over at him, catching his arm. "Michael?"

He took a step forward. "Kitty … how could you?"

Kitty's façade faltered, but she quickly recovered. "I'm sorry Michael. It wasn't my choice."

"They told me you were … d-d-dead," he said, his voice quaking. Lauren thought he was going to buckle, but he stood tall, his hands balled into fists as if that would steady him.

"It wasn't my choice. I was … *extracted* … I let my … *personal feelings* interfere with my mission. Poor judgement on my part; totally my fault, but I don't like it any more than you do," she said, stoically. "I have a job to do. I know there are no words I can say that can make it up to you, Michael." She took a deep breath, steeling herself. "I'm sorry, but I have to take your data … everything."

"Oh yeah?" Michael's brow clamped down hard. "I don't think so."

"That document says I can." She pointed to the pages of paperwork India was reading. His boss sunk back against the conference table, her hand going to her mouth as she read.

Michael took a step back, turning away from Kitty. "You're dead to me." The poison in his tone seemed to sting as Kitty froze and paled.

"Michael," Lauren said as he turned into her. "Perhaps we could all just take a seat? Let's just sit down and we'll figure all this out."

"I'm not turning over my project," Michael said, eying her defiantly, glancing back at Kitty with fire in his eyes.

"I don't see that you have a choice," India said, looking up from the document.

Rowan stepped up. "I think Lauren has the right idea. Sit. Maybe we can reach some kind of a … compromise."

"A compromise?" Kitty gasped. "There's no room for compromise here. I have a warrant to collect and confiscate any and all data you have. Your work is funded by the US Government through NASA. You're mandated to comply with every and all government orders issued as part of your grant agreement."

"Kitty, this is Michael's work," Lauren said. "If you need to classify it, that's understandable. He has security clearance … surely there's a path through all this that doesn't involve taking his work away from him."

"I'm afraid this is non-negotiable. My orders have been issued and I am obligated to carry them out. This isn't personal … and I am deeply sorry." She turned to her colleague. "Mr. Malakoff will need every paper and computer file in your possession. He will also oversee scrubbing your computer systems of any latent records."

Michael stepped up to Kitty, lowering his head so he could hold her gaze. In a low tone, and between clenched teeth he said, "You can have my project when you pry it out of my cold, dead hands."

"I'm happy to arrange that." The Estonian agent stepped forward and drew a weapon, leveling it at Michael.

Clearly startled by the weapon, Kitty gasped. "Mr. Malakoff! Put that away! This is a peaceful enforcement of security protocols. I won't have you brandishing a weapon here."

He held the gun trained on Michael. "I beg to differ," he grunted. "Your orders might be to sequester the data, but *my orders* … are to destroy it."

"What?" Lauren gasped, as did half the team. "You can't …" She took a step forward but stopped when the gun trained on her.

"Malakoff!" Kitty pursed her lips and lowered her tone, clipping his name.

"I assure you, Dr. Pierce," he said. "I can." Lauren gasped. "Yes, Dr. Pierce, I am familiar with your work. All the more reason to ensure this information is … destroyed."

"But why?" India demanded. "Dr. Donovan … you can't let him."

"Yevgeny," Kitty's ire had grown to near its limits. "You are in violation of our orders from NATO."

"I don't take orders from NATO," he sneered.

"Mr. Malakoff," Kitty demanded, her cheeks flaming pink. "A word?" She tilted her head to the door.

"The word, Dr. Donovan is actually two," Malakoff said, turning the weapon on her. "Hostile takeover."

"Technically that's three," Rowan snarked. Lauren shot a dark eye in his direction, and he realized his error and melted back behind her, turning Henry away from the scene.

"I would expect better from an agent of the Estonian government." Kitty's upper lip pinched beneath her perfectly upturned nose.

"I would, too." A wicked grin crossed his angular face. "But I am not Estonian … though this fact is not well known."

"Freakin' KGB!" Michael snarled. "I knew it."

"That's ridiculous," Kitty said. "The KGB was disbanded in 1991 when the USSR was dissolved."

Malakoff's brow lifted. "Yes, KGB, Dr. Grayson … Dr. Donovan," he said. "Most people assume that the *Komitet Gosudarstvennoy Bezopasnosti* was shut down. I assure you, however, we just took things … in a different direction." Malakoff scanned the assembly, pausing a moment on Henry. Michael and Lauren both took a step closer to one another, blocking him; shielding the child from danger. Malakoff's eye moved on to Kitty, then India, and lastly Lubanzi, taking in the scene. Lauren suspected he was sizing up the resistance, trying to decide who was going to give him the most trouble. "I have spent the last twenty years in Estonia, working as *a friend to the cause*. When Dr. Budnikov began publishing blog posts about these signals, the KGB realized he had information he wasn't supposed to have … wasn't supposed to share. I was asked to … *investigate*."

Michael stepped forward, bowing up. "*You* killed Alexei!"

"He was a discredit to his profession, Dr. Grayson." Malakoff eyed him down. "As are you … as are you all." The gun waved past each of them. "While Dr. Donovan and I disagree on the methods, the purpose behind my work is not dissimilar. If *they* are out there, and if *they* come here, *we* will be ready for war."

"War?" Kitty started, but froze when Lubanzi leapt from his chair, charging the Russian operative.

Everything happened so fast that it seemed to move in slow motion. Lauren heard the deafening concussion of the weapon firing. She smelled the gunpowder and the tang of iron as Lubanzi lunged toward the Russian operative. Kitty began shouting orders as she moved in to help the astronomer. Henry began wailing.

The gun went off a second time, and dots danced in Lauren's eyes as Michael pushed past her, knocking Lubanzi off his trajectory, shoving Kitty aside. Lauren realized India had fallen, a pool of crimson began to grow on the carpet around her unmoving form. Lauren felt frozen, unable to move as she witnessed the whole ordeal as it happened around her. Kitty sat on her rump, her hand going to her forehead where she'd hit the table.

Michael tackled the Russian and the two wrestled for the gun. Rowan shoved Henry into Lauren's arm, starting to press past her, but she grabbed his sleeve and pulled him back.

"Rowan, no." He pushed her back as he turned to face the enemy, undaunted.

Henry wrapped his arms around his mother's neck, his sobbing intermixed with weak and trembling cries for his Mama. Rowan, heedless of her pleas plowed into Malakoff, tackling him around the waist. Lauren moved closer to Kitty, side stepping flailing arms and kicking feet, nearly getting up-ended herself, as she shielded Henry, turning her back on the melee, but watching it over her shoulder.

A strange sense of tunnel vision passed over her as Lauren turned and realized Lubanzi had fallen and wasn't getting up. Michael had Malakoff by one arm, as Rowan swung, catching him in the jaw with a left hook. Malakoff used Michael's weight for leverage and kicked Rowan in the gut, knocking him back. He staggered and went down hard at Lauren's feet, disconcerted and clearly disoriented.

Malakoff got a blow in on Michael, and a moment later, he was on the floor next to Rowan. Lauren knelt beside them, checking on Rowan before turning to her brother. His nose was bleeding and the cut over his eye had opened up too. Malakoff had managed to keep the weapon in his hand and now stood with it hanging by his side, his hand trembling. Lauren suspected Michael had done enough damage to have at least pinched a nerve or torn a ligament in the effort to get the gun away.

"Not a wise move, Dr. Grayson." Malakoff shook his head at Michael. "Not wise at all." He slowly raised his hand.

"Yevgeny!" Kitty shouted as the goon made to raise the weapon towards her former lover. He caught the movement out of the corner of his eye as she came at him brandishing the fire extinguisher from the wall. The powdery discharge blinded and stung his eyes as she directed it at his face. When the flow ebbed, she braced herself and brought it down hard over his head. Michael, recovering from the blow, leapt to his feet … just as the gun went off.

"Mama!" Henry wailed. "Mama … go!"

Lauren found herself lying flat on her back, with Henry safely wrapped in her arms. A heavy weight lay atop of her lower torso. Henry sobbed, his tears falling on her face as he crawled off of her, sitting up beside her. Rowan lay in a heap nearby. She rolled her head towards him and put a hand on Rowan's back. He stirred, groaning as Henry crawled over to him, muttering "Dada …"

The room spun around her. The water-stained ceiling tiles and light fixtures from Michael's office were gone. Above her now, the surface was smooth, but had a soft glow to it. The chaos of a few moments ago was now replaced with an ethereal hum and a sense of calm passed over her. She felt safe, where moments before she'd been terrified. As her vision blurred, she considered the fact that she must have hit her head when she fell; her pulse throbbing in her skull.

"Lauren?" Rowan's face appeared over her; concern knitted in his brow as he held Henry over his shoulder. "Honey? Are you okay?"

"Rowan?" She hesitated, blinking rapidly, trying to clear her vision.

She tried to move and found she couldn't. She glanced up and realized Michael was laying over her legs. "Michael." She tried to sit up, grabbing him, pulling him into her lap. Her hand found a damp spot that was spreading across the front of his black shirt. She drew her hand away and her heart stopped. "Michael!"

Suddenly Kitty was at her elbow. "Michael?" She peeled up his shirt. Blood oozed from a hole in his abdomen. "He's been shot!"

Rowan shoved Henry into Kitty's arm's and moved around to the other side so he could get to him. He pressed his hand on the wound. "Lauren, I have to check for an exit wound," he said. "I'm going to roll him over. When I do, I need you to move out from under him so you can help me."

Lauren nodded. "Help him," she insisted. "Whatever you have to do."

Rowan nodded and carefully moved him, finding the corresponding, and much larger exit wound he was expecting. Lauren's own shirt was blood-soaked, and she started to move, but a yelp escaped her throat, and she clutched her own side. "Rowan …" she panted, lifting her own shirt. He forgot all about Michael's injuries. A similar entry wound marred her flesh, even with her navel. He clamped his hand over the wound, laying her back. He stripped out of his jacket and found a tear just under the arm pit. With effort, the fabric gave way and he ripped it into several pieces. He folded one of them up and held it over the wound. "Can you hold this?"

"Yeah," she squeaked.

"Put pressure on it," he said.

"I'm fine …" Lauren said, unconvincingly. "Just help Michael."

Rowan's heart broke at the pain in her eyes. He thought about how he would feel if it were Cassandra, his sister, laying wounded in a growing pool of blood. He turned back to his brother-in-law, assessing his condition. His pulse was weak and his color poor. Rowan wished he had his medic kit, but he couldn't linger on the thought. He had to make do with what he had, which wasn't much.

"Mama!" Henry wailed and reached for her, fighting against Kitty's grasp.

"Here," Lauren said, lifting one hand. "I'll take him. Kitty, help Rowan."

Lauren lay flat on her back, pressing the make-shift bandaging down, wincing as she did. "Do you have an exit wound?" Rowan asked as he worked the bandaging under her brother's limp form.

"I don't think so …" She winced, pinching her eyes shut.

Henry lay his head on her chest, patting her. "Mama …"

Lauren put a hand on his arm. "Mama's going to be okay, sweetie." She tried to reassure him.

"Keep pressure on that wound, Honey," Rowan instructed her.

"Where are we?" Lauren muttered, feeling like her voice was farther away than it should be. Dots were dancing in her eyes now and the lights began to dim.

"Hold this," she heard Rowan say to Kitty, then he appeared over her. His features were out of focus, but her hand went to his chest. "Lauren?"

"I'm … so sleepy …" she whispered.

"No!" Rowan shouted. "You can't sleep yet! Stay with me." He patted her cheek, trying to hold on to her. His hand went to the wound on her side, and he lifted the bandage to inspect it. Blood welled up from the hole, an indicator that there was no arterial bleeding. That was a good sign, but she wasn't out of danger. "Lauren?" her head rolled to the side but righted as her eyes seemed to focus on him. "Come on, talk to me."

"Just help … my brother," she insisted, weakly trying to push him away.

In desperation, Rowan pressed the cloth down against her stomach, probably harder than he had to. The pain that shot through her brought her back to the moment and she fought to move his hand away. "I'm sorry," he said. "You have to stay with me. I won't lose you."

"It's just a … a flesh wound …" She forced herself up on her elbow, realizing pain was the one thing keeping her conscious. "Michael?"

"He's losing a lot of blood," Kitty said. Her complexion had gone pale as she glanced down at the blood pouring from between her fingers.

"I'm afraid the bullet nicked his spleen … maybe hit his liver, too," Rowan said. "I don't have a triage kit … no *Quik Klot*, nothing to stop the bleeding." He paused, checking for a pulse. "Christ!" He gasped and folded his hands over her brother's chest, beginning compressions, instructing Kitty to keep pressure on the wound.

"Michael," Kitty called his name as she followed instructions. Against her pale skin, her eyes reddened, and Lauren considered for a moment that she looked a bit like a white rabbit, then also considered her own grip on consciousness might be slipping as she laid back down, gazing up at the odd ceiling.

"Do something …" Lauren pleaded. He glanced up at her as he tried to do what he could, which wasn't much. "Save him …" Her voice trailed off.

"Lauren?" Rowan's voice echoed in her head.

"I can't lose him … I have so many things to tell him … so many things to make right." Tears welled up in her eyes. She knew it was just a matter of time. Michael was dying.

"Lauren?" Rowan's voice moved farther away. "Lauren!"

"Mama …" Henry caught her braid as he buried his face in her shoulder. "Mama …"

A whooshing noise broke the eerie silence. Lauren craned her head around. An invisible door opened, and a shadowed figure stood at the threshold. Rowan gasped and slumped down onto his rump as he fell back. A horrified gaze overtook his face.

Lauren's grip on her son tightened. She should have been afraid, but an odd calm washed over her. Kitty's eyes rolled back, and she went limp. She collapsed in a heap on the floor beside Lauren.

16

The figure stepped into the room, and the lighting lifted. Lauren's vision cleared, and she got her first good look at it. The being was nothing like the image she had in her mind of an alien — yet it was everything she'd imagined; and more. It appeared exceptionally tall. Its smooth skin was a gentle silvery blue-gray, almost sparkly in the dim light. Lauren was enraptured by its large black eyes that seemed kind as it peered down at her. It had an elongated skull, around which it wore a circlet of gold and precious gems. There were two vertical slits for a nose, and barely more than a horizontal slit for a mouth.

Unlike many images of extraterrestrials, this being wore adornments, and a robe that hid its intimate secrets. It appeared to be bipedal. It was tridactyl … three fingers on each hand. In the long cloak, she couldn't tell what its feet might look like. She wanted to see if they were cloven, like the body of the infant god-child they had found in Peru.

A bizarre piercing click echoed around her and she struggled to clamp her hands over her ears, wincing at the pain in her head, as well as the pain in her body. Henry wailed, and

Lauren realized Rowan was in a similar position. The being backed up a moment and the noise stopped. "F … F … F… For … forgive …" the words didn't appear to come from the creature, but rather was a part of the air around them. Its tone was soft, warm, and rich. The being's speech was soothing, even as the being seemed to struggled to form the words. "W … w … we forget …" Lauren lowered her hands as she realized she could understand the speech. "We forget how fragile you are …" the being seemed to have communicated. Lauren didn't know if anyone else could understand it. She kept it in her peripheral vision as she focused on Michael.

Her husband reached over and caught Lauren's hand. Her gaze returned to Michael as she realized Rowan wasn't working on him. "Is he?" she looked to Rowan with pain in her eyes.

Rowan pursed his lips and shook his head. "I'm sorry …" he said. "No pulse … he's gone. I couldn't save him." He reached for her, but a pained gasp escaped Lauren's throat.

Before tears could escape her eyes, the entity moved towards them, lifting a hand. Michael's form levitated off the floor, and Rowan jumped back, nearly falling over Kitty who roused. Henry squealed brightly, pointing at Michael. "My my!" He tried to say his uncle's name.

Rowan knelt back beside her. At her bidding, he helped her sit up, supporting her in a reclined position, taking over the effort to hold pressure on her wound as her hands went limp beside her. Her head fell back into his shoulder and she sighed contentedly.

"Can you help him?" Lauren asked as the being made a motion with its other hand, and a table rose from the floor beneath Michael's limp form. A warm light radiated from the pedestal, blinking in a slow thudding pulse that throbbed audibly.

"Faith, curious one," the being seemed to say.

"Do you understand it?" Rowan asked. "What's it saying?"

Lauren realized she was alone in her comprehension. "I do." Henry reached for his father, who pulled the baby up into his arm with his free hand.

The being turned pointing a hand at Lauren. "You too are … broken."

Lauren gasped as she felt herself being lifted off the floor by an unseen force. Rowan released his grip, scooping up Henry and scrambling to his feet as a second table lifted up. The force moved her to its surface. Lauren melted onto the table as a warm feeling of safety came over her. Rowan caught her hand as the being moved between the two beds, placing a hand on Michael's head, then put the other on Lauren's.

As a scientist she wanted to study the being, but as a wounded mother, in what should have been a terrifying situation, her instincts told her she should take her child and flee, but all fear seemed to escape her. A sense of contentment and calm filled every fiber of her being.

The three-fingered hand ran down her arm, and took her hand, squeezing it reassuringly. Lauren stilled when she realize the fingers had tiny suction cups that massaged her flesh as they probed. "Be of good heart, you are among friends," the disembodied voice spoke.

"You can hear that, right?" Rowan asked. "You understand it?"

"Yes," she said, as he took a step forward. She glanced at Rowan, gauging his reaction, not sure if he was ready to run or put up a fight; she suspected the latter. "They won't harm us."

"The curious one is correct," the voice said softly.

Rowan took a step back. "Oh, that I understood."

"Your languages have changed since we were last here," it said. "It is hard to … adapt."

"Who are you?" Rowan asked, glancing back over at Kitty, who'd come to and rolled up onto her elbow, glancing up, studying the room. When she saw the entity, she gasped. Scrambling up against the wall, she cowered in horror as the scene unfolded around her.

"You might know our kind as Messengers …" The voice answered.

"Angels?" Lauren's brow furrowed, even as the pain in her side lifted.

"We have been called that."

"We?" Rowan asked. "Who's this *we*?"

"We," the voice began, but hesitated as the creature lay a hand on its own chest. "We are not like you. We are … The Three."

"Clearly," Rowan clipped.

"There is a triality to our kind," The Three said. "Your own people referred to us as Father, Son, Holy Spirit. Maiden. Mother. Crone."

"The Trinity …" Lauren gasped.

"But that is not wholly true." The Three turned its attention to Michael for a moment as the throbbing tone that rose from the bed seemed to soften and increase in tempo. He turned back to Lauren, offering her a hand. "We are past, present, and future. We are space, time, and matter. We are the here, the now … and the never."

Lauren's brow furrowed as she was lifted into a sitting position, the bed adjusting as she moved. She reached down and found the spot where her flesh had been damaged just moments before. There was nothing to suggest anything had ever been amiss. The hole in her t-shirt and the blood on her clothes and skin were the only evidence that she'd been injured. Even the throbbing in her head seemed to abate.

The table lowered and her feet found the floor. She was standing without knowing how she'd come to do so, as she gazed down at the curious creature who still held her hand.

"He will be restored," The Three said with a nod to Michael. "But it will take more time. His broken … his injury is more severe."

Lauren felt at ease, as she extracted her hand and turned to Rowan, who put a protective arm around her. "We …" she hesitated. "I have so many questions …"

"As we are sure you would, curious one," The Three said. "But we have many thanks to bestow upon you. Answers are among the many gifts you will receive … when the time is right."

Lauren realized Kitty had found her feet and had come to stand at her elbow. She attempted some kind of a polite bow, a bob of the head and perhaps even the bend of a knee. "I bring you greetings from the United Nations of the Planet Earth." Clearly she'd recovered from her shock and found her courage.

The creature lifted its hand and placed it on her head. When it withdrew, the goose egg on her forehead was gone. Then it dismissed her with a wave of the same hand. "We recognize your governments, but doubt you speak for all those who dwell below."

"Dwell … *below*?" Rowan puzzled.

Lauren paused, trying to find her place in three dimensions. She tried to sense where she was at the moment, but knew she could not, because she was not on Earth. This was a vessel of some sort, but what kind or where it was, was outside of her grasp of cognition.

"When he is mended, we will explain all," the being turned, and waved a hand for them to follow. The unseen door opened, and the creature passed through it. "We have chosen our own champion, one who will speak for us."

Lauren took a tentative step, but hesitated, caught by Rowan's hand on her arm. "Do you think it's wise to trust … I don't know what to call it?"

"We have nothing else to go on but trust," Lauren said,

and turned to follow. Rowan hesitated a moment, glancing at Kitty, who stood fast. He muttered something under his breath about what Lauren had gotten them into this time, but he fell in behind her. When Kitty realized they were leaving her alone, she followed too.

17

The vessel, or whatever this place was, was nothing like the *Starship Enterprise*, which was what Lauren had always expected a spaceship would be. Yet, in some ways, it was. The room was pristine, the seamless and rounded walls, as well as the floor seemed to glow blue-white; illuminating the room softly. A table lifted from the floor as they entered. Other furnishings, including chairs appeared as well, and something akin to a sofa or chaise.

"You will rest here," The Three said. "Be … comforted. We will return when the *other* is mended." It turned and left them; the door whooshed shut behind it.

"Please tell me I'm hallucinating," Kitty said, holding her head in her hands. "I know I hit my head in the scuffle. My head should be hurting, but … it isn't. Please tell me I have a concussion and I'm lying unconscious on the floor in Michael's office." She took a few steps over to the chaise and collapsed onto it.

"If you're hallucinating about being on an alien spaceship, then I have a concussion, too." Rowan's hand went to the spot on his jaw where the Estonian thug had punched him. The being hadn't offered him healing; perhaps he didn't need it.

To be sure, he ran his tongue along the line of his teeth to check if any were loose or broken before he sank into one of the chairs at the table. It seemed to mold to his tall frame as he relaxed.

"I can't tell where we are," Lauren admitted. "My … bump of direction … my spatial orientation … it's completely off-kilter." She sat, too. Henry snuggled up against her, seemingly content as he rested his head on her chest and babbled happily to himself.

Rowan reached for her hand. "Are you okay?"

She leaned back and lifted her shirt, showing him the lack of any injury. "Apparently, I'm fully healed."

"I was terrified," Rowan confessed, inspecting Henry. He turned to his dad and held out his arms. Rowan took him and continued his assessment, finding nothing amiss.

"You and me both," she said. "What happened to the KGB guy?"

Kitty sat up. "I clobbered him with the fire extinguisher," she said. "I hope I broke his freakin' neck."

"What about Lubanzi and India?" Rowan asked. Lauren just shook her head, conveying her certain fear that neither appeared to have survived the attack. "Dammit."

There was a long awkward pause as each of them processed what had just happened.

"Are we actually on an alien spaceship? Like … in outer space?" Kitty asked.

"I have no evidence of that," Lauren said. "But neither do I have evidence to the contrary."

"Is this the first contact our government has been planning for?" Rowan asked.

Kitty's expression darkened. "It's not anything like what we anticipated," she said. "But I know what my orders are, and given time, I'll begin a dialogue, find some common ground, start working towards the *yes* we need to move forward."

"The *yes*?" Lauren asked.

"The ultimate goal of any diplomatic process is to obtain an *initial yes* through finding a common perspective on an issue, and to develop an appreciation of the culture and interests of the foreign diplomat." Kitty stood and peeled off her suit jacket. "A *yes*, in this case, is an agreement that we are not enemies, but rather allies. That we can aid one another in some capacity. We can begin by coming to a mutually beneficial accord."

"So you're mission is to establish a treaty with an alien race?" Rowan asked.

"An accord, by definition, is a voluntary agreement that entities enter into first while they try to work out terms of a treaty. Accords are just one of the many forms of the diplomatic process, along with alliances, conventions, and treaties. NATO was technically formed as an Alliance. You're probably familiar with the Geneva Convention?"

"Yes," Rowan said.

"The Revolutionary War ended with the Treaty of Paris in 1783. That's the highest level of diplomatic agreement in the hierarchy of diplomatic tools."

"That's assuming they're willing to negotiate." Rowan stood, patting Henry, and walking the floor behind the table.

"Or that there's anything we can offer that they can't just take by force," Lauren said.

"I suspect they need us for something … or we wouldn't be here," Kitty said.

Rowan paced, lulling Henry into a light slumber as the hours passed. Lauren alternated between sitting and standing, pacing some herself. Kitty sat, silent, sullen.

LAUREN TURNED WHEN A WHOOSHING SOUND BROKE THE weary silence. The door opened. Michael staggered in leaning heavily on the wall. He took two steps in and stumbled. Lauren and Rowan both jumped to catch him, but Lauren got to him first and his momentum took her down with him. "What are you doing out of bed?" she asked. "I don't think you're supposed to be up." Rowan, still with his child in his arms, helped Lauren out from under him. He handed Henry back to his mother. Michael might have been taller than Rowan, but he was lean and rail thin. Rowan got his injured brother-in-law up and helped him over to the chaise Kitty vacated, getting him settled.

"I'm okay," Michael insisted as Lauren came over and sat down on the edge of the chair beside him. "I'm okay."

"But … you were … dead," Lauren said. Henry reached for his uncle, but Lauren held him back.

"Well I'm not dead now," Michael grunted, laying back, wincing, and clutching his stomach. "Though I'm not sure which is better, at the moment."

Rowan peeled back his shirt, finding a mending wound just below his ribs. "What the hell?" he muttered. Lauren leaned over, inspecting her brother.

"What?" Michael groaned, lifting his head.

"The wound is practically … healed," Rowan said.

"My!" Henry fussed. "My my!" He reached for Michael, but Rowan took him and held him.

Lauren lifted the tail of her own shirt. "The bullet passed through you and hit me. But I'm healed." She looked down, her hand searching for the hole that was no longer there. A fading pink mark was all that marred her abdomen.

"What's going on?" Michael lifted his head and tried to focus his eyes to gain his bearings. "Where are we?"

"I'm not sure I can tell you," Lauren said, glancing at Kitty. She seemed intent on Michael.

"No, I've been here before." Michael said. "Lauren, remember … what I told you?" He said, as if he didn't want to repeat it in front of Kitty.

Lauren nodded and turned to Kitty. She said softly, "I think he's hallucinating."

"He's been through a lot," Rowan said. He patted Michael's shoulder. "Just get some rest, buddy."

Michael nodded weakly, surrendering to oblivion.

AFTER SOME TIME, WHICH COULD HAVE BEEN MINUTES, HOURS or days, food appeared on the table, but no one made a move toward it. Not even to inspect the bowl of fruit or loaf of bread. Even the jug of what appeared to be wine went untouched. Kitty paced around the table but said nothing as Lauren finally sank onto one of the chairs, exhaustion catching up with her. Rowan sat down across from her but neither spoke.

Henry leaned back against his mother, her braid in his fist, as he rocked against her and tried to coax her to play. "Nana …" he grunted reaching towards the table. Lauren glanced over and realized there was a banana among the offerings. Henry patted her leg. "Nana, Mama."

"It might not be safe to eat," Kitty said, unbidden.

"I'm inclined to agree with her," Rowan said. "It could be … a trap."

Lauren frowned at both of them and reached for the banana. It was pale green around the edges, with a perfect unblemished yellow peel. Rowan took it from her hand. "You can't give that to Henry."

Her expression turned sharp as she snatched it back and handed Henry over. Henry didn't protest but watched his mother as she peeled the fruit and sniffed it cautiously. Lauren found the perfume pleasant, and familiar. She took a bite and chewed, analyzing the texture as well as the taste. Finding nothing off putting, she swallowed and took another bite.

"They brought us here," Lauren said. "If they wanted us

dead, we'd already be dead. I sincerely doubt they mean to poison us."

Henry reached for it, grunting. "Na na na."

Lauren broke off a piece and handed it to her son. He squished it in his chubby hand before shoving it into his mouth. "Thanks a lot, Eve. We're sure to get banished from the garden now." Rowan quipped bitterly.

"Or trapped here like Persephone in Hades," Kitty quipped.

"It's not an apple," Lauren snipped in return, shoving a bite of banana into Rowan's mouth, too. "Or a pomegranate," she added to Kitty. "It's delicious." Rowan chewed but didn't seem happy about it. He could have spit it out if he'd wanted to, but he didn't. Lauren took another bite and gave the rest to Henry to gnaw on.

KITTY FINALLY GOT UP THE NERVE TO GO SIT BESIDE MICHAEL, taking his hand, inspecting his healing knuckles. Bruises were fading and the cuts from the fist-fight had turned to pink scars.

Michael opened his eyes, lifting his head looking around, confused. He calmed and laid his head back down. Before she could speak, he sneered, "Did you try to kill me?"

"What?"

"The crash? Did you arrange that? Did you try to kill me?" He enunciated each word individually, so as to be clear.

She turned her back, crossing her arms over her legs, leaning on her elbows. "No. I didn't try to kill you. I could never hurt you. I was … betrayed."

"Uh huh," Michael drug the words out. "Because I'm the love of your life. You never forgot me after college, and the few days we had together in Houston were so special. The best you ever had…" He snarked.

She turned and narrowed her brow. Her blue eyes burned

like laser beams. "Stop it, Michael!" she ordered. "I never meant to hurt you … it wasn't my idea to make you think … I'd died. I was following orders. They told me it'd be better if you thought I was gone. I didn't like it either. I hated every minute of it … because I knew … I could never see you again."

The pain in her voice was genuine, but Michael found himself trying to gauge her acting skills. "Why, Kitty?" His words had a bite to them that was undeniable.

"Michael, I didn't know you were working on Project Morning Star when I ran into you that day at NASA. Last I heard you were working on telemetry systems for the next generation of space craft. I was working undercover with the Hubble Team to see what NASA knew about contact with alien life. Rumors of these signals has been spoken in whispers around the world for the past few years. I was watching for any of the radio telescope projects to report back on the signals. Several did, but none seemed to be close to finding the truth … the truth we suspected but could not confirm … 'til now."

Michael's eyes averted away from her, staring at the wall that seemed illuminated from within. "Did you have something to do with Alexei? With his murder?"

"What?" She looked affronted. "No! God, Michael. No." She stood and turned her back to him a moment, before continuing.

"Then who did?" he demanded. "Your hired goon? Malakoff?"

"Not every government out there has joined our Alliance. There are countries who don't believe in a peace accord … with …" Her eyes jutted towards the ceiling; her finger pointed upward. "With them." It took her a moment to continue. Michael was still fuming. "There are countries out there who would rather strike pre-emptively and will stop at nothing to interfere with our efforts, silence our champions and keep the population oblivious to the real situation for a completely different reason."

"Keep people oblivious? Maybe you should tell us more about your … Alliance." Rowan hadn't been invited into the conversation, but it didn't stop him from jumping in.

"And the forces working against you," Lauren added.

Kitty gazed up at them as they came to stand over her. She motioned to the empty chairs, indicating it would not be a short story. Rowan and Lauren both sat down. She rose from the edge of the chaise and paced a moment. She seemed to collect her thoughts before she began.

"It started in a NATO secret session over a three decades ago." Kitty crossed her arms and took a deep breath. "It's been a carefully guarded secret since Bill Clinton volunteered the US to lead the effort."

"Bill Clinton?" Lauren's brow lifted. "President Clinton?"

"He wasn't always in favor of an intergalactic peace accord. But, in an interview on national TV, Clinton said … and I quote, *a battle with aliens may be the only way to unite this incredibly divided world of ours.* He was one of the most progressive presidents when it came to a policy on alien relations," Kitty said. "It's just that most Americans don't know it. He went on to say, *think of how all the differences among the people on earth would seem small if we felt threatened by a space invader.*"

"And there is a threat," Michael said. "If your translation is correct."

"He hoped it wouldn't end up like Independence Day," Kitty said. "But, you seem to know more about these … creatures than anyone. You tell me. Are they a threat?"

Michael seemed contemplative for a long moment. "I don't know. I want to trust them, but … I'm as scared as you are. At the moment though, I don't think it's *them* that I fear."

"What do you mean?" Kitty pursed her lips.

"My friend was murdered," he snarled, his eyes gazing up to the ceiling as he lay back. "My project was threatened …

my life and my family have been threatened. I thought you died … and I had to think it was no coincidence." There was a definite bite to his words as he rolled up onto one arm, then pushed himself up to sitting. "But now, I realize, it's not the aliens or some foreign government trying to stop me. It's *you*."

Kitty seemed wounded by the vitriol in his tone. She took a step back, fighting for words, but unable to come up with anything to placate him. Lauren watched the uncomfortable tension between them thicken.

"Are there other projects listening in?" Lauren asked, trying to make peace. "I mean, trying to find these … alien signals?" She moved close enough to Michael to put a hand on his back to steady him.

"Sure," Kitty said. "You're not the only one with a radio telescope picking them up."

"But why stop Michael's?" Lauren asked. "Why so much attention on Project Morning Star?"

"While I had no idea you were working on Morning Star when I met you in Houston," she said directly to Michael. "I did see something in your eye when we were looking at the feed from Hubble in my office that day … and I was afraid … I knew then … if anyone would figure it out … it'd be you. I had to report it to my superiors."

Michael stared, stone-faced as she spoke. "Now we've done it," she said, lifting her hand to the room around them. "We've made first contact."

Michael's expression didn't change. "You didn't make first contact. We did. Lauren and Rowan, and me. Not you. We found the aliens. We made first contact … over three years ago. Her in Peru … me, here."

Lauren realized Michael hadn't made good on his lifelong promise to find aliens before she did. If his timelines matched up with hers, they'd done it at practically the same time. He began having his experiences about the same time she found the godchild in Peru. But suddenly, that no longer mattered.

All those years of bickering and fighting didn't mean anything anymore.

"It doesn't matter who made contact *first*," Kitty stated. "But this ... *this* ... it has to be managed," she muttered. "I have the authority to negotiate a peaceful accord with these beings. This is my job. I need you all to let me do my job so we can avoid a situation that could lead to ... intergalactic war ... to the very destruction of our planet."

"There haven't been any threats ..." Michael started angrily but froze.

"Yet," she added.

As if summoning the creature from the heavens, and before there could be any debate, the door hissed opened and the creature entered, carrying what appeared to be clothes. It paused at the entry way, scanning the room, its eyes coming to settle on Michael. It came over to him and lay the clothing on the chaise beside him. "We have prepared you something clean to wear while you heal," The Three said.

Before Michael could protest, the clothes appeared in place upon his person, and any evidence of blood, sweat or soil was gone from his body. His hair swept back as if being lifted by the wind. The tresses seem to lengthen as it appeared to be tied by unseen hands and was scooped back into a queue, tied with a length of what appeared to be a leather thong. Lauren glanced down. Her own hands that had been stained in blood were now pristine. She found no evidence of blood or grime, even beneath her short nails.

"You will eat, and we will talk," the creature said, turning with a wave to the table. "If this food is repugnant we will provide other nourishment." Without so much as a wave the of its hand the table cleared, and a carafe and cups appeared on the table. The perfume of coffee found its way to Lauren's nose. Her stomach growled. She couldn't be sure how long it had been since she last ate.

"Nana," Henry reached for the table. Much to Lauren's

surprise, a bowl appeared with what looked like, of all things … Cheerios.

Lauren took one of the oat circles and put it in her mouth, testing it. Rowan watched with interest. Satisfied with the results, she reached for a plate she hadn't seen before. She scooped a handful of Cheerios and put them on the plate for him, before taking a banana and peeling it for Henry. He grabbed it and shoved it into his mouth, using the newly erupted teeth to gnaw on it.

Rowan looked skeptically at Lauren, and at the creature, but reached for the carafe and sniffed it. He poured two cups, adding what appeared to be cream and sugar from separate containers. He took a sip and pushed a cup over to his wife who accepted it with thanks. "Anyone else?" No one took him up on it.

"Michael," the being summon with a raised hand. "You need to regain your strength." Michael rose slowly, but once he was confident of his footing, he moved without effort to come sit at the table with his sister and her family. Steak and cheesecake appeared among the offerings, as each of them found a plate in front of them. The perfume of fried chicken and mashed potatoes joined in as Lauren found her plate prepared.

Rowan's plate appeared to contain his favorite meal, red beans, and rice. He sniffed at it cautiously, then took a tentative bite. Lauren watched for his reaction. "It's not as good as yours," he said in sidebar to her. "But it's not bad."

Kitty hesitated to join, but when a plate appeared for her, she finally gave into her hunger and came to sit next to Michael. The creature seemed satisfied when everyone settled in to eat. It took the last empty seat next to Michael and allowed them to make short work of the food.

Lauren found herself engrossed in watching the dynamics of the table around her. Paying little attention to her own food, she tended to Henry first. She recognized the effort of casual diplomacy; ply your guests with a nice meal and set them at ease in an environment you control. Watching Michael devour everything on the plate, she couldn't help but notice that it didn't seem to empty until he was sated. Clearly his injuries required energy to mend, and his color seemed much improved when he pushed back the plate. As each guest finished, the plates disappeared. Cups were refilled and everyone seemed to relax. Lauren's plate remained the last on the table, as she fed small bites to Henry with her fingers.

Lauren wasn't surprised when Kitty made her move.

"Thank you for your hospitality." She folded her napkin and lay it on the table. "Your technology is impressive."

The Three, however, did not appear to fall for her not-so-subtle efforts to develop rapport. Its eye caught Lauren's as it turned to her brother. "You, Michael, Champion of the gods, your place is secured among the stars," the being said. "You will speak for us, if you are willing."

"Me?" Michael seemed stunned.

"I don't think you understand," Kitty said. "I represent an alliance of world leaders who have designated *me* to serve as a liaison between our world and … and yours."

The Three turned and looked to her. "We recognize your world's desire to choose your own champion. We have chosen Michael."

"Champion?" Kitty recoiled. "What do you think this is? Mortal Kombat?"

If the creature understood the reference to the video game, it gave no indication. "Combat is inevitable," The Three said. "I believe you have a saying; the enemy of my enemy is my friend?"

"Yes," Michael said. "We're not your enemy?"

"Nor am I yours," The Three said. "Which makes us friends, does it not?"

"Does it?" Lauren screwed up her face, trying to make

sense of its words. The Three seemed to be speaking in riddles.

"We have an enemy," the Three finally explained. "One who would wish to destroy you, just as they would wish to destroy *us*. My enemy. Your enemy."

"Our enemy?" Kitty said. "Who is this enemy?"

"The feud has raged for a millennia. This enemy will stop at nothing to destroy what it has created … you have spoken of this in whispered tones with your sister," it addressed Michael.

"Enlil?" He asked.

"That is one of many names used by the darkest of all forces," The Three said. "It is an enemy who will stop at nothing to be restored to favor with the Most-High, Anu."

"Would one of your names be Enki?" Lauren asked, retrieving her braid from Henry's grasp.

"We have many names," the creature blinked its large dark eyes. "This is one you may use if you prefer to assign a more simple moniker to this vessel." Its hand seemed to gesture to its own body.

Rowan turned and looked at his wife. She nodded, recognizing the need for understanding in his gaze. "Enki." She tried the name out. "Why are you telling us now?" Lauren turned her attention back to their host.

"We fear the dark forces of Enlil are gathering," Enki said. "We fear you will not survive if we do not intervene … and we cannot defeat Enlil without your aid."

"What do you need from me?" Lauren looked perplexed. "How can we help?"

"We have come only for Michael," Enki said. "He has much to learn before the war comes to this place. There are spells and incantations to bind the fallen son of Anu. Michael has been chosen."

"Wait, what?" Rowan turned.

"It is no mistake that the moniker assigned to this vessel,"

Enki waved a hand towards Lauren's brother. "Is the name of the ancient heavenly warrior, a minion of the Most-High. Chief Warrior, Protector, Healer and Peacemaker."

"Wait. What?" Michael recoiled. "What do you mean you came for me?"

"War is coming, and we cannot fight it alone. We need a warrior to champion our cause. But we cannot fight a war on two fronts. We need the peacemaker to strengthen the bonds between the Heavens and Earth."

"Wait, if you need … an ambassador … that's my job," Kitty protested, finally able to get the words out. "I speak for the United Nations Task Force. I'm …" The creature raised its hand and Kitty's mouth closed. The look on her face spoke volumes as she scowled angrily.

"You have a role to play as well, Catherine," it said. She took a step back. Lauren moved to Michael and snaked her hand in his. They shared a concerned look, but their attention returned to their host. "It would not be kindly received for us to take a respected scientist. He must come with us of his own will. Witnesses must know the heart of the … *ambassador*." It used her words. "Catherine, your role will be to serve as his intermediary. He will speak for us. You will speak for him."

Kitty opened her mouth as if to interject herself into the conversation, but no words came out, as the creature lifted a three-fingered hand like Darth Vader using *The Force*. It turned back to her, fixing those large dark eyes on Lauren's. Lauren suddenly chilled at the creature's gaze. She had been told she was Chosen. The Bigfoot Shaman had told her as much. *Had she lost her status? Had she failed in some way?*

"Lauren, *Truth Seeker*, your time will come." Lauren's brow lifted. No one called her that except … Tsul'Kalu. "Your mission will surpass the call of all others, but your place is here. Blessed are you and blessed is your purpose here. Maiden, mother … magi." His hand went to her head, but then went to Henry's.

"Mama … go." Henry eyed the alien defiantly.

"Hush, little one," Enki's façade seemed to brighten, though it's face seemed to lack the ability to smile. The large eyes blinked. "When it is time, you may take your mother home."

"Wait. What?" Rowan puzzled. "What do you mean he can take his mother home?"

"My do," Henry patted his own chest, and then leaned into Lauren and patted hers. "My go."

"Wait? Is … Henry doing that?" Rowan stumbled over the words, and Lauren gasped when she realized what he was thinking. "He's the one teleporting you. No wonder you didn't know how it happened."

"Henry?" She didn't know who to direct the question to, Enki or Henry. "No. No. That can't be right." She turned to Rowan. "But … he's just … he's just a baby?" Lauren gasped, her hand going to his back. "But …" Lauren seemed to pale.

"The child is his mother's son," Enki said. "As she is blessed, so blessed is her offspring. Lauren," Enki's voice softened. "While your powers were bestowed, those of your children are ordained."

"Children?" Lauren's brow lifted.

"There will be many," Enki said, that beatific expression she was accustomed to seeing on Tsul'Kalu's face passed over the alien features of their host. Enki turned his gaze to Rowan. "A love such as this … how could there not be? Protector, your job will not be easy. She is your ward, and you are hers."

"I wouldn't have it any other way," Rowan said, forcing a smile onto his face, his eyes going to his wife's.

"Lauren," the being spoke softly, turning to her. "You who have sought truth, found it, and used it wisely. You are to serve as our hand, our eyes. When the time comes, your role will require the greatest sacrifice."

"Sacrifice?" Lauren gulped hard. Her eye went to Rowan

first, then Michael, but the being came forward and lifted its long hand to her head, placing it on her crown, then caressing her cheek.

"We will not ask more of you than you can give, and we will guard over your family, and your children." The hand moved down to her stomach and came to rest over her womb. "But fear not. We will send aid when help is warranted. We will not abandon you in your hour of need … and you are never alone. You have been given all the gifts you need to complete your mission … when the time comes."

"But …" Lauren's face contorted as she struggled to make sense of the message and what it could possibly mean. Enki's strange hand came to her chin and lifted her face. She was transfixed as she gazed into the large dark eyes and could see all the wisdom of the universe contained within. The questions no longer mattered; faith took hold, and she knew whatever the challenge, she would be equal to it.

The creature's thin lids closed in a slow blink and the spell was broken. She took a faltering step backwards, finding Rowan's hand in the small of her back, his arm came to wrap around her protectively.

"There is little time," Enki said calmly, turning to Michael. "You must consent. But I will give you a moment to … discuss."

With a bow of its head, it blinked, the door hissed open, then whooshed closed just as softly as the being left them. Michael's eyes followed it, then turned back to his sister. "What just happened?"

"I'll tell you what happened," Rowan smirked. "We got abducted by aliens … and they want to keep you." The shock of it all seemed to hit him suddenly. He let go of Lauren and turned to pace. Lauren found herself standing numbly.

"You can't seriously be considering staying with that … those … that … thing?" Kitty protested as she marched over to Michael. He stood, facing her without flinching. "You don't know what they'll do to you."

"If they were going to hurt me," Michael said, glancing at Lauren, but not meeting her eye. "They'd have done it by now." His hand went to where he'd been injured and he added, "That doesn't appear to be the point."

"But …" Kitty started to protest. Lauren felt her anguish. She didn't want to leave Michael here either, but she was starting to see the logic in it. She didn't know what was ahead for any of them, but she had to believe this was part of a bigger plan. Something bigger than any of them, especially bigger than herself.

Michael drew Kitty into him. He took a deep breath; the perfume of her shampoo made his knees weak. "You're not the only one allowed to have secrets," he said. "I've made my decision."

"You're staying." Lauren knew he would. He had found his purpose. She couldn't deny him that. She didn't want to leave him behind. They'd finally come to an accord of their own. They still had work to do to rebuild their relationship; to fix their family.

"No!" Kitty stamped her foot like a spoiled child. "You can't stay here. You can't go with these … things. I can't authorize it! I won't allow it! I won't!"

"I don't think you have a say in this," Lauren said, stepping in between them. "Michael has to stay with them, and it's the best way for him to help you establish an accord with these beings. You want them as your allies, don't you?"

Kitty gasped. It was plainly written on her face. She was stunned at the sudden realization that they were both against her, and oddly enough, maybe they were both right. "Michael, we have to go back and let the authorities know about the Estonian operative's betrayal. Someone has to explain what happened to India, Lubanzi … Alexei," Lauren said, seeing him pale as he realized his boss and his mentor had met a similar fate as his Russian colleague. He nodded.

The color of the room suddenly changed, and the soft blue-white light dimmed to an almost purple tone. The doors swept open. The creature returned, but this time, it was not alone. A compliment of three entered the room.

"We have come for your answer," Enki said.

"How will we communicate with my brother?" Lauren asked. "We may need his help to convince our governments of this enemy and the war that is coming. We need some way to get a message to him."

"You need no devices," Enki said. "When a message is true and urgent, we will know. Michael will know."

"How long will he need to stay?" Kitty's voice trembled.

Enki reached for her hand, lowering its head. "You may consider it a lifetime appointment. Though to us, a year is but a day."

"I'll never see him again?" Kitty gulped, her eyes shimmering as tears gathered within the dam of her lashes. Lauren felt a pang in her own chest but refused to allow her emotions to well to the surface.

"Perhaps," Enki said. "But his place will be with us, among the stars."

"So what are we supposed to do?" Rowan asked, standing, pacing behind the table. "Am I supposed to stand by while my infant son blinks us from place to place?"

"Your job is to protect your wife," Enki said. The being turned to Lauren. "Your job is to prepare."

"And what about me?" Kitty's face had grown red, and she was distraught.

"You will prepare your governments," Enki said. "You must make peace among your own people. We will show you the way."

"But … I can't tell them about you …" Kitty said.

"Our presence is …known."

18

Yevgeny Malakoff came to on the floor of the office building where Michael Grayson had made his discovery. The Estonian operative had a wicked headache and couldn't get the room to stop spinning. The spent fire extinguisher lay nearby, it's bright red color clearly visible through his blurred vision.

He rolled his head to one side and made out the body of one of the scientists he had shot. He lifted his head, finding the other a few feet away. *Two. He only got two?* Malakoff blinked back the dots in his eyes and made out the shadow of the weapon he'd brandished earlier. His hand grasped for the gun but missed.

He lay a moment longer, willing his vision to clear. The blur of papers scattered on the floor gave him something to focus on, rather than the bodies that lay around him. Malakoff sat up, fighting a wave of dizziness as his vision began to clear and he realized there were words and symbols scribbled haphazardly in blue ink. The operative got to his knees, forgetting about the gun, focused on the documents. None of it made much sense, but he wasn't sure if that were a result of the blow to the back of his head or the language, but he gathered the papers together deciding he could study them more later. A cell phone lay beneath the table. Yevgeny took it and switched it on. There was no passcode on it, and only one audio file and one photograph. The operative's heart flipped in his chest as he recognized the picture, and he came to realize what he was holding in his hand. This had belonged to the Russian Cosmonaut he'd been sent to deal with. He'd searched the man's apartment before going to the television studio.

A shuffling from the hallway made him freeze and he pocketed the phone in his jacket and slid back to the floor, curling up into a ball, groaning as the door opened. "Help … me," he feigned as a woman shrieked. The housekeeper turned and ran from the room, abandoning her cleaning cart in the doorway.

Yevgeny managed to snag the gun and use the tail of his shirt to wipe the prints before tossing it over by one of the bodies. He could hear the footfalls of feet running towards the room; feel the vibrations of it through the tiles. He collapsed and prepared to play the role of his life. "Help …" he moaned as the door flew open and security rushed into the room. "Help me …" he grasped the hand of one of the guards who stopped to check on him.

"What happened?" the security officer asked. "Who did this?"

"An American spy … Kitty Donovan …" he said. "She pulled a gun on the team … she double crossed me …"

"Is that … Director Cameron?"

The lieutenant nodded, kneeling beside her. "She's dead."

"So is Dr. Dlamani," another said.

"Where's Dr. Grayson?" The lieutenant asked.

"With her …" Malakoff said. "He's her lover. They conspired to … to take the data from his project … they're going to sell it to the Russians …" Malakoff felt a flutter in his stomach as he delighted in his clever delivery as he clutched his supposedly wounded shoulder. It was injured, but not to the degree he exhibited. "His sister too … they conspired against me."

"Call the embassy," the guard at his side said to the lieutenant. Clearly this was the man in charge. "The authorities need to be alerted … and get this man a medic!"

~

Frank White sat, bleary-eyed, in the emergency operations center staring down the Estonian Security Forces Director. It was after midnight and it was too much effort to make coffee, considering the urgency of the matter at hand. He ran a weary hand down his face as he listened to the wild story the director wove.

"Mr. Jääger, I am having a hard time believing what I'm hearing," he said. "While Kitty Donovan is a lot of things, she's not a traitor."

"She turned on our operative and shot two scientists to get her hands on the data," Jääger clipped. "The South African Consulate has directed local authorities to issue a BOLO for her and her accomplices."

"Accomplices?"

"Dr. Michael Grayson, his sister and her husband."

"His *sister*?"

"You may recognize her name," Jääger sneered. "Dr. Lauren Grayson … and her husband, Rowan Pierce."

Frank sat back in his chair. He did recognize the name. Too well. "Christ…" he muttered under his breath. "Was your operative injured in the attack?"

"Yes," Jääger said. "He's being treated in hospital as we speak."

"I can have agents on the ground in hours," Frank said.

"Nyet," Jääger sneered. "South African officials won't even let me send my teams. They assure they will take care of it."

"I want to talk to them before anyone else," he said. "I am enacting Article 3 of the Bishop Convention for my personnel and parties associated. I want International Mediation Services to resolve this conflict."

"This is not a war, Secretary White." Jääger said curtly. "Enacting this branch of NATO is reserved for matters of impending war."

"It isn't yet," Frank said. "My goal is to keep it that way. If anything happens to any of these US Citizens — especially a government official — it could easily escalate into an international conflict ... even a war."

"You fail to mention the obvious, Secretary White." Jääger glared at him through the camera. "If your scientist has achieved his goal, this could be an intergalactic conflict ... *that* is the real hazard here."

"Which is why I want to talk to my people first."

19

That gut-wrenching feeling of disorientation hit Lauren before she was ready for it. She found herself standing in a meadow, surrounded by trembling aspen trees, a cool mountain breeze lifted her disheveled hair. Immediately, her sense of place put her in the meadow where she and Rowan had been married.

"What the hell?" She heard Kitty behind her. She turned, relieved to find Rowan stood with Henry a few feet away. "Where are we?

Rowan studied the trees and turned his gaze towards the babbling river a dozen yards away. "Is that …?"

"The Big Thompson River," Lauren said. "Yes."

"Colorado?" Rowan seemed to sway. Lauren stepped over to him and put a hand on his arm. "We're home?"

"Mama go," Henry reached for Lauren. She took him, holding him tightly, relieved they were out of harm's way … for now. "My go."

"We can't be in Colorado!" Kitty stormed, pacing towards the river, but turning abruptly. "How am I going to explain this to my superiors? How do I …"

"I don't know," Lauren said. "But we are going to need help."

"What do you mean?" Rowan asked.

"Considering Dr. Cameron and Dr. Dlamani were shot, and we don't know what happened to your Estonian counterpart, we have to assume the worst." Lauren patted her pocket. "I don't have my phone," Lauren said, realizing she'd left hers on the table in Michael's office. Rowan fished in his pocket and withdrew his, holding it out to Lauren. She took it and handed it to Kitty. "Who's more likely to help us?"

Kitty pondered it a moment, looking blankly at the device. She handed it back. "If I could remember his number, I'd call Jack White, but … all my numbers are programmed in my phone.

"Where was your phone?" Rowan asked.

"In my suit jacket," she said, running her hand up her bare arms, the cool breeze eliciting goosebumps on her flesh.

"Mama." Henry patted Lauren's chest.

Lauren turned to Rowan, handing him the phone back. "Do you have internet? Can you do a Google search?" She put a second hand on Henry's back, trying to get him to stop squirming.

"Mama!" Henry fussed.

"What, baby?" She turned her attention to him.

"Fishy …" he pointed up. "Fishy …" His tone was urgent. "My go."

One minute, they were in Colorado, the next, they were back on the ship in the room they had waited in earlier. Kitty's jacket still hung on the back of a chair. Henry's stuffed shark lay on the table nearby. "Fishy!" Henry reached for it, nearly slipping out of his disoriented mother's grasp. "Fishy! Mama! Fishy!"

Lauren recovered enough to grab Kitty's jacket, feeling the weight of the phone in her pocket. She thought to find Michael and say the goodbyes she hadn't had a chance to say earlier, but again, the world seemed to blink out from around her, and she stumbled into Rowan.

"Lauren? Jesus Christ…" He startled, catching her before scooping Henry out of her arms as she stumbled a few steps away and collapsed to her hands and knees, retching. Kitty went to her side, catching her braid and pulling it out of the way as she puked repeatedly into the grass. Rowan came around to the other side, offering a hand when she tried to stand, gathering her wits, and allowing her body to orient itself to the sudden change of location.

"Mama?" Even Henry sounded concerned.

"I'm okay." She turned and spat trying to get the foul tang out of her mouth. "Sheesh." She bent over and put her hands on her knees to steady herself. "I hate that feeling …"

"You'd think you'd get used to it," Rowan said. Clearly, it hadn't affected him the same way it did her. Of course, she'd done it more than he had, and with each *episode* it got worse.

"You'd think," Lauren said. She stood back, taking a deep breath, then moved in leaning on his arm. Resting her face against his bicep she seemed to recover quickly enough. "Kitty, make the call."

~

"THE SECRETARY OF HOMELAND SECURITY?" LAUREN lowered her tone as they sat on the patio outside the Starbucks in Estes Park. "That's your boss?"

"Frank White," she said. "He's up to speed on everything."

"How did you explain how we got back to the US?"

"Aliens," she said. "I'm pretty sure he thinks I'm crazy, but I told him it was aliens."

"Welcome to my world," Lauren said, reaching for the cup of coffee Rowan brought her. "I've been called everything from crazy to a complete crackpot."

"Do you ever get used to it?" Kitty asked.

"The more evidence I gather, the more truth I learn, the less it bothers me," Lauren said. "Let the ignorant talk all they want."

"How long do we have to wait?" Rowan asked.

"Frank told us to wait here," she said. "It could be several hours before an extraction team reaches us."

"Dr. Donovan?" A voice behind her made her wince. She froze a moment, her eyes locked with Lauren's. She turned slowly and Lauren's eyes lifted. "Agent Bryce Anderson. The extraction team is meeting us at the airport."

Kitty stood, and Lauren wasn't certain her knees would hold her. "What's the password?"

"Frank sent me," the agent said.

"Really?" Rowan pinched his lips dubiously. "Isn't that kind of lame?"

Kitty turned. "He's right."

"The car is this way." He held out a hand.

Lauren stood, holding Henry on her shoulder as he napped. Whatever had happened, the boy seemed drained and lay like a heavy limp doll in her arms. She stopped a moment. "We don't have a car seat for Henry."

"I've taken care of it," Agent Anderson said.

Any protests Lauren had melted away. With Henry safely strapped in the middle of the back seat of the SUV, Lauren buckled up beside him. She knew how he felt. A wave of exhaustion washed over her, and no sooner were they underway, she nodded off.

~

WHEN LAUREN AWOKE, THE LARGE BLACK SUV WAS PARKED inside a brightly illuminated hanger. The agent got out of the car and came around and opened her door. "Dr. Pierce," he offered her a hand. "Are you okay?"

"Hm?" Lauren was still weary and moved slower than usual. "Yeah," she yawned. "I'm fine." Rowan collected Henry who woke with a start, fussing as his dad unhooked the straps on the car seat.

A jet was parked nearby. The crews were busily preparing for takeoff, inspecting the key components, making sure it was safe for the journey. A man dressed in a white shirt with blue and gold epaulets on the shoulders, obviously the captain, made his own inspection, working from a checklist on a clipboard.

Anderson handed her the toy shark that had slipped from Henry's hand as he popped his head back in and retrieved the car seat, knowing they would need it again. "You must have children, Mr. Anderson," Lauren observed. Henry saw the shark in her hand and started fussing.

"Fishy!" His voice echoed in the high-ceilinged hanger. Lauren tossed it to Rowan, who caught it with his free hand, handing it to Henry, who hugged it and smiled brightly.

"My kids are grown," he said. "Won't be long before I'm a grandpa."

"You don't look old enough for grandkids," Rowan said.

"You flatter me, Mr. Pierce."

"Where are we going?" Kitty asked, reminding them that there was serious business still needing attention.

"Classified," Anderson said, directing them toward the plane with a lifted hand.

The pilot met them at the base of the stairs. "Welcome aboard," he said. "Make yourselves comfortable, we'll be underway in about twenty minutes."

"You've received the flight instructions?"

"Yes sir." The pilot nodded. "I filed the flight plan and I'm just waiting for approval."

"Good," the agent said.

Rowan let Lauren and Kitty mount the stairs first and fell in behind them. He ducked at the door but paused there to listen to the conversation 'til Henry tugged on his beard. "Dada!" He bopped him in the face with the stuffed shark.

"Henry," Lauren scolded, and the baby looked at her, recoiling sheepishly. "That's not very nice." She reached for him and he gave her a devilish grin as he held up his arms to her.

The cabin was larger than Lauren had expected. There were six seats, all upholstered in white leather, trimmed with gray piping and cherry-wood trim that was lacquered and polished to a shine. They pivoted to face one another, and a short pub table sat between two of them on each side. Lauren took one, her back to the cockpit. She settled in to nurse Henry. He suckled greedily, clearly hungry. Lauren was too, and her stomach growled audibly.

"I hope there are some peanuts or pretzels served on this flight," she muttered to Rowan who took the seat across from her.

Anderson finally came into the cabin and took a seat at the back of the plane, followed by a man in a uniform who peeled out of his jacket, and hung it in the small closet off the galley. "Change of plans," the steward said, with a bob of his head. "I've just gotten word from the Captain, there's a bit of weather coming in. We're going to have to push off a bit early to get ahead of it and we've just gotten clearance to take off. I have just enough time to get everyone a beverage," he lay a couple of napkins on each of the tables in front of Lauren and Rowan. "I'm Victor, by the way. I'm your cabin steward for the flight."

"I don't suppose you have a snack?" Rowan asked. "We haven't eaten in … well, a while." They hadn't eaten since … he couldn't believe he was thinking this … since they were on an alien space craft.

"Of course, Mr. Pierce," he said. "Dr. Grayson?"

"I'll take whatever you have," she said.

"Let's start with drinks. Perhaps some sparkling water or a glass of wine?"

"Sparkling water, actually."

"I need a beer," Rowan groused.

"Import or domestic?"

"Honestly, I don't care," he said. "Surprise me."

"Dr. Donovan?"

"Scotch, whatever you have."

"Irish or Domestic."

"Scottish, if you have it."

"Excellent choice," he said, and went on to ramble on about the Glenfiddich and how it was distilled while he prepared a drink for each of them.

"Agent Anderson?" The steward asked.

"I'm fine." He waved the steward off as he placed a glass of sparkling water on ice in front of Lauren. There was a wedge of lime to go with it.

"Your beer, sir," he placed an empty pilsner glass on the table next to the bottle of beer that was icy cold when Rowan picked it up. He inspected the label, pleased to find it was a local IPA he hadn't tried.

The steward served Kitty's drink then brought over a plate of appetizers, crudités, and cheese. He took a smaller plate over to Kitty.

The pilot came running up the stairs, turning and pulling the cabin door behind him. "Victor did you brief them on the situation?"

"I did," he said.

"Secure for takeoff, then."

There was a quick safety briefing as Victor was locking up the cabinets that held the refreshments. "Buckle up, and we'll be off in a moment," he said, as the plane began to move.

~

ROWAN SAT WATCHING OUT THE WINDOW. LAUREN AND HENRY were both asleep again. Watching the flaps on the wing as they lifted, he noticed the airspeed decreased noticeably. He looked over at Kitty, who fidgeted nervously.

Rowan peered back down, as the ground gradually came closer. Flashing lights appeared on the landing strip below. Something was going on. He looked down at his watch. It'd been a couple of hours since they'd left the airport in Denver, if his time piece were accurate, though he wasn't sure it was. All sense of time had been warped since the spaceship and the sudden teleportation to Colorado. He regretted there hadn't been time to go see his parents. They'd postponed a visit home to see Lauren's family first. How long ago had it been? A week? Maybe. He couldn't remember. Rowan had lost count of the days.

"What's going on?" Kitty asked, gazing down.

She turned back, looking at the agent in the back seat. Anderson folded his newspaper closed and gazed out the window. He looked back at Kitty and shrugged. "Hmm." He grunted noncommittally.

"Okay folks," the pilot came on the intercom. "We're coming in for a landing." Victor got up from his jump-seat and collected the empty plates and glasses, smiling at the sleeping mother and child as he passed, careful not to bump either of them.

Rowan puzzled over the choice of landing sites. This didn't appear to be a commercial airport, international or regional. This looked like a military base, but there was only one building, and it was set out in the middle of nowhere. He hadn't seen a major city since they'd taken off. He glanced back to the west, noticing the sun was setting. The plane touched down with a lurch and the squeal of tires.

Lauren sat up abruptly, looking around, startled. Rowan smiled at her, reaching over, and catching her hand. "Okay?"

"Fine," she muttered, trying to move the arm Henry was

laying on, stretching out her numb fingers, and making a fist repeatedly. "Where are we?"

"I don't know," he said. "But … I have a bad feeling."

Lauren's head snapped up. She was immediately on guard. "What?" Her gaze went to the window. A dozen military vehicles with flashing red and blue lights were parked alongside the landing strip where the plane was pulling in. Anderson stood as the plane came to a stop. Victor was already unlatching the door and dropped the stairs.

"Dr. Cameron?" Anderson turned and indicated for her to come along.

Kitty looked at Rowan, then Lauren, and rose with trepidation. Lauren fumbled with her seatbelt as she passed. Rowan took Henry, making certain they had his stuffed shark.

As Kitty stepped onto the tarmac, a contingency of military police crossed the tarmac to greet them. Rowan was still at the top of the stairs when an MP stepped up to Kitty. "Dr. Donovan?"

"Yes," she said. "I'm Dr. Donovan."

He opened an envelope and gazed down at it. "On the orders of the NATO Security Council, I am placing you under arrest on the charge of treason and two counts of murder in the first degree; assault and battery, and attempted murder with a deadly weapon. You have the right to remain silent. You have the right to an attorney."

Lauren froze at the bottom of the stairs. Rowan was at her elbow a moment later. Kitty was handcuffed and led into the building and the rest of the troops returned to their vehicles leaving Lauren and Rowan standing alone on the runway.

"What's going on?" Lauren asked, as much to the universe as to Rowan.

"I don't know."

Another vehicle pulled up and an older man in khakis and a blue zip-up jacket got out of the back seat. His jacket had a government seal embroidered on it. "Dr. Grayson,

Mr. Pierce, I'm Frank White, Secretary of Homeland Security."

"What's going on?" Lauren asked as he took her hand.

"I was hoping you could tell me," he said. "Let's go inside. I'd like to have a word."

"Why was Kitty arrested?" Lauren asked, stunned as he took her arm and led her toward the building. Rowan fell in behind them, watching. He was as uneasy as Kitty had been on the plane. Perhaps she'd seen something like this coming.

"It's complicated," he said.

Lauren stopped in her tracks. Rowan nearly plowed into her. "Simplify it."

Lauren and Rowan were taken to different rooms. Henry pitched a fit about being separated from his mother, but the MPs refused to allow the infant to be sequestered with Lauren. They left her alone in a small room with only two wooden chairs that looked like something from the 1940s. The wait seemed unnecessarily long, and she spent it pacing; growing more and more angry.

By the time the Secretary of Homeland Security came in, her blood was boiling. She could feel the heat in her cheeks as she turned on him and gave him the same tongue lashing she'd given her brother. When she finally finished in a choking profanity, the secretary looked at her flatly and asked, "Are you done?"

"I've spoken my mind," she said, without flinching.

"Then have a seat," he said. "I have questions."

"I'm certain the first is probably *What happened in Michael's lab*?" Lauren posed.

The man lifted a shoulder. "It's as good a place as any to start." He sat back with a notepad on his knee and a pen in his hand.

Patiently, she started at the beginning, providing only the

information that was pertinent to the events that transpired leading up to and including when Kitty and the Estonian goon had shown up. She explained how Malakoff had pulled a gun on the team and tried to destroy Michael's work rather than allow Kitty to confiscate his data.

"Malakoff turned on Kitty?" The Secretary's brow lifted as he paused in his scribbling. "Not the other way around?"

"What do you mean?"

"Kitty didn't pull a gun?" He asked.

"I never saw Kitty draw a weapon," Lauren shook her head. "He's the one that shot Dr. Cameron and Dr. Dlamani."

"Okay, so what happened next?" he asked. The story continued with the melee between Rowan and Michael against Malakoff and Kitty getting knocked into the table. "So, how did Malakoff get injured?"

"Oh, Kitty did do that," Lauren said proudly. "She sprayed him in the face with a fire extinguisher, then clobbered him over the head with it."

"What happened next?"

"I don't know if I can answer that." Lauren sat back, crossing her arms.

"Why not?"

"I got shot," Lauren said. "Michael, too."

Frank looked up at her sharply. "Shot?"

"Malakoff shot Michael … and I got hit, too." She lifted her shirt, intending to show him the mark, but her flesh was unmarred. No evidence remained of the bullet wound.

"I'm sorry, Dr. Pierce, but the math just doesn't add up." He shook his head, putting his pen down, scratching his cheek. "A bullet each in Dr. Cameron and Dr. Dlamani, and a bullet hit you and one hit your brother? The ballistics doesn't support that."

Lauren sat shaking her head. "Same bullet that hit me, hit Michael."

"But you don't have a mark? You're a scientist, Dr. Pierce, surely you respect the evidence I'm working with."

"I understand your logic," she said. "But there's more going on than meets the eye."

"You said your brother was shot? Where is he now?"

Lauren's eyes lifted to the ceiling. "Up there."

His expression dropped. "Oh, Dr. Pierce, I'm sorry for your loss." His tone dropped, too.

"He isn't dead," she said.

"Wait, what?"

Lauren's expression said more than her words ever could. The man paled as it sunk in what she was implying, and she was quite confident she'd just blown his mind.

FRANK FINISHED INTERVIEWING DR. PIERCE AND HER HUSBAND and paced the now empty tarmac in the moonlight, smoking a cigarette and trying to take it all in. He was trying to make sense of it all before he began the interrogation of his own operative. Rowan had told almost the exact same story his wife had told, almost verbatim. He'd seen people try to synch up their stories and do a worse job than these two had. While the perspectives were different, the chain of events matched up. Anyone else, he might have pressed harder, or harassed more, but he'd seen their show, and knew the mission of their work; the truth. He did not expect that either would lie to him.

He glanced up at the night sky. The moonless dark was spattered with stars that weren't typically visible in DC. He thought about those summer fishing trips with his grandpa when they'd sit by the fire after a day on the river and watch the stars overhead. He wanted to believe there was something out there bigger than them, but he also feared for the human race if Dr. & Mr. Pierce were telling the truth.

He dropped the cigarette butt and crushed it under his shoe before going back in to take care of the last matter at hand. An MP met him at the door. "A problem, sir."

"What?"

"Dr. Pierce is insisting she needs to nurse her son," he said.

"Fine," Frank said, dismissively. "I'm done talking to them. I'm going to talk to Dr. Donovan."

WHEN THE DOOR OPENED, KITTY POPPED UP FROM THE CHAIR in the otherwise empty room. "Sir."

He waved her off. "Have a seat, Dr. Donovan," he instructed. She sank back into the chair. "What happened in South Africa? I want to know everything, start to finish."

"Sir." She hesitated. "You're not going to believe half of it."

"Try me," he said. "And don't try to sugar coat anything. You've been accused of treason, murder, and assault. I'm not going to go to battle for you if I can't trust you to tell me the truth."

"Have you talked to Lauren and Rowan already?"

"I'm talking to *you*," he said curtly. "Now, spill it."

Kitty eyed him for a moment and finally took a deep breath, letting it out in a wavering sigh. She sat back, and told him everything. Her version was no different from that of the Pierces'. Frank had no reason not to believe them, any of them.

"Malakoff all but admitted to killing Alexei Budnikov," Kitty added. "He has to be brought to justice," she said, eyeing down the secretary, trying to figure out how well received her tall tale had been. He finally sat back and nodded, and no words were needed. Kitty was finally able to relax.

MPs came to the door, and escorted Kitty into the room where Rowan and Lauren were waiting. Rowan looked like he was about to drop, but Lauren was playing pat-a-cake with Henry and his Fishy.

"Wheels up in thirty," Frank said, pausing at the door.

"Wait." Rowan stood. "What's going on? What is this place?"

"This is a space port," Frank paused. "Western Oklahoma. It was an emergency backup landing site for the Space Shuttle program before it was shuttered. We use it now for clandestine meetings and other emergency landing situations," Frank explained. "Malakoff alleged Dr. Donovan had turned on him, and that she and Dr. Grayson were trying to steal the data from his project to sell to the Russians. He said Kitty tried to kill him."

Rowan looked to Kitty, then his wife. "Well that's a load of crap."

"I'm with you on that," he said. "We're going to DC to settle this once and for all."

"Suppose there's a McDonalds drive through on the way?" Rowan asked.

"Corporal," the secretary turned to one of the MPs. "Rouse the KP team. Rustle up some sandwiches for the trip, or something."

"Yes, sir," he said and turned to carry out the order.

Dinner on the plane was a feast. There were a half-dozen boxed meals that included sandwiches on fresh hoagie rolls, there was potato salad, baked beans, freshly baked cookies, and fruit salads. There was even a box for Henry that included fresh carrots that had been cooked 'til tender, tiny bites of diced hot dogs, a banana and a zip-top bag of crisp rice cereal.

Victor made sure they had beverages and offered up additional snacks to compliment the meal and the mood seemed to lighten in the absence of the MPs. Even Frank seemed to relax some, visiting with the company as they ate, handing Henry nibbles of his cookie, with Lauren's approval.

"And what did you think of the aliens?" Frank finally asked, directing the question to Kitty.

She almost choked on her sandwich at the abruptness of his question. "Uh …" she paused to cough and clear her throat. "I … uh …" She hesitated. "Well," she hemmed. "I'm not sure, sir."

"Well were they freaky or scary? Did they look like little green men from Mars? Come on, spit it out." He scoffed.

"They were everything you would expect, and more," Lauren volunteered. "Taller than *The Grays* you see so often in pop culture. Their skulls were elongated … like they just stepped off a Sumerian tablet or an Egyptian Hieroglyph."

"Did they speak English? French? Russian?"

"Not at first," Lauren said, remembering the piercing scream that had nearly ruptured her eardrums. "But they seemed to adapt easily. I understood them either way, but … they adapted for the sake of the others."

"You speak alien?"

"You have no idea how often I've had to ask that question," Rowan chortled. "She's been able to speak practically any language for the past three years or so."

"What happened three years ago?" Frank asked.

"I had an encounter …" Lauren said, but stopped and started over. "This isn't the first time I've met *them*. Somehow, they gave me the ability to understand all human language."

"Any language?"

Lauren nodded.

"That could be useful." Frank turned back to Kitty. "Do they seem amicable to establishing a diplomatic process?"

She lifted her shoulder. "I suppose you could say they seemed agreeable," she said.

"Good," he said. "As soon as Estonia is dealt with, the NATO Task Force is going to need to be briefed."

"Of course," Kitty said.

"I want you to prepare your case to take to the Task Force," he instructed.

"Of course you do." She yawned.

21

Jääger was not at all happy when Frank finished presenting the evidence to the NATO task force. The accusation that their operative had turned on Kitty Donovan and had killed two civilians and tried to kill two more was not well received. "The ballistics match the first-hand accounts provided by those present. We have teams on site in South Africa working to collect video from security cameras. The story your operative has told is full of holes, filled in with lies and half-truths," Frank said, stoically. "He is officially wanted by Interpol as a person of interest in the murder of Dr. India Cameron, Dr. Lubanzi Dlamani … and Dr. Alexei Budnikov."

"The Estonian government will not stand for this!" Jääger sputtered, red-faced and furious at the accusation. "Your evidence is flimsy at best."

"We're continuing to build our case, but in the meantime, this is the least of our worries," Frank said, addressing the entire audience. He hesitated to ensure he had their full attention "Dr. Michael Grayson and Dr. Kitty Donovan have made first contact … and the news isn't good."

Chaos washed over the audience.

NATO representatives from around the world began shouting questions, shouting accusations, and in some cases, just shouting. Frank glanced over at Kitty, just off screen. He'd been fully briefed during the journey to DC.

When the discord settled, Frank stood, taking center stage in the middle of the room. "According to Dr. Donovan, there are two warring factions out there, and Earth could be ground zero for an intergalactic feud that has been raging for centuries. We have begun peaceful negotiations with one of these factions."

"Kitty Donovan doesn't speak for me!" Jääger slammed his hand on his desk, standing so that only his midsection was visible in his camera shot. He leaned down, glaring directly into the camera. "This is an outrage! An outrage, I'm telling you!" Again chaos broke out.

Kitty took the opportunity to step into the camera shot, coming to stand by Secretary White. "I will not be the Ambassador to this alien race," she said. "They have chosen another avatar to speak for them. We have no say in the matter." She had to wait while the assembly shouted their protests. For a collection of peacemakers, they certainly liked to yell a lot, Kitty thought. "The being, who suggested we refer to as Enki, has chosen Dr. Michael Grayson as his representative. They will only allow him to speak for their race."

"What about this other faction?" someone shouted clearly enough for her to make out.

"We know very little about the second race," Kitty admitted. "Dr. Grayson is currently working to learn their role in this bizarre passion play. With any luck, we can learn this information, but ladies and gentlemen, I cannot tell you how important it is that we find a path through this conflict … together. There is no way we can expect to defeat an alien enemy when we bicker amongst ourselves." She had to raise her voice over the din. "You have come together to form this task force. For decades we have said we are united. If your countries feel differently now that the threat is a clear and present danger, you're too late. Speaking for the United States of America … we need you. We need each of you."

"The other thing we need is for this information to remain classified," Frank added. 'The general public does not need this burden. As agreed upon in our original charter, this information is expected to be held in the strictest confidentiality … under penalty of death."

The shouting began in earnest as Kitty turned away from the camera and walked back to the dark corner where Lauren sat, holding Henry. Rowan stood beside her, his hand on her shoulder.

"Peacemakers, my Aunt Fanny." She shook her head as she turned and leaned against the wall next to Rowan, smiling as she gazed at Henry.

He reached for her, shaking his toy shark. "KiKi," he called to her. She reached over and took him, giving his tired mother a break. "KiKi … go."

LAUREN AND KITTY LOOKED AT EACH OTHER, AS THEY FOUND themselves on the spaceship. Michael sat on the floor with his eyes closed, his hands resting on his knees. While his eyes didn't open the corners of his lips curled up. "My-My!" Henry squealed, fighting to get away from Kitty. She sat him down on the floor and he crawled over to his uncle and climbed up into the void created by his folded legs. "My-My."

Michael opened his eyes abruptly. "Peek-a-boo!" He grinned at the boy. Henry squealed in delight as Michael's gaze lifted to the two women. "Welcome back," he said.

Lauren waited for him to collect Henry and rise before she came over and held open her arms to him. "Michael." She sighed as he hugged her tightly, transferring Henry into her arms. He kissed her head, then turned to Kitty and held his arms open. She hesitated then rushed into his embraced and melted as she leaned her head back, pressing her lips to his. He tightened his grip on her and dipped her back as he kissed her with a fever that came from desperate longing and a genuine love.

Henry leaned back to eye his mother, grinning devilishly at her, then turning back to Michael and Kitty. Lauren couldn't help but be pleased. They were cute together, and clearly, he cared very much for her. Any animosities between them had been resolved or … forgotten. Lauren waited, but the kiss lasted longer than the kiss she planted on Rowan at the altar, or any kiss before or since. Finally, she cleared her throat overtly.

Michael glanced up and smiled, despite his lips on Kitty's. He came up for air, freeing Kitty, but keeping his hand in the small of her back to support her as she caught her breath and returned to her senses, her knees rubbery for a moment longer. She reached up and smoothed down her honey blonde hair, blushing as she turned to face Lauren.

"Sorry to interrupt," Lauren said, bemused as his fingers wove between Kitty's and she leaned against him. "I'm assuming we're here for a reason."

"Of course," Michael said, leading them over to a table that rose from the floor, along with a chair for each of them.

Lauren took a deep breath, realizing this space had a unique odor that she hadn't been able to pinpoint before. It was a mixture of pure oxygen, synthetic materials, and something she couldn't quite identify.

Michael lay his hands flat against the table, glancing at Kitty before turning to Lauren. "I've spent the last couple of years learning about my benefactor's history, and the conflict between him and his brother."

Lauren did a double-take. "Wait." She put a hand up. "The last couple of *years*?"

He tilted his head in her direction, giving her credit for

catching him in something she couldn't have possibly known. "I'm sorry," he said. "Time passes differently here."

Lauren's brow lifted as her gaze slipped over to Kitty, who mirrored her expression. They both turned back to Michael.

"Where is *here*?" Kitty asked.

"Another valid point," he said. "This isn't exactly a simple concept. Your scientists call it the *Einstein Rosen Bridge*. I think you'll both understand though. Time and place are concepts that have never been fully understood, not as they truly are. Some, like Einstein, have gotten close, but The Three have come to understand that time and place are unified, and separate."

"You're talking in riddles." Lauren furrowed her brow.

"You were onto something when you said time was circular and eternal," Michael said. "And yes, I know you said that because I came to visit you in San Diego before Henry was born. You didn't know I was there, but I was listening in. Anyway, time is also like a blanket, woven in four dimensions. The farther from the center point of creation, the slower time moves, until it hits the Apex. There it gains momentum and can essentially slingshot to a much faster speed. I realize it's a higher concept, but you have plenty of time to think on it."

Lauren and Kitty's eyes darted from one another again, before they turned back to Michael. "Tell us about the Dark One," Lauren said. "Enki said there was a war coming."

Michael nodded, knowing this concept would be easier for them to comprehend. "The brothers have been at odds. You know the legends," he said, lifting a hand. "What you don't know, is that while Enki retreated to the heavens to prepare for the coming war, Enlil took shelter where no one would think to find him." He glanced to each of them. "Earth."

Kitty practically recoiled, even as Lauren slumped back into her chair. "He's … on Earth?" Kitty gasped.

"Where there is famine, there is apathy, also the mark of the Dark One. Where there is hatred, Enlil is the instigator. In a world where children are abused and husbands raise a hand to their wives, the Dark One reigns supreme. This is how he gains his power. As the gods above gather their forces, and build their allies, Enlil bides his time, allowing others to fight his wars to fuel his war-machine."

Lauren caught Michael's hand. "But …" She struggled to form her thoughts and find her words. "How do we defeat that?"

"Through peace," he said, his sidelong gaze going to Kitty. "Through love. Through forgiveness." He returned his eye to Lauren. "The world has time. Right now, that is the greatest weapon we have. But Kitty, the peace accord falls to you to broker, not with Enki and The Three … but on earth. You must bring the nations together. You must navigate the many factions into one accord."

"Might as well ask me to move the tides, or stop the sun from rising," Kitty said.

"I will teach you," he said. "Stay with me a while. I will help you learn how to use the power of your voice to broker peace."

"How long?" Kitty asked, looking afraid.

"It will not take long," he said, turning to Lauren. "I will send for you when it's time for Kitty to rejoin your time-place."

"When you say we have time …" Lauren stiffened. "What do you mean? A week? A few months? A few years?"

"He comes as a thief in the night," Michael's voice went dark. "The Most High will grant you the full armor of the gods, so that you will be able to stand firm against the schemes of the Dark One. I cannot promise you the hour, but there is time. Years most likely, decades perhaps, but the time you have must not be squandered."

Lauren stood, holding Henry to her chest. Michael rose and came to stand behind her, his hand on her back. "I'm afraid," she admitted.

"Fear not, for I will be with you always."

Lauren nearly tumbled over as she found herself standing beside Rowan. He caught her limp form as blackness enveloped her. He lowered her and Henry to the floor, catching her hand as he knelt beside her. "Lauren? Where'd you go? Where's Kitty?" She fought to get back to him, following his voice.

"I'll call for a medic." She heard Frank say.

"I am a medic," Rowan said, taking Henry. The boy put his arms around his dad's neck. "Lauren!"

She swatted him away as she took a deep breath and returned to the present and her own place within it. She rolled over onto her side, clutching her arms around her stomach. "I'm gonna be sick …" she muttered.

Frank jumped up and grabbed the wastepaper basket by the door and put it in front of her. She got to her knees and leaned over it, hesitating a moment before she vomited, then vomited again. After that she sat back on her knees. Frank disappeared and came back a moment later with a damp cloth and a bottle of water. Rowan took both. She leaned back against him, and he pressed the cloth to her forehead, and the bottle of water to the back of her neck.

"Oh that's good." She let out a breath. She closed her eyes, inhaling repeatedly until her stomach settled. "Thank you, that's better," she said, taking the bottle of water, cracking it open and taking a sip, swishing it around in her mouth, spitting it out in the trashcan. She drank greedily and mopped her face with the towel. "I'm fine."

"You sure?" Rowan asked.

"Yeah," she said. "I think all this space hopping messes with my internal gyroscope or something."

"Where's Kitty, Dr. Pierce?" Frank asked.

"With Michael," she said. "He had information to give her. He said he'd call me back when he was done teaching her what she needed to know to ensure a lasting peace."

"I have a ton of questions." Frank hooked an arm under Lauren's and lifted her to her feet. "But they can wait. Come on," he said. "I'll make arrangements for a hotel and we'll get you a place to rest. I'll have dinner sent to the room and we can talk more tomorrow. I've got agents hunting for Malakoff, and there's little more I can do here tonight myself."

22

"I know where you dwell. I know where Satan's throne lies," Yevgeny stood bare-chested in an abandoned building, a burning stick in his hand. His tattooed body bore the marks of dark incantations and symbols of the highest dark arts from religions and cultures around the world.

He scrolled a pentagram on the rotting floorboards, searing the mark into the dried lumber. "I call upon thee, O, Morning Star! By all thy names I call thee: Lucifer. Abaddon. Mephistopheles. Asmodeus. Shiva. Diabolus. Enlil. Come to me, my Master!"

Outside, the rush of wind lifted in the trees, raking the limbs against the dilapidated roof. A rumble of thunder broke across the landscape, and the very building itself seemed to tremble. Flames erupted from an empty fireplace, and a rush of something passed his body so silently he felt it more than heard it.

A dark silhouette filled the room, outlined by the flickering firelight. The perfume of sulfur and brimstone hit him full in the face, and he dropped to one knee, his hands on the floor at his side as he bowed. "My Lord." He kept his eyes averted to the floor. "I come with ill-tidings; troubling news. I seek your guidance."

"Speak …" A deep voice rumbled, chilling him to the core.

"Your brother has returned and has chosen his Champion," he said. He had a mole inside the Estonian Security Council who had briefed him on the secret meeting. "Forces in the Heavens are gathering and I fear a shift in the balance of power."

"My power continues to grow," the Dark One thundered.

"Your book must be made whole if you are to regain your rightful place and seize dominion over the heavens and the earth."

There was a moment of silence, as the Dark One gathered his thoughts. "Peace is the enemy of discord," he growled. "Discord is food for my soul. Your mission is to ensure I am fed, and my power grows. In the same effort, you must put a stop to this champion, or all will be lost."

The man bowed to the shadowed being. "I will not fail you," he said. "But aid is needed. I cannot find the Chosen One or the Champion for your enemy has hidden them from me."

"All will be revealed once my strength is restored," the shadow growled.

"I shall feed you well, my lord."

~

MALAKOFF HAD BEEN BACK IN ESTONIA LESS THAN A FEW hours before returning to his hideout, a place where the veil of time and space was most thin, where the Dark One could be summoned. He returned to his home just as the sun was rising. He knew it would only be a matter of time before his deception was discovered, but he figured he had time enough to create enough chaos to set things in order.

His first call was to a reporter at one of the lesser reputed world news organizations, offering up an exclusive story, almost too good to be true. He spun a tail of drama and international intrigue. A reputed scientist working for NASA was selling classified documents to foreign governments, who were all conspiring to conceal evidence of an extraterrestrial presence on Earth. Fear was the first fruit of the dark spirit. Fear led to anger. Anger led to conflict. Conflict led to suffering. Suffering was mana from … hell, in this case.

His next call was to his superiors.

"You idiot!" Jääger shouted. "How could you be so stupid? You allowed the American agent to escape! She went straight to her superiors and told them everything! Everything! Your orders were to seize the data, eliminate the scientists and ensure there were no witnesses! I can't believe the incompetence I am forced to work with! You know the consequences if we fail?"

"I do," Malakoff finally got a word in edgewise. "Which is why I've called in my reinforcements. I just need to get to Donovan, her boyfriend … and his family."

"I can arrange that, but … you're not going to like it," Jääger intoned.

FRANK WHITE SAT BEHIND A MAHOGANY DESK; HIS PHONE tucked under his ear. Lauren sat across from him, stirring a generous dose of cream into her coffee. Rowan had taken Henry for a morning walk in the crisp autumn air.

"Dr. Pierce," he said, hanging up. "I've just gotten word; Yevgeny Malakoff has been turned over by the Estonian Government for questioning."

Lauren sat up. "What?"

"He's also facing charges of treason in his own country,

but in the interest of international relations, the Estonian Security Council is escorting him here."

"Here? To DC?"

"To this office," he said. "We're going to get to the bottom of this."

Lauren sat, gazing into her coffee a moment. "With everything you know now … what happens next?"

"Hard to say," he said. "I briefed the President this morning and I have a meeting with the National Security Advisor. I'll make recommendations, but something of this magnitude … it's hard to say." Frank paused for a long moment. "If you had a say in what was to follow, what would you advise?"

Lauren's brow lifted. "You're asking me? On matters of national … global security?"

"Intergalactic security." He noted.

She conceded with a nod. "Valid point." Lauren sat back and thought about this for a moment. "I am a scientist," she said. "First and foremost. I believe what I can prove. Or … I did."

"Did?"

"In the past three years, I have seen some unexplainable things; been able to do things I can't quite explain. I have no empirical data to fully elucidate what's happened to me, or how it's changed me. I don't consider it magic, but I have a hypothesis."

"Oh?"

"My theory is there is a force in the universe that is woven of matter, energy, time and space. There are those who can command these forces; some will use them for good … others for evil."

"Kinda sounds like the plot to Star Wars." He chuckled.

Lauren lifted a shoulder and nodded. "Perhaps," she said. "But I have to think there is a purpose in all of it. A balance of power must be maintained. Good cannot dominate every-thing; nor can evil. Homeostasis … now *that* is the goal."

"I'm afraid I can't take that to the Security Advisor, Dr. Pierce."

"Then I'm afraid I can be of little help to you," she said. "Kitty told you what they said. You have to decide what to do with that."

He nodded. "I can't keep but thinking about a quote I saw on a t-shirt though."

"Oh?" She lifted a curious brow. "What did it say?"

"*Every disaster movie starts with a scientist no one will listen to,*" he said. "I was hoping you'd provide me with some council, some words of wisdom I could use that would convince them. We have to listen to our scientists, because God knows, our politi-cians can't be trusted."

The revelation shocked Lauren, but a sudden realization came over her. "Okay," she said. "Here's the best I have: To everything, there is a season. For every force there is an equal and opposing force. A body in motion tends to stay in motion."

Frank looked puzzled. "I'm sorry?"

"Balance," she said. "The key to everything in the universe is balance. If you want to avoid war, you must embrace peace. If you wish to defeat the enemy, you must surrender. The cure for hate … is love."

He pursed his lips as he considered her words for a long moment. "Why do scientists always speak in riddles?"

"Because a wise man will seek the truth in them," she smiled, and sipped her coffee.

He picked up his cup and sat back, pondering this for a moment. He finally met her eye. "I like you, Dr. Pierce. I like you a lot."

Lauren sat in the observation room with Henry laying against her, a limp form in her lap. Rowan had worn him out, and she was grateful that he was sleeping. Rowan sat beside her, taking in everything as Malakoff was led into the adjoining interrogation room in handcuffs. He had a black eye and a bruise on his jaw, and Lauren suspected Rowan took a great deal of pride in those marks. He'd made at least one of them; had the busted knuckles to prove it.

Lauren felt the pressure in the room shift and wasn't a bit surprised to find Kitty standing beside her. Rowan, however, nearly leapt out of his skin, but managed to keep the yelp choked down. Henry never flinched.

Kitty's hand went to her shoulder, steadying herself. "That doesn't get any easier, does it?" She chortled. Rowan caught her and helped her into his chair.

"I didn't expect you to be back so soon," Lauren put a hand on her arm. She'd been prepared to hate her, for Michael's sake, but she found herself growing more fond of the scientist.

"So soon?" Kitty puzzled. "It seemed like … a month, at least."

"You just left yesterday," Rowan said.

"Well, Michael did say time moves differently ..." Lauren's eyes lifted. "Up there."

"So what did you learn?" Rowan grabbed another chair and pulled it over. He sat backwards on it so he could lean his arms on the backrest.

"So much," she said. "I'm not even sure where to start." She turned to the window where Malakoff had been seated at a table and left alone; his hands cuffed behind him. Kitty's whole expression dropped. "What is *he* doing here?" She started to rise, but Lauren's hand tightened on her arm.

"The Estonian government turned him over to US authorities," Lauren said. She couldn't help but notice Kitty's reaction as she stiffened, her eyes fixed on the KGB spy. When she spoke, her voice was dark, like a soothsayer in a trance. "The Dark One has agents who serve the master. They create chaos upon which the Dark One feeds."

"Enlil?" Lauren leaned forward, catching her eye. Kitty softened slightly as she nodded. "Is ... is Malakoff one of these agents?"

"I believe so," she said. "I don't have the same ... what do we call it? *Magic*? I don't have the same *magic* you have?"

Lauren sat back, lifting Henry into a more comfortable position. "*Magic* doesn't seem like an adequate term," she said. "But I don't know what else to call it."

Lauren watched as Malakoff's gaze seemed to settle on her. The one-way mirror ensured he couldn't see her, but her heart chilled at the devious grin that spread across the villain's face as he gazed at what could only be his own reflection in the mirror. She felt his dark eyes burn into her. A sharp pain pierced her skull and the room tilted.

Rowan caught her elbow. "Easy there. You okay?"

The gaze broke and Lauren turned and looked at her husband. "Oh, yeah," she muttered. "He's a baddy."

Malakoff stood and walked over to the window, the

motion catching Lauren's eye. Rowan turned. Lauren rose, and Malakoff's gaze locked on hers. They stood staring each other down. Henry slipped out of her grasp and Kitty took the sleeping baby, hoisting him onto her shoulder.

"Lauren?" Rowan said. "Lauren?"

She took a weak step forward, coming to stand even with the KGB operative. She could feel a warm light build in her core, as she stared into the cold eyes that seemed to grow darker. The smell of sulfur and brimstone found its way to her nose just as Malakoff let out a beastly roar, straining the chain between the cuffs on his hands, which shattered. His arms went up with the force of his effort, and Lauren realized the cuffs were glowing bright red, sparks flying from the molten metal as it dripped from his wrists. Lauren didn't flinch. Suddenly, the man drew back his arm, like a demon possessed, and smashed his palm through the glass. Kitty shrieked. Rowan snagged Lauren and pulled her down. He tackled her to the floor; shielding her from the shattering glass, even as shards cut his own flesh.

Lauren pushed him off of her and scrambled to her feet, shouting at Kitty to get Henry out of there. She hoisted Rowan to his feet and shoved him towards the door. "Go!" she shouted as she turned to face Malakoff. The KGB agent had taken on a dark aura, his boiling eyes completely black, his chin seemed more angular, his bared teeth appeared as fangs. "Go!" She shouted at Rowan, sensing he was still in the doorway. "Go! Get Henry somewhere safe!"

She could hear the baby's cry down the hallway as he called for her, frightened from his sleep by the sudden noise and excitement. But Lauren's full attention was on the enemy before her.

"The taint of goodness on your flesh offends me," the man snarled, his deep voice resonated in her core. "You are not worthy to be the Champion for the gods."

She didn't know what he was talking about. Michael had

been named Champion, but she didn't have time to think on it. "I'm not afraid of you." Lauren stood her ground, realizing she hadn't been unscathed by the breaking glass. Blood ran into her eye and she pushed it away, wiping her hand on her jeans.

"You should be, Dr. Pierce," he said. His Slavic tongue clipped the words. He withdrew and a rumble of thunder crashed around them. Lauren's hands went to her ears to protect them from the crash, but the remaining wall between them fragmented and blew out towards her. Bits of drywall and metal studs struck her, nearly taking her knees out as she staggered back.

The door behind Malakoff flew open and two federal agents charged into the room, their weapons drawn. Malakoff never turned his head, but his hand rose and sent a blast of dark energy towards them. Their guns went red hot and they yelped collectively as the weapons turned to molten metal. Then, the bullets in the chamber exploded in the agent's face. Both dropped where they stood, one clawed at his eyes, screaming in pain. The other gasped, clutching his neck, blood gurgling up from between his fingers.

Lauren stood her ground as Malakoff turned back to her. His eyes flickered red now, fueled by the bloodlust and the suffering around him. "So you think you're a demon?" She spat blood from her mouth, realizing her lip was cut; iron mingled with her saliva and she spat again.

"You think yourself a witch?"

"I don't know what I am," she said, uncertain where the words came from.

"*Thou shall not suffer a witch to live*," Malakoff sneered.

"Really?" Lauren quipped. "You're going to quote the Bible to me?"

His grin deepened. "Whatever works, *da?*"

"So, what are you?" Lauren asked, her hands up as if to shield herself if he made any move. Malakoff stood seething, and she had to wonder if he were buying time or sizing her up. "An agent of Enlil?"

"I am the very Hand of the Dark One Himself."

Lauren swiped at the blood running down her face, to clear her vision. The room tilted and she widened her stance to steady herself. She wasn't sure what she was doing. A woman her size couldn't fight a man of his stature, demon, or no. Her mind was racing trying to come up with a defense, something she could say or do to stop him in his tracks. She couldn't risk something happening to her. Henry needed her. Rowan did too, and she knew it.

Enki's words reverberated in her head, but she couldn't reconcile the being's words with the horror that faced her now. Where was Michael when she needed him? When she needed a Champion, where was her older brother?

Malakoff straightened a moment. "It isn't you? You're not the Champion." It wasn't a question. Suddenly Lauren realized he'd thought she had been chosen to speak for the gods.

"Yes, where is the Champion? I came for you, but I will use you to get to him." His hand went up and she could feel her feet slipping on the tile floor as an unseen force drew her to him. "I will destroy everything he loves ..." he said. "The pretty blonde ... the baby ... and you."

Lauren's anger grew, her face contorting with it, even as she struggled to free herself from his unseen grasp. The fetid breath of the KGB operative, now fouled with this dark entity that seemed to overtake the man, became sickening as she drew closer.

"Lauren!" Rowan raced into the room, charging the operative, pushing her aside as he rushed to tackle Malakoff. The monster raised his hand and Rowan's body violated the laws of physics when it flew back and slammed into the wall. The thud of his flesh on drywall was sickening but the demon rushed in, reaching for her throat.

Lauren threw her hand up without thinking. Heat built in

her shoulder. She could feel the metal pins from the injury she'd sustained in Washington State go painfully hot against her bone. The surge of energy traveled down her arm culminating into a power she'd never experienced. The force caught Malakoff in the chest, pushing him away so hard it knocked her off her feet. It cast her opponent aloft.

The cry that erupted from the operative's throat was gut-wrenching as he hit the wall, leaving an impact crater in the crumbling drywall. He fell to the floor, his body seizing, smoke rising from the center of his chest. Beneath the scorched shirt, the blackness in his heart seemed to ignite into flames, burning a hole in the man's body. A moment later, the smoldering embers of flesh, bone, and ash were all that were left in the charred void.

Lauren sat stunned, terrified, and confused; trying to make sense of what had just happened. Her fingers tingled and her shoulder throbbed. For a moment she felt as if her humerus had split down the middle. Gazing down at her hand, lightning bolts danced between her digits and dissipated into sparks.

Regaining her wits, she took in the devastation all around her. Panic rushed through her and her heart skipped a beat as she realized her husband lay unmoving by the door. "Rowan!" She grabbed his shirt and tugged on him, rolling him over. He moaned, as his face scrunched up. Cuts marred his flesh and spots of blood stained his skin and clothing. "Rowan, honey?" she asked, a little more calmly. He looked up at her, his face softening. "Are you okay?"

He hesitated a minute, wincing. "Define okay."

"Are you going to die?"

"I don't think so," he said.

"Do you want to?" She tried to lighten the mood.

"I'm not going anywhere without you." He caught her hand, reaching for her face.

She cupped his hand to her cheek and brightened with relief.

Lauren turned as she heard voices in the hallway and realized help was coming. Then she realized Rowan wasn't the only one injured. "Be right back." She jumped up and went to check on the agents who'd faced the KGB operative and lost.

Frank White burst into the room and froze, recoiling at the devastation he witnessed. "Jesus Christ!" He gasped, taken aback by the destruction, wincing as he looked over at the KGB operative. "What the hell happened in here? It looks like a war zone."

Lauren looked up at him. "This was just a skirmish," she said. "Call 911. Your agents need medical attention." Lauren barked orders, doing what she could for the two. One had shrapnel wounds to the neck, the other to the face. "Rowan?" She was surprised when he managed to crawl over to see what he could do to help. He jumped in, and took over, despite the fact that he was clearly in pain.

Lauren sat back on her heels, looking up as she heard her son crying. Kitty hesitated at the door, but Henry was screaming and kicking against her, writhing as he struggled to get to his mother; tears cascading down his red face. Henry slid out of Kitty's arms into Lauren's. "Are you okay?" She inspected him and was quickly satisfied that he had not been harmed.

"Mama …" Henry pointed to the body of the dead KGB operative as Frank walked back in the room followed by paramedics. "Bad. Bad."

"Yes," she said, approving of his new word. "He was a very bad man."

Henry gave her a toothy grin that reminded her so very much of his father when she'd first met him. She glanced over at Rowan as he stood, letting the medics help the fallen agents first. Two more agents entered from the interrogation room, pausing at the destruction that had been wrought. "What the hell …?" One of them muttered, walking over to the body by the wall. "What happened to this guy?"

Rowan and Lauren exchanged glances. "He raised a hand to my wife," Rowan said.

"Did you do that?" Frank asked, looking at Rowan.

"I didn't have to," he said. "You mess with the bull; you get the horns. You mess with my wife … you get a body bag."

"But …" The two agents puzzled over the corpse. "How …"

"I'm not confident I know how," Lauren said, directing it more to Frank. "The only thing I can guess is … divine intervention."

~

THE CUT ON LAUREN'S FOREHEAD TOOK SIX STITCHES TO close. Rowan's injuries took a few more, most of his were on his shoulders and the back of his head. He had a few contusions from hitting the wall, but it wasn't as bad as Lauren had feared. Frank took them back to his office after the medics were done with them and put a pot of coffee on. Henry wrapped his arms around his mother's neck, twisting her braid in his little hands, refusing to let go of her once he had her.

He tucked himself into her when she finally sat down across from Frank's desk. Rowan pulled his chair closer to his wife, and put his arm around her, drawing her in. She leaned against him, physically drained. Kitty paced behind them.

"Dr. Donovan?" Frank asked, causing her to pause and turn her gaze to him. "Do you have something to share? A message for us, perhaps?"

Kitty nodded, pulling another chair over, sitting down. "I learned everything I could from Dr. Grayson … Michael," she said. "My brain is still trying to process it all, but he told the story of two brothers, one betrayed by his father, and angry at his brother; the other, a protector of mankind. The two fought a war for control over the earth and the angry one lost. He was cast from Heaven and banished to Hell; enslaved in the world he sought to destroy. The Protector vowed to return and cast out the other brother; to free mankind from the destruction his brother wrought."

Frank listened patiently, folding his hands, laying them on the desk. He nodded as she spoke.

"In Russia, there is a little known religion that arose because of the Russian's need to win the space race. A cult of the cosmos, if you will. It started with Yuri Gagarin."

"Gagarin?" Rowan puzzled.

Kitty nodded. "In a movie called, *The Moon*, made in 1965, there was a line that went something like *We had made it to the stars and there was no bearded old god there. Only science. Only the Soviet System*. But as Russians turned away from the more mainstream Christian religion, the fallen brother began to gain power, and a darker cult began to grow. Malakoff was an agent of the fallen brother, or the Dark One, as he is sometimes called. There will be more of these minions after him," she said, her tone growing dark as she glanced at Lauren. "Michael says this is only the beginning. We have to continue the work our NATO Task Force has begun, but we have to work to build our relationships here. We will all need to work together if we are going to face this threat in the future."

"How much time do we have?" Frank asked.

"It's hard to say," Kitty said. "All we can do is prepare."

"Did Michael say ..." Lauren started, but hesitated. "What my role is in all this?"

"What makes you think any of this has anything to do with you, Dr. Pierce?" Frank asked.

Lauren looked to her hand as she remembered the feel of the energy racing through her bones. "I don't believe in coincidences." She lifted her eyes to him. "I have a gift ... gifts ... I have to think there's a reason for it."

"He said, you are the Hand of the gods." Kitty said. "Here to do their work and to find the truth in all things."

"That's not very specific," Lauren said.

"Well you're work *here* is done," Frank said. "Once the agents have taken your statements, that is."

"What do you want me to tell them?" Lauren gulped. "I used *magic* given to me by the gods to defeat a demon?"

"Dr. Pierce," Frank had an impish grin in his eye. "This is Washington D.C. That won't even be the craziest thing any of us have ever heard."

Lauren puzzled a moment, her nose wrinkling. "I'm not crazy."

"No one said you were."

"Sister." Lauren rolled over in her sleep, finding Rowan's warm body against hers. She snuggled into him and drifted back to sleep. "Lauren."

"What?" she said, turning to find Michael standing on the fallen log at the edge of the river behind the home where they'd grown up. The moonlight made his raven tresses glow blue in the darkness. "Michael! What are you doing here?"

"*We* couldn't leave things … unsettled between us," he said as she approached, still dressed in the oversized cotton t-shirt she'd fallen asleep in.

"Kitty told us most of what you taught her, but … what am I supposed to do? What's my purpose?"

"You are to be a good wife and mother. Seek the truth and make wise use of it. Stay curious, always." Tsul'Kalu's words came back to her in a rush that left her feeling oddly disconcerted. "When the time comes, you will know what to do, and will have all the tools you need to accomplish your task. Allies will come to your aid, and you need not fear, for *We* will be with you." He hopped down off the log and walked towards her. "In the meantime, *We* have some things *We* need to ask of you."

"What can I do?" Lauren asked.

"Take care of our mother," he said. "Time is too short to spend it being angry, for not speaking one's mind, and not letting go of the past. Can you do that, Lauren?"

"I can try," she said.

"*We* know you and Rowan have a job that needs to be done, one you haven't been able to do," Michael said, changing gears. "Go to your husband's home. Take Kitty with you. *We* will provide aid. Watch for a package *We* will send you."

"But what am I going to tell our mother about you? Where you've gone … what you're doing?"

"No one can know," he said. "This is a secret that must remain between us. *We* trust Rowan and Kitty to guard this secret, too."

"Of course they will," Lauren said. "But …" she hesitated. "What do we tell people?"

"Just don't tell anyone your brother died," he said. "It was too much to bear when he thought he lost Kitty. He doesn't want to put anyone through that."

"But what do I tell people? Tell our mother?" It didn't even register in her brain that he'd yet to speak of himself in the first person, or singular.

Michael smiled, drawing her into his arms. "*We* are sure you can come up with something," he said. "Do your best to make certain it's a … *good story*."

"And Kitty?"

"Care for her as a sister," he said. "She will need your aid as much as you need hers."

Lauren nodded and hugged him fiercely. She hesitated to let him go, and felt tears welling up in her eyes. "Can we stay here a little while longer? I don't want to say goodbye yet."

"We will not say goodbye, Lauren." He kissed her head. "We will simply say, *sigwu do na dagwa do'hv*."

∼

"YOU HAD AN ANCESTOR RUN FOR PRESIDENT?" ELEANOR SAT at Martha Pierce's dinner table going through the stacks of white three ring binders. They contained everything she knew about Rowan's family history.

"He might have won, too, if he hadn't been so … gregarious," Martha mused.

"That's a nice way of saying he was an asshole," Charles said, gruffly in side bar to Lauren.

"Charles!" Martha gasped. "Do you want your grandson to hear you talk like that?"

"Pshaw!" Charles bounced the boy on his knee, delighted with his first grand-child. They'd spent the day in the back yard playing with Mr. Buttons, the Pierce's Boston Terrier. Henry had been delighted and took a quick liking to both the dog and his grandparents, especially Charles. Henry giggled, blowing bubbles and making faces at his grandpa, who returned the favor.

"Your work here is quite impressive." Eleanor kept flipping pages. "How far back have you gotten?"

"I have documentation going all the way back to Robert the Bruce." Martha beamed. "Once you get into the royal lines, it gets much easier. I can trace us back farther, but I'm just going to have to go to Europe and get those records myself. The oldest documents can't always be found on-line."

"How do you feel about going with us to Scotland?" Rowan asked, wincing when Lauren's head shot up. "Once we get done with Lauren's family tree, of course."

"Well I'm sure that would be nice, but … we just bought an RV and intended to hit every National Park in the US," Charles said. "After that, we're headed to Canada."

"Oh," Lauren reached for her coffee cup. "Too bad."

"Maybe next time." Rowan shrugged, sitting back in his chair. Lauren insisted she liked his parents, but he could tell her mother was starting to get on her nerves. Four days ago they'd arrived in Denver, following her brother's instructions. Clearly, Lauren's limit was three days; maybe two. Lauren and Kitty had managed to sneak out for a few hours the day before to do some shopping. Their bags from South Africa had been delayed. They arrived in Colorado with little more than the clothes on their backs, and the few things they'd gotten in DC to get by with. Henry needed diapers and the Pierce house wasn't exactly child proof, so Lauren had picked up some plug covers and a few other things to keep Henry safe as he crawled around the house.

"Rowan, you have enough here for a whole season, just on your family tree," Eleanor beamed. "Did you know if you can get to Robert the Bruce, you can get to Charlemagne the Great?"

"Charlemagne is my middle name," Rowan said.

"It's an old family name on my side of the family," Rowan's dad said. "It was my grandpa's name, and my great grandpa's name," Charles said. "They had to call me Charles so they wouldn't get confused."

"Did you figure out what you're going to do about Lauren's family tree?" Eleanor asked.

"I got some good information from my cousins and my brothers," Lauren said. "Not as much as Martha has, but … turns out, my family is pretty interesting after all."

Eleanor's bookish face brightened. "See, I told you so."

～

JUST AS THE FAMILY SAT DOWN TO DINNER, THERE WAS A knock at the door. "Rowan, dear. Could you get that?" Martha asked, passing Charles the basket of dinner rolls.

Rowan nodded and stood to do his mother's bidding. It had always been his job as a kid. He paused as he opened the door, finding a man in an unmarked brown shirt and shorts, despite the chilly night. "Rowan Pierce?"

"That's me," he said, brightly.

The man held out an envelope with Lauren and Rowan's names written on it. "Have a good day," the delivery man said, as Rowan took it.

"Thanks," Rowan said, studying the envelope, turning to close the door. He hesitated and turned back. There was no one there. Rowan's brow narrowed as he stepped out onto the front porch, trying to see down the cul-de-sac, but there was no delivery truck; no traffic at all.

Rowan scratched his head as he returned to the table and sat down.

"What was that?" Lauren asked. He handed the envelope to her. She recognized the handwriting, and her eyes brightened. "It's from Michael."

"Your family records, dear?" Martha asked.

"Maybe," she said, laying them aside, returning her attention to feeding Henry his dinner.

Rowan could tell it was everything she could do not to rip the envelope open right then and there. Only Martha Pierce's meatloaf kept him from doing it himself. His mother was an excellent cook.

AFTER DINNER WAS DONE, LAUREN PITCHED IN AND HELPED with the dishes, then made excuses about needing to get Henry ready for bed. She gathered him and the envelope up and headed upstairs to Rowan's old room. She did get Henry ready for bed, before tearing the envelope open. Inside, she found an unusual device. It looked like the cord for an iPhone, but it had a strange block at the end, unlike anything she'd seen before.

She found the new iPhone she'd gotten to replace the one

she'd left behind in South Africa. She'd been due for a new one anyway, and this one had all the bells and whistles, and enough storage to film a whole season of *The Veritas Codex* on. Collecting Henry, she lay down to nurse him while she fiddled with the device.

Rowan came in and stood at his dresser, emptying his pockets, removing his watch and ring, and preparing for bed. It was a ritual she'd watched him do every night for almost ten years, and she smiled to herself as he turned, peeling out of his plaid shirt, still in his t-shirt and jeans as he kicked off his shoes.

Rowan's room had changed little since he'd gone into the military. His books were all still in the shelves, his plastic model of the Starship Enterprise still hung in the corner along with a Styrofoam planet. According to Rowan, the only thing different was the queen size bed with navy blue sheets and a plain comforter. She watched him as he took a book off the shelf and came over to lie down beside her.

"So what is it?" he asked.

"Some kind of storage device," she said, as she scrolled through the strangely configured icons. They were more like Sumerian glyphs than anything she'd ever seen on her modern device. Lauren scooted in, moving Henry so she could feed him and show Rowan the phone. She tapped on one of the icons, surprised to find it was a video clip. While Rowan hadn't taken a lot of film during their time at Michael's lab. This video showed the scene of her and Michael from the airplane as he'd played her the audio file of the signals from space. It was as if the camera had been mounted over the flight attendant's station.

"What the ..." Lauren gasped, closing that file; opening another. There were files of videos from Lauren's trip home, and the family reunion, but something was different. In this video, Lauren was sitting beside her mother and they were holding hands, talking, and laughing in a way they never had.

It gave Lauren hope. It was a promise from Michael that everything would be made right, given time and attention. Lauren found herself looking forward to returning home. She didn't know when that would happen, but she'd be ready when time permitted.

"Do you realize what this is?" Rowan sat up, taking the phone from her hand, scrolling through the videos. "Michael gave us our episode …" he said. "This is the story of you two … working together." He ran his hand down his beard.

There was a tap at the door. "Come in," Lauren said.

The door opened and Kitty stepped in, looking sheepish. "Sorry to bother you," she said. "Another delivery arrived, and your mother keeps talking about trying to teach us how to play canasta and bunko. Am I disturbing you?"

"Of course not," Rowan said, waving her in. She came in and held out the package. "Let me guess, message from Mars?"

"Actually, this one is from Tahlequah," she said. "Fed Ex just dropped it off."

Henry had nodded off, and Lauren picked him up and moved him to the travel crib she'd gotten at the mall. She returned and patted on the foot of the bed, encouraging Kitty to sit as she took the package.

"It's from my mother," Lauren said, studying it. She glanced up at Rowan. "Wonder how she knew where to find me?"

"If your Mom is anything like you or Michael, then I don't think you need to wonder." Kitty mused. "What is it?"

"I don't know," she said. Rowan stood and went to the dresser, picking up his Swiss Army knife and brought it to her.

Carefully, Lauren used it to slit the packaging, doing her best not to cut what was inside. She closed the knife and handed it back. Reaching in, she pulled out a bundle of cloth wrapped in tissue. There, she found a beautifully crafted ribbon skirt; made from navy blue calico and satin ribbons in a variety of colors to match the red flowers, and green stems in the fabric's print.

"That's pretty," Rowan said with an arch of his brow.

"Beautiful," Kitty added.

Lauren smiled, beaming with pride. "Mom said she was going to send it to me … so I'd have it when I needed it."

"I guess you're going to need it soon then." Rowan shrugged. "Knowing your mother."

Lauren nodded, turning to Kitty. "Any luck thinking of a way to explain what happened to my brother?" She addressed the question to both Kitty and Rowan. "I don't think my mother will buy he's in the witness protection program."

"It has to be something pretty spectacular if we're going to fool anyone," Rowan scratched his chin, leaning his elbow on his knee.

"The secret to any good undercover project is to try and keep as close to the truth as you can," Kitty said. "It's too easy to get caught in a lie if you stray too far from reality."

"Have you done many undercover projects?" Rowan asked.

"I infiltrated a top job at NASA, and you question my abilities as a spy?" Kitty feigned indignation. "I have gone on dozens of clandestine projects. I know my way around an undercover job."

"So how do we use your abilities to hide my brother in plain sight?" Lauren asked.

Kitty sat up straight, as if a light bulb had just come on over her head. "I just might have an idea …"

EPILOGUE

Lauren beamed, watching Rowan's expression as they walked into Mission Control in Houston. Jean-René had the cameras on him, capturing that expression as he totally geeked out. His eyes were filled with wonder as he gasped, "Wow! This is incredible!" The words escaped from deep in Rowan's chest.

The videographer had returned from France with hours of footage from his parent's retelling of their family history. Once his father's health-crisis was addressed and they were sure he was out of the woods, their secondary mission had taken over. He'd taken Bahati to all the places his mother had identified with their family's long and well-documented past. If her research and records were accurate, the Toussaint family was descended from French nobility; nobility that had taken part in the Crusades, as well as several notable wars. While Rowan's family tree made it to Charlemagne the Great through the Merovingian line, Jean-René's tree met Rowan's through the Carolingian line. He came from the branch of French royalty through Phillip VII, who had been aided by none other than Joan of Arc, the Maid of Orleans. They truly were blood-brothers ... well, more or less.

Today's program, a complete left turn from their original mission, had taken nearly two months of working with Kitty, and NASA, to get to this point. Jean-René too, had been working covertly with some of his buddies that did special effects for the movies, and today was the culmination of their efforts. They were all confident they'd be able to pull it off, and the world would be watching.

Kitty appeared at Lauren's elbow. "I hope all this works," Lauren said. Her stomach was in knots and she was fighting to keep her morning coffee down.

"It'll work," Kitty said. "Everything ready on your end?"

"Yeah." Lauren took a deep breath.

"Let me introduce you to the mission team." Kitty took them around the room. Rowan and Lauren shook hands with everyone in Mission Control, while Jean-René and Bahati set up cameras, lighting, and audio equipment in front of a small set that had been constructed off to the side of the main command center. *The Veritas Codex* team had come up the day before to work out logistics and complete required security briefings while Lauren got Henry settled with his grandparents in their RV, parked in one of the visitors parking lots at the Johnson Space Center.

They'd had a long day already. They had to report early for makeup and wardrobe, and then there had been one last security briefing before they went over the last minute changes to the script that NASA required. It was only then, that they'd been escorted to Mission Control and gotten their first look at the place where the magic would happen.

"Lauren? Are you ready?" Jean-René called her over. "Rowan?"

"Here we go," Lauren said to Kitty with a faint smile, excusing herself from the conversation. She paused to pick a spec of lint off her navy blue blazer and smoothed down her red blouse. The colors matched her ribbon skirt perfectly, and she was pleased at how patriotic they were. Lauren had found a beautiful silver necklace in a shop in Santa Fe that had lapis lazuli stones, as well as a matching bracelet and earrings; finishing off her ensemble.

She smiled at Rowan who wore an embroidered Exploration Channel dress shirt that was a beautiful French blue and dark blue dress slacks. His necktie was almost the same shade of red as the ribbons in Lauren's skirt.

Once they were seated in front of the cameras, Bahati moved in with a light meter to check the light-levels and made a few adjustments to the circle lamps that nearly blinded them. Once satisfied with everything else, she pulled a compact from her pocket and did a quick fix on Lauren's make up, including touching up her lipstick. "You look great," she said, smoothing her hair. Then she turned to Rowan and powdered his forehead and nose too. He didn't have on much makeup, but he was already starting to sweat under the lights. It was essential with this much lighting to keep the shine to a minimum. "You look great, too." She patted his cheek and slipped back behind the cameras.

The opening of their scripted introduction appeared in the teleprompter as the light flashed on the camera. Jean-René stepped out from behind it. He wore a set of headphones and Lauren knew he was getting instructions from the control room back in San Diego as they prepared to go on. "And we're live in 5 … 4 … 3 … 2 …" He didn't speak after that, but gave them the go sign and the teleprompter kicked in.

"Welcome to Mission Control. I'm Rowan Pierce from the Exploration Channel's *The Veritas Codex*."

"And I'm Dr. Lauren Grayson." She used her maiden name for her on-air personae. It was one of her last connections to her brother, and today, she was grateful for it. "We are your hosts for today's historic launch of the first manned mission to the International Space Station in over two years."

"But this is no ordinary mission." Rowan picked up the narration. "This is a joint effort between the United States and Russia. Once opponents in the race to reach outer space, today's launch represents a new spirit of cooperation, and the cherry on top is that this mission includes one of our own. Mission Specialist Dr. Michael Grayson is none other than the brother of my lovely wife." Rowan smiled as he turned to Lauren. With no active U.S. Space Missions scheduled to launch since the shuttle program had been shuttered, the only active space program was in Russia. Despite the top secret revelation that the KGB were still working, they had no choice but to use Russia as a cover. Kitty's diplomatic connections had made today's ruse possible. "Tell us, how exciting is it for you to see your older brother launched into outer space?"

Lauren laughed on cue. "There was a time I'd have liked to hit the red button myself," she joked. "But today, I couldn't be prouder. Michael has been working for decades on radio-telescopes and this mission will afford him the opportunity to oversee the construction of a new sub-orbital radio telescope that could very well exceed the capabilities of Hubble."

"Our technology has improved since Hubble was launched," Rowan continued. "Since its launch in 1990, the Hubble Telescope, named for the trailblazing astronomer, Dr. Edwin Hubble, has made over 1.4 million observations in its lifetime. For more, let's turn to our colleague Dr. Kitty Donovan, Senior Program Administrator of the Hubble Project here at the Johnson Space Center in Houston." Kitty had a seat at the desk with mission control behind her. Jean-René just had to pivot to get the shot. No one would ever know she was less than 10 feet away from Rowan and Lauren's set. "How excited are you to have Dr. Grayson on this project, and more importantly, how badly needed is this new telescope?"

"We couldn't be any more thrilled, and to have a colleague like Dr. Grayson leading the team is truly a joy. There's no one more qualified than Michael." She grinned. "Hubble has been working with makeshift repairs — essentially contact lenses for a telescope — so a new space-based system is long overdue."

The shot came back to Rowan. "Well, we'll come back to Dr. Donovan in a little bit, but with a little less than two hours 'til launch, let's take a look at the life and career of Dr. Michael Grayson leading up to this moment." Rowan moved seamlessly to the other camera. As he finished his lines, the show segued to a pre-recorded piece on Michael's history. Jean-René and his team had put it together from the footage Michael had provided, showing false scenes of Michael and Lauren at the homecoming, with Michael across the fire as Rowan told ghost stories, watching his sister through the firelight. Nothing showed the animosity between the siblings, or even implied it. They put forward a unified front.

It made Lauren smile. This was the way it should have been, had their egos not gotten in the way of their relationship. This would be the legacy of their twelfth-hour détente.

Lauren had to emotionally detach herself from the footage to keep the tears from forming in the corners of her eyes. As soon as it ended, she was on. "Aww, I love that knucklehead." She had to say it, it was on the teleprompter, but it was everything she could do to make it jovial. She missed him terribly. "Now, as Rowan mentioned earlier, this mission is a joint effort with Russia, and the launch is actually taking place in Siberia, where it's just after dinner time. The crew of the Russian rocket, named *Ангел I*, from the Russian for *Angel,* has been preparing all day for this nighttime launch. For more on that, let's go to our intrepid reporter in the field, Pavel Smirnov."

A hired actor had been cast to play a Russian reporter. In reality, Russia *was* launching a rocket to the International Space Station today, but of course, Michael wasn't on it. The Russians were in on the ruse, but only the necessary officials were clued in.

All the video of the astronauts preparing for the launch had been digitally remastered. Jean-René had superimposed Michael's face over another astronaut's image from the 1980s and the reconstructed image had been superimposed into actual footage of the crew as they walked out to the launch pad. The video was so convincing even Lauren couldn't find flaw with it.

"Congratulations, Dr. Grayson. Your brother is about to make history," the reporter said after Lauren made introductions.

"Thanks," she said. "We're very proud of Michael."

"Pavel, tell us, how's it going at Mission Control in the remote regions of Russia?" Rowan asked. The Russian government's one and only requirement for this whole smoke-and-mirror's event was that they were not allowed to know the location of the launch. As a result, Rowan had written the scripts to be intentionally vague.

A picture-in-picture window appeared over Pavel's shoulder and expanded as he stepped out of the camera shot on the display to Lauren's left. The Siberian tundra was visible beyond his shoulder and it looked bitterly cold; the sky, gray. "It's been a lovely day here, but the sun will be setting soon, and this will be a spectacular night launch. The cosmonauts have been buckled into the Soyuz and are beginning their final systems checks."

"Have there been any issues that could delay today's launch?"

"Engineers have been concerned about a seal when they began trying to pressurize the fuel system, and they spent several hours this morning working on it, but as of now, everything appears to be in working order, and we are currently go for launch, unless something changes."

"Let's hope nothing changes." Lauren turned back to the camera. "But now it's time for a commercial break. We'll be back after a word from our sponsors."

"And we're out," Bahati said. "Four minutes."

Lauren stood and stepped out from behind the hot lights that had blinded her. Kitty stepped out from behind one of the cameras and met her at the edge of the dais, handing her a bottle of water. Lauren took it and drank greedily. "Thank you," Lauren said, yawning. "Early call to set," she said in explanation.

"You're telling me? I had briefings with my team this morning. They had more questions than I anticipated."

"Everything good?"

Kitty nodded, stifling her own yawn. She glanced over her shoulder to the team who were now in their places at the various computer terminals that filled the room, theater style. A dozen or so large display screens filled the front of the room, each showing a different view of the launch pad in Russia. "Wow," Lauren's gaze went to one of the images, of the sun setting behind the *Soyuz* on the launch pad. A wide expanse of emptiness spread out around it, and a golden glow illuminated everything. The shadows filled the void. The tall winter-dry grasses that claimed the land beyond the base waved in the light evening breeze. A shiver ran down her spine.

Kitty half-turned, then pivoted all the way around, crossing her arms over her silk blouse. "Spectacular, isn't it?"

"Truly." Lauren nodded, glancing back at her.

"Michael would have loved to see this day," Kitty said softly. "He'd be nerding out over all of this."

Lauren's eye went to Rowan, as he stood talking to some of the mission team, not sure who was more excited as they took turns signing autographs for each other. "Yes, he would," she answered absent-mindedly. "I just hope …" she started but hesitated. "I hope he can get a message home once in a while."

"We're negotiating the communication plans now," Kitty said, turning back around.

The corner of Lauren's lip twitched before lifting into a smile. "Do you think he's watching all this?"

"I know he is," she said, leaning in. "He said to tell you …

good story." The initial idea had been Kitty's, but it was Lauren and Rowan who had been the authors of this day. They'd worked out the story and all the subtle details. Kitty used her resources to facilitate it.

~

A THREE-HOUR LIVE SHOW WAS EXHAUSTING. BUT WHEN THE launch was delayed at the last minute due to a weather issue, Lauren began to think the rocket would never breech the atmosphere. It took a good forty minutes for a storm south of the launch site to pass far enough as to not interfere with the trajectory of the rocket's path. It was mid-morning before they were able to sit back and go silent as the rockets fired. The craft lifted tentatively at first, then with gusto, above the few buildings surrounding the launch pad and up into the sky.

"And we have lift off," Rowan said. "The Angel has taken wing. Godspeed, my brother. Godspeed." Lauren was supposed to take the next few lines, but her voice caught in her throat and she froze. Rowan reached over and caught her hand, continuing with her lines. "Congratulations to NASA and the Russian Space Agency on the successful launch of the Angel 1, including American Astronaut Dr. Michael Grayson, and Russian Cosmonauts Serova, Tarilyn, and Pavlova who will be aboard the International Space Station for the next eighteen months. Docking with the ISS is targeted for 27 hours from launch." Rowan's hand went to his earpiece, and Lauren turned to look at him with surprise in her eyes. "I've just been informed, the ashes of Russian Cosmonaut Dr. Alexei Budnikov are included among the craft's payload, where they will be jettisoned into space. Dr. Budnikov will spend eternity … among the stars."

"As he should," Lauren said, smiling through the tears that threatened to escape her lashes. "Godspeed Alexei. Godspeed Michael and Godspeed to the crew of the Angel I."

~

JACOB WAS WAITING BEHIND THE CAMERAS WHEN LAUREN AND Rowan came off the set for the last time. He waited 'til they saw him before he began to clap. He beamed, grinning brightly. "Congratulations! And job well done. Lauren, once again you've managed to surprise me. I wasn't sure you could pull this one off."

For once, a coy grin lit her face. "Me?"

"And you said your family was boring," he said.

She lifted a shoulder. "I've been wrong before."

Jacob turned and gave a nod to Rowan. "I'm afraid she's got you beat. An astronaut on the International Space Station beats Robert the Bruce any day in my book."

"Well." Rowan shrugged. As long as Jacob wasn't chewing them out for a couple plane tickets to South Africa, they were golden. Little did he know how golden they were. "Suit your-self." He chuckled. "Honestly, I can't disagree."

"So," Jacob said, putting a hand on Lauren's arm. "How likely are we to get your brother to do some interviews for Space Week next summer?"

"I don't know." Lauren tried to keep her face passive. "I understand he's going to be pretty busy up there."

"But surely…" Jacob started, but Lauren looked past him, as her in-laws appeared with Henry.

"Mama!" Henry squealed, reaching his arms out for her. Rowan's parents had driven them down from Denver to Houston in their RV and had taken over babysitting duties so Lauren and Rowan could work today. They had plans for the rest of the day, but with the launch being delayed, a mimosa brunch wasn't likely to happen at this point. Lauren rushed over and took Henry who hugged her. "Mama! Mama, eat."

"Are you hungry?" Lauren asked, poking him in the tummy, paying little attention to her boss.

"I've seen the preliminary film for the episode on you and

Michael." Jacob fell in beside her but turned to Rowan. "How long before you can get the rest of it done? And what about Jean-René and Bahati's family trees?"

"We wanted to incorporate some of the film from today's live event in Lauren's episode," Rowan said. "But it shouldn't take more than a few more weeks to finish all the postproduction work, now that this is out of the way."

"Outstanding." Jacob clapped his hands together like a maniacal evil-villain.

"My mom has a lot of the research done for my episode. We'll have to discuss our travel budget if we're going to go to Scotland and France. Give us a couple of weeks and I'll be able to give you a better idea. Jean-René's episode should go first though. He already has a lot of film in the can. If there's any additional film we need for his episode, we can grab it while we work on mine."

"Too bad you didn't know about your French connection before. Jean-René could have filmed some video for you. Saved the Network some cash."

Rowan just shrugged. "We'll do our best to be efficient," he said. "Maybe we can get everything ready for Bahati's episode before we leave the states, save any unnecessary flights across the Atlantic."

"Who gives a flying fig? You just gave America an exclusive front row seat to a Russian Soyuz launch during sweeps week!" Jacob enthused. "You basically just wrote yourself a blank check, my friend." Jacob slapped his shoulder. "Just let me know when you're ready to sit down and talk about your *next* project." He winked.

"Uhhhh," Rowan drew the word out. "Can we finish this project first?"

Jacob ignored the question, still basking in the glory of the moment. "A live special at NASA. An epic episode about Lauren and her astronaut brother. And an episode on each of your family histories. Maybe an interview with an astronaut for Space Week. This might be one of my best ideas ever." Jacob was muttering as he slugged Rowan in the shoulder and headed off to meet the NASA team and give his kudos to Jean-René and Bahati too.

Rowan stood with his hands on his hips, gazing down at the toe of his dress shoe. "Your idea indeed," he muttered to himself. "I'm pretty sure it was Curt's idea!" he called after Jacob, as he went to join the celebrating scientists each slapping each other on the back. Someone had opened a bottle of champagne and a cake had been wheeled in on a cart.

Rowan shook his head and went to catch up with his family. He put an arm around Lauren and bopped Henry playfully on the nose.

"Are you ready to go get something to eat?" Lauren asked.

"I'm starving," he said. "What about you, Henry?"

"Mama. Go," Henry said, showing off the shine of a couple new teeth. "Go eat, Dada."

"Yes, I want to go, too," Rowan said. "I'm starving."

"Now if we could just find your father," Martha said to Rowan. "Where did that man go? I'm sure he is hungry, too. This is just like your father … always wandering off …"

"Eat." Henry grunted, licking his lips. "Mama! Eat! Go, eat."

"Just a second, sweetie," Lauren said. She turned to Rowan. "Ask Bahati and Jean-René if they want to come with us. We can go to the commissary and come back and break down the equipment after we've eaten."

"Mama, go," Henry said urgently, rocking against her, tugging on her jacket. "Mama. Go … eat." He grabbed a hand full of her hair and yanked it.

"Ow!" She protested.

~

Rowan turned to see about the rest of the team but paused when his mom called his name. "Honey, fetch the Colonel," she called after him. "He's probably in there telling war stories with his Air Force buddies."

Rowan hadn't seen his dad slip off. "Dad's in Mission Control?" Rowan hesitated, realizing Lauren wasn't standing there anymore. He scanned over the crowds that were beginning to gather in the hallway outside. She wasn't anywhere.

"Oh goodness! Where did that girl go?" Martha turned. "Lauren?" she called, turning to chase after her. "Hurry up, Rowan. I'll go catch up with Lauren. We'll meet you in the commissary."

Rowan stood dumbfounded as he looked after his mother, but his eye went to the horizon searching. He grimaced and shook his head. *Mama, Go*, indeed.

ABOUT THE AUTHOR

Betsey Kulakowski has thirty years of experience as an occupational safety professional and recently completed her degree in Emergency Management. She lives with her husband and two teenage children in Oklahoma. Betsey has been writing since she could, and created her first book at the age of six—cardboard cover, string binding and all.

The Veritas Codex (Book 1 of The Veritas Codex Series)

The Jaguar Queen (Book 2 of The Veritas Codex Series)

The Alien Accord (Book 3 of The Veritas Codex Series)

ABOUT THE PUBLISHER

Babylon Books is a division of Bernhardt Books, a family-owned publishing house founded in 1999 that showcases emerging authors and compelling fiction.

Editor-in-Chief: Alice Bernhardt

Chief Financial Officer: W. Harrison Bernhardt

Marketing Director: Ralph Bernhardt

Learn more at: www.babylonbooks.net